## SPEC  MESSAGE  ADERS

## THE ULVERSCROFT FOUNDATION
### (registered UK charity number 264873)

was established in 1972 to provide funds for research, diagnosis and treatment of eye diseases. Examples of major projects funded by the Ulverscroft Foundation are:-

- The Children's Eye Unit at Moorfields Eye Hospital, London
- The Ulverscroft Children's Eye Unit at Great Ormond Street Hospital for Sick Children
- Funding research into eye diseases and treatment at the Department of Ophthalmology, University of Leicester
- The Ulverscroft Vision Research Group, Institute of Child Health
- Twin operating theatres at the Western Ophthalmic Hospital, London
- The Chair of Ophthalmology at the Royal Australian College of Ophthalmologists

You can help further the work of the Foundation by making a donation or leaving a legacy. Every contribution is gratefully received. If you would like to help support the Foundation or require further information, please contact:

**THE ULVERSCROFT FOUNDATION**
**The Green, Bradgate Road, Anstey**
**Leicester LE7 7FU, England**
**Tel: (0116) 236 4325**

**website: www.foundation.ulverscroft.com**

Earl Derr Biggers was born in Warren, Ohio in 1884. He graduated from Harvard University in 1907, and lived for many years in California. Biggers wrote six novels featuring detective Charlie Chan, who became a staple of the movies. He died in Pasadena, California in 1933.

# KEEPER OF THE KEYS

Charlie Chan of the Honolulu Police is in
Lake Tahoe when the glamorous opera
singer Ellen Landini is shot dead at the
party he's attending. Sheriff Don Holt is
relieved to have Chan's assistance. There
are four suspects — Landini's widower
and her former husbands — and a paucity
of clues. However, Chan finds clues from a
galley proof of Landini's forthcoming
autobiography. And it appears that Ah
Sing, an elderly Chinese houseboy and
'Keeper of the Keys', is an important
piece of the puzzle, although he is fiercely
traditional and uncooperative. However,
Chan's cultural knowledge works to his
advantage in solving the case.

Books by Earl Derr Biggers
Published by The House of Ulverscroft:

THE HOUSE WITHOUT A KEY
THE CHINESE PARROT
BEHIND THAT CURTAIN
THE BLACK CAMEL
CHARLIE CHAN CARRIES ON

EARL DERR BIGGERS

# KEEPER OF THE KEYS
## A CHARLIE CHAN MYSTERY

*Complete and Unabridged*

# ULVERSCROFT
*Leicester*

First published in
the United States of America in 1932

This Large Print Edition
published 2013

A catalogue record for this book is available
from the British Library.

ISBN 978–1–4448–1568–9

Published by
F. A. Thorpe (Publishing)
Anstey, Leicestershire

Set by Words & Graphics Ltd.
Anstey, Leicestershire
Printed and bound in Great Britain by
T. J. International Ltd., Padstow, Cornwall

This book is printed on acid-free paper

# 1

## Snow on the Mountains

The train had left Sacramento some distance behind, and was now bravely beginning the long climb that led to the high Sierras and the town of Truckee. Little patches of snow sparkled in the late afternoon sun along the way, and far ahead snow-capped peaks suddenly stood out against the pale sky of a reluctant spring.

Two conductors, traveling together as though for safety, came down the aisle and paused at section seven. 'Tickets on at Sacramento,' demanded the leader. The occupant of the section, a pretty blonde girl who seemed no more than twenty, handed him the small green slips. He glanced at them, then passed one to his companion. 'Seat in Seven,' he said loudly. 'Reno.'

'Reno,' echoed the Pullman conductor, in an even louder tone.

They passed on, leaving the blonde girl staring about the car with an air that was a mixture of timidity and defiance. This was the first time, since she had left home the day

1

before, that she had been so openly tagged with the name of her destination. All up and down the car, strange faces turned and looked at her with casual curiosity. Some smiled knowingly; others were merely cold and aloof. The general public in one of its ruder moments.

One passenger only showed no interest. Across the aisle, in section eight, the girl noted the broad shoulders and back of a man in a dark suit. He was sitting close to the window, staring out, and even from this rear view it was apparent that he was deeply engrossed with his own affairs. The young woman who was bound for Reno felt somehow rather grateful toward him.

Presently he turned, and the girl understood, for she saw that he was a Chinese. A race that minds its own business. An admirable race. This member of it was plump and middle-aged. His little black eyes were shining as from some inner excitement; his lips were parted in a smile that seemed to indicate a sudden immense delight. Without so much as a glance toward number seven, he rose and walked rapidly down the car.

Arrived on the front platform of the Pullman, he stood for a moment deeply inhaling the chilly air. Then again, as though irresistibly, he was drawn to the window. The train was climbing more slowly now; the landscape, wherever he looked, was white. Presently he was conscious of some one standing behind him, and turned. The train maid, a Chinese girl of whose guarded glances he had been conscious at intervals all afternoon, was gazing solemnly up at him.

'How do you do,' the man remarked, 'and thank you so much. You have arrived at most opportune moment. The need to speak words assails me with unbearable force. I must release flood of enthusiasm or burst. For at this moment I am seeing snow for the first time.'

'Oh — I am so glad!' answered the girl. It was an odd reply, but the plump Chinese was evidently too excited to notice that.

'You see, it is this way,' he continued eagerly. 'All my life I can remember only nodding palm trees, the trade winds of the tropics, surf tumbling on coral beach — '

'Honolulu,' suggested the girl.

He paused, and stared at her. 'Perhaps you have seen Hawaii too?' he inquired.

She shook her head. 'No. Me — I am born in San Francisco. But I read advertisements in magazines — and besides — '

'You are bright girl,' the man cut in, 'and your deduction is eminently correct. Honolulu has been my home for many years. Once,

3

it is true, I saw California before, and from flat floor of desert I beheld, far in distance, mountain snow. But that was all same dream. Now I am moving on into veritable snow country, the substance lies on ground all about, soon I shall plunge unaccustomed feet into its delicious cold. I shall intake great breaths of frigid air.' He sighed. 'Life is plenty good,' he added.

'Some people,' said the girl, 'find the snow boresome.'

'And some, no doubt, consider the stars a blemish on the sky. But you and I, we are not so insensible to the beauties of the world. We delight to travel — to find novelty and change. Is it not so?'

'I certainly do.'

'Ah — you should visit my islands. Do not think that in my ecstasy of raving I forget the charm of my own land. I have daughter same age as you — how happy she would be to act as your guide. She would show you Honolulu, the flowering trees, the — '

'The new police station, perhaps,' cried the girl suddenly.

The big man started slightly and stared at her. 'I perceive that I am known,' he remarked.

'Naturally,' the girl smiled. 'For many years you have been newspaper hero for me. I was

4

small child at the time, but I read with panting interest when you carried Phillimore pearls on flat floor of desert. Again, when you captured killer of famous Scotland Yard man in San Francisco, I perused daily accounts breathlessly. And only three weeks ago you arrived in San Francisco with one more cruel murderer in your firm grasp.'

'But even so,' he shrugged.

'Your pictures were in all the papers. Have you forgot?'

'I seek to do so,' he answered ruefully. 'Were those my pictures?'

'More than that, I have seen you in person. Two weeks ago when the Chan Family Society gave big banquet for you in San Francisco. My mother was a Chan, and we were all present. I stood only a few feet away when you entered the building. True, I was seated so far distant I could not hear your speech, but I was told by others it was brilliant talk.'

He shrugged. 'The Chan family should have more respect for truth,' he objected.

'I am Violet Lee,' she went on, holding out a tiny hand. 'And you — may I speak the name — '

'Why not?' he replied, taking her hand. 'You have me trapped. I am inspector Charlie Chan, of the Honolulu Police.'

5

'My husband and I recognized you when you came aboard at Oakland,' the girl went on. 'He is Henry Lee, steward of club car,' she added proudly. 'But he tells me sternly I must not speak to you — that is why I cried 'I am so glad!' when you spoke first to me. Perhaps, said my husband, inspector is now on new murder case, and does not want identity known. He is often right, my husband.'

'As husbands must be,' Chan nodded. 'But this time he is wrong.'

A shadow of disappointment crossed the girl's face. 'You are not, then, on trail of some wrong-doer?'

'I am on no trail but my own.'

'We thought there might have been some recent murder — '

Charlie laughed. 'This is the mainland,' he remarked, 'so of course there have been many recent murders. But I am happy to say, none of them concerns me. No — I am involved only in contemplation of snow-capped peaks.'

'Then — may I tell my husband that he is free to address you? The honor will overwhelm him with joy.'

Chan laid his hand on the girl's arm. 'I will tell him myself,' he announced. 'And I will see you again before I leave the train. In the

6

meantime, your friendly words have been as food to the famished, rest to the jaded. Aloha.'

He stepped through the door of the car ahead, leaving his small compatriot flushed and breathing fast on the chilly platform.

When he reached the club car, the white-jacketed steward was bending solicitously over the solitary passenger there. Receiving the latter's order, he stood erect and cast one look in the direction of Charlie Chan. He was a small thin Chinese, and only another member of his race would have caught the brief flame of interest that flared under his heavy eyelids.

Charlie dropped into a chair and, for lack of anything better to do, studied his fellow traveler, some distance down the aisle. The man was a lean, rather distinguished-looking foreigner of some sort — probably a Latin, Chan thought. His hair was as black and sleek as the detective's, save where it was touched with gray over the ears. His eyes were quick and roving, his thin hands moved nervously about, he sat on the edge of his chair, as though his stay on the train was but a brief interlude in an exciting life.

When the steward returned with a package of cigarettes on a silver tray and got his money and tip from the other passenger,

Chan beckoned to him. The boy was at his side in an instant.

'One juice of the orange, if you will be so good,' Charlie ordered.

'Delighted to serve,' replied the steward, and was off like a greyhound. With surprising speed he returned, and placed the drink on the arm of Charlie's chair. He was moving reluctantly away, when the detective spoke.

'An excellent concoction,' he said, holding the glass aloft.

'Yes, sir,' replied the steward, and looked at Chan much as the Chinese girl on the platform had done.

'Helpful in reducing the girth,' Chan went on. 'A question which, I perceive, does not concern you. But as for myself — you will note how snugly I repose in this broad chair.'

The eyes of the other narrowed. 'The man-hunting tiger is sometimes over-plump,' he remarked. 'Still he pounces with admirable precision.'

Charlie smiled. 'He who is cautious by nature is a safe companion in crossing a bridge.'

The steward nodded. 'When you travel abroad, speak as the people of the country are speaking.'

'I commend your discretion,' Charlie told him. 'But as I have just said to your wife, it is

8

happily unnecessary at this time. The man-hunting tiger is at present unemployed. You may safely call him by his name.'

'Ah, thank you, Inspector. It is under any conditions a great honor to meet you. My wife and I are both longtime admirers of your work. At this moment you seem to stand at very pinnacle of fame.'

Charlie sighed, and drained his glass. 'He who stands on pinnacle,' he ventured, 'has no place to step but off.'

'The need for moving,' suggested the steward, 'may not be imminent.'

'Very true.' The detective nodded approvingly. 'Such wisdom and such efficiency. When I met your wife, I congratulated you. Now I meet you, I felicitate her.'

A delighted smile spread over the younger man's face. 'A remark,' he answered, 'that will find place in our family archive. The subjects are unworthy, but the source is notable. Will you deign to drink again?'

'No, thank you.' Chan glanced at his watch. 'The town of Truckee, I believe, is but twenty-five minutes distant.'

'Twenty-four and one-half,' replied Henry Lee, who was a railroad man. The flicker of surprise in his black eyes was scarcely noticeable. 'You alight at Truckee, Inspector?'

'I do,' nodded Charlie, his gaze on the

9

other passenger, who had evinced sudden interest.

'You travel for pleasure, I believe you intimated,' the steward continued.

Chan smiled. 'In part,' he said softly.

'Ah, yes — in part,' Henry Lee repeated. He saw Chan's hand go to his trousers pocket. 'The charge, I regret to state, is one half-dollar.'

Nodding, Charlie hesitated a moment. Then he laid the precise sum on the silver tray. He was not unaware of the institution of tipping. He was also not unaware of the sensitive Chinese nature. They would part now as friends, not as master and menial. He saw from the light in Henry Lee's eyes that the young man appreciated his delicacy.

'Thank you so much,' said the steward, bowing low. 'It has been great honor and privilege to serve Inspector Charlie Chan.'

It chanced that at the moment the detective's eyes were on the foreign-looking passenger at the other end of the car. The man had been about to light a cigarette, but when he overheard the name he paused, and stared until the match burned down to his finger-tips. He tossed it aside, lighted another and then came down the car and dropped into the seat at Charlie's side.

'Pardon,' he said. 'Me — I have no wish to

10

intrude. But I overhear you say you leave the train at Truckee. So also must I.'

'Yes?' Chan said politely.

'Alas, yes. A desolate place, they tell me, at this time of year.'

'The snow is very beautiful,' suggested Charlie.

'Bah!' The other shrugged disgustedly. 'Me, I have had sufficient snow. I fought for two winters with the Italian Army in the North.'

'Distasteful work,' commented Chan, 'for you.'

'What do you mean?'

'Pardon — no offense. But one of your temperament. A musician.'

'You know me, then?'

'I have not the pleasure. But I note flattened, calloused finger-tips. You have played violin.'

'I have done more than play the violin. I am Luis Romano, conductor of the opera. Ah — I perceive that means nothing to you. But in my own country — at La Scala in Milan, at Naples. And also in Paris, in London, even in New York. However, that is all finished now.'

'I am so sorry.'

'Finished — by a woman. A woman who — but what of this? We both alight at Truckee. And after that — '

'Ah, yes — after that.'

11

'We travel together, Signor Chan. I could not help it — I heard the name. But that was lucky. I was told to look out for you. You do not believe? Read this.'

He handed Charlie a somewhat soiled and crumpled telegram. The detective read:

'MR. LUIS ROMANO, KILARNEY HOTEL, SAN FRANCISCO: DELIGHTED YOU ARE COMING TO TAHOE TO VISIT ME. OWING TO VERY LATE SPRING, ROAD AROUND LAKE IN POOR CONDITION. LEAVE TRAIN TRUCKEE. I WILL TELE-PHONE LOCAL GARAGE HAVE CAR WAITING. YOU WILL BE DRIVEN TO TAHOE TAVERN. AT TAVERN PIER MY MAN WILL WAIT FOR YOU WITH MOTORLAUNCH. BRING YOU DOWN TO MY PLACE, PINEVIEW. OTHER GUESTS MAY JOIN YOU IN CAR AT TRUCKEE, AMONG THEM MR. CHAR-LIE CHAN, OF HONOLULU. THANKS FOR COMING.

    DUDLEY WARD'

Chan returned the missive to the eager hand of the Italian. 'Now I understand,' he remarked.

Mr. Romano made a gesture of despair.

'You are more fortunate than I. I understand to the door of this place Pineview — but no further. You, however — it may be you are old friend of Mr. Dudley Ward? The whole affair may be clear to you.'

Charlie's face was bland, expressionless. 'You are, then, in the dark yourself?' he inquired.

'Absolutely,' the Italian admitted.

'Mr. Dudley Ward is no friend of yours?'

'Not at all. I have yet to see him. I know, of course, he is a member of a famous San Francisco family, very wealthy. He spends the summers at his place on this high lake, to which he goes very early in the season. A few days ago I had a most surprising letter from him, asking me to visit him up here. There was, he said, a certain matter he wished to discuss, and he promised to pay me well for my trouble. I was — I am, Signor, financially embarrassed — owing to a circumstance quite unforeseen and abominable. So I agreed to come.'

'You have no trace of idea what subject Mr. Ward desires to discuss?'

'I have an inkling — yes. You see — Mr. Ward was once the husband of — my wife.' Chan nodded hazily. 'The relationship, however, is not very close. There were two other husbands in between us. He was the

13

first — I am the fourth.'

Charlie sought to keep a look of surprise from his face. What would his wife, on Punchbowl Hill, think of this? But he was now on the mainland, with Reno only a few miles away.

'It will be perhaps easier for you to understand,' the Italian went on, 'if I tell you who is my wife. A name, Signor, known even to you — pardon — to the whole world. Landini, the opera singer, Ellen Landini.' He sat excitedly on the edge of his chair. 'What a talent — magnificent. What an organ — superb. And what a heart — cold as those snow-covered stones.' He waved at the passing landscape.

'So sorry,' Chan said. 'You are not, then, happy with your wife?'

'Happy with her, Signor? Happy with her!' He stood up, the better to declaim. 'Can I be happy with a woman who is at this very moment in Reno seeking to divorce me and marry her latest fancy — a silly boy with a face like putty? After all I have done for her — the loving care I have lavished upon her — and now she does not send me even the first payment of the settlement that was agreed on — she leaves me to — '

He sank into the chair again. 'But why not? What could I expect from her? Always she was like that. The husband she had was never the right one.'

Chan nodded. 'Ginger grown in one's own garden is not so pungent,' he remarked.

Mr. Romano wakened to new excitement. 'That is it. That expresses it. It was always so with her. Look at her record — married to Dudley Ward as a girl. Everything she wanted — except a new husband. And she got him in time. John Ryder, his name was. But he didn't last long. Then — another. He was — what does it matter? I forget. Then me. I, who devoted every waking hour to her voice, to coaching her. It was I, Signor, who taught her the old Italian system of breathing, without which a singer is nothing — nothing. If you will credit it — she did not know it when I met her.'

He buried his head emotionally in his hands. Charlie respected the moment.

'And now,' went on Mr. Romano, 'this boy, this singer — this what's-his-name. Will he command her not to eat pastries — seeking to save that figure once so glorious? Will he prepare her gargle, remind her to use it? Now I recall the name of the third husband — he was Dr. Frederic Swan, a throat specialist. He has lived in Reno since the divorce — no doubt she flirts with him again. She will flirt with me, once she has hooked this boy.

15

Always like that. But now — now she can not even send me the agreed settlement — '

Henry Lee approached. 'Pardon, Inspector,' he announced. 'Truckee three minutes.'

Mr. Romano dashed for the door, evidently bound for the Pullman and his baggage. Charlie turned to his compatriot.

'So happy to know you,' he said.

'Same for you,' replied Henry Lee. 'Also, I hope you gain much pleasure from your journey. In part,' he added, with a grin. 'I am going to watch newspapers.'

'Nothing about this in newspapers,' Charlie assured him.

'If you will pardon my saying it,' replied Henry Lee, 'I watch newspapers just the same.'

Charlie went on back to his Pullman. Swift dark had fallen outside the windows, the snow was blotted from view. He gathered up his bags, turned them over to the porter and proceeded to don the heavy overcoat he had purchased for this journey — the first such garment he had owned in his life.

When he reached the car platform, Mrs. Lee was awaiting him. 'My husband has told me of his happy moment with you,' she cried. 'This is notable day in our lives. I shall have much to tell my small man-child, who is now well past his eleventh moon.'

'Pray give him my kind regards,' said Charlie. He staggered slightly as his legs were struck from behind by some heavy object. Turning, he saw a tall man with a blond beard, who had just snatched up a bag from the platform — the object, evidently, which had struck Chan so sharp a blow. Expectantly Charlie waited for the inevitable apology. But the stranger gave him one cold look pushed him ruthlessly aside and crowded past him to the car steps.

In another moment the train had stopped, and Charlie was out on the snowy platform. He tipped his porter, waved good-by to the Lees and took a few steps along the brightly lighted space in front of the station. For the first time in his life he heard the creak of frost under his shoes, saw his own breath materialized before his eyes.

Romano came swiftly up. 'I have located our motor,' he announced. 'Come quickly, if you will. I secured a view of the town, and it is not even a one-night stand.'

As they came up to the automobile waiting beside the station, they beheld the driver of it conversing with a man who had evidently just left the train. Charlie looked closer — the man with the blond beard. The latter turned to them.

'Good evening,' he said. 'Are you Dudley

17

Ward's other guests? My name is John Ryder.'

Without waiting for their response, he slipped into the preferred front seat by the driver's side. 'John Ryder.' Charlie looked at Romano, and saw an expression of vast surprise on the Italian's mobile face. They got into the rear seat without speaking, and the driver started the car.

They emerged into the main street of a town that was, in the dim light of a wintry evening, reminiscent of a moving picture of the Old West. A row of brick buildings that spoke of being clubs, but behind the frosted windows of which no gaiety seemed to be afoot to-night. Restaurants with signs that advertised only the softer drinks, a bank, a post-office. Here and there a dusky figure hurrying through the gloom.

The car crossed a railroad spur and turned off into the white nothingness of the country. Now for the first time Charlie was close to the pines, tall and stern, rooted deep in the soil, their aroma pungent and invigorating. Across his vision flitted a picture of distant palms, unbelievable relatives of these proud and lofty giants.

The chains on the tires flopped unceasingly, down the open path between the snow-banks, and Charlie wondered at the sound. On their right now was a tremendous cliff, on their left a half-frozen river.

The man on the front seat beside the driver did not turn. He said no word. The two on the rear seat followed his example.

In about an hour they came upon the lights of a few scattered houses, a little later they turned off into the Tavern grounds. A vast shingled building stood lonely in the winter night, with but a few lights burning on its ground floor.

Close to the pier entrance the driver stopped his car. A man with a boatman's cap came forward.

'Got 'em, Bill?' he inquired.

'Three — that's right, ain't it?' the garage man inquired.

'O.K. I'll take them bags.'

Bill said good night and departed, strangely eager to get back to town. The boatman led them on to the pier. For a moment Chan paused, struck by the beauty of the scene. Here lay a lake like a great dark sapphire, six thousand feet above the sea, surrounded by snow-covered mountains. On and on they moved down the dim pier.

'But,' cried Romano — 'the lake — it does not freeze.'

'Tahoe never freezes,' the guide explained scornfully. 'Too deep. Well, here's the launch.' They paused beside a handsome boat. 'I'll put your stuff aboard but we'll have to wait a minute. They's one more coming.'

Even as he spoke, a man came hurrying along the pier. He joined them, a bit breathless.

'Sorry,' he said. 'Hope I haven't kept you waiting, gentlemen. I stopped at the Tavern for a minute. Guess we might as well get acquainted. My name is Swan,' he added. 'Dr. Frederic Swan.'

One by one he shook hands with each of them, learning from each his name. As this newcomer and the man with the blond beard climbed aboard, Romano turned to Charlie and said softly:

'What is it? What is it you call it when you reach a town and all the hotel rooms are filled?'

'So sorry,' Chan said blankly.

'All right — I will get it. It has happened to me so often. A — a convention. That is it. A convention. My friend, we are about to attend one of those. We are going to attend a convention of the lost loves of Landini.'

He and Chan followed the others aboard, and in another moment they were skimming lightly over the icy waters in the direction of Emerald Bay.

# 2

## Dinner at Pineview

The mountains were breathlessly still under the black sky, the wind blew chill from their snowy slopes and as the spray occasionally stung Charlie Chan's broad face, he reflected with deep inner joy upon the new setting to which fate had now transplanted him. Too long, he decided, had he known only the semi-tropics; his blood had grown thin — he drew his great coat closer: his energy had run low. Yes — no doubt about it — he was becoming soft. This was the medicine that would revive him; new life was coursing in his veins; new ambitions seethed within him; he longed for a chance to show what he could really do. He began to regret the obviously simple nature of the matter that had brought him to Tahoe; the affair was, on the face of it, so easy and uncomplicated that, as his son Henry might have phrased it, he had come just for the ride.

Though the moon had not yet risen, he could discern the nature of the lake shore on their starboard side. The dim outlines of one huge summer home after another glided by; each without a light, without a sign of life. Presently, in the distance, he saw a lamp burning by the water's edge; a little later and it multiplied into a string of them, stretched along a pier. The boat was swinging inshore now; they fought their way along against the wind. As they reached the wharf, the passengers in the launch looked up and saw a man of about fifty standing, hatless and without an overcoat, above them. He waved, then hurried to help the boatman with the mooring ropes.

Evidently this was their host, Dudley Ward, debonair and gracious even in a stiff wind. He greeted them as they came ashore. 'John, old boy,' he said to Ryder, 'it was good of you to come. Doctor Swan, I appreciate your kindness. And this, no doubt, is Mr. Romano — a great pleasure to welcome you to Pineview. The view is a bit obscured, but I can assure you the pines are there.'

The boat was rocking violently as Charlie, always politely last, made a notable leap for the pier. Ward received him, literally, in his arms.

'Inspector Chan,' he cried. 'For years I have wanted to meet you.'

'Desire has been mutual,' Chan answered, panting a bit.

'Your native courtesy,' Ward smiled. 'I am sorry to remind you that you heard of me only — er — recently. Gentlemen — if you will follow me — '

He led the way along a broad walk from which the snow had been cleared toward a great house set amid the eternal pines. As their feet sounded on the wide veranda, an old Chinese servant swung open the door. They caught the odor of burning wood, saw lights and good cheer awaiting them, and crossed the threshold into the big living-room of Pineview.

'Sing, take the gentlemen's coats.' The host was alert and cordial. Charlie looked at him with interest; a man of fifty, perhaps more, with gray hair and ruddy pleasant face. The cut of his clothes, and the material of which they were made, placed him at once; only a gentleman, it seemed, knew the names of tailors like that. He led the way to the tremendous fireplace at the far end of the room.

'A bit chilly on Tahoe to-night,' he remarked. 'For myself, I like it — come up here earlier every year. However — the fire won't go so badly — nor will those.' He waved a hand toward a tray of cocktails. 'I had Sing pour them when we sighted you, so there would be no delay.'

He himself passed the tray. Ryder, Romano and Swan accepted with evident pleasure. Charlie shook his head and smiled, and Ward did not press him. There was a moment of awkward silence, and then the irrepressible Romano, posing with feet far apart in front of the blaze, raised his glass.

'Gentlemen,' he announced, 'I am about to propose a toast. No other, I believe, could be more appropriate at this time. However little she may mean to you now, whatever you may think of her at this late day — '

'One moment,' Ryder spoke, with his accustomed cool rudeness. 'I suggest you withdraw your toast. Because, as it happens, I want this drink.'

Romano was taken aback. 'Why, of course. I am so sorry. Me — I am too impetuous. No one, I am sure, has more to forgive than myself.'

'Beside the point,' said Ryder, and drained his glass.

Swan also drank, then laughed softly. 'We have all much to forgive, I fancy,' he remarked. 'And to forget. Yes, it was always herself Landini thought of first. Her own wishes — her own happiness. But that, of course, is genius. We ordinary mortals should be charitable. I myself have supposed for many years that I hated the very name of

Ellen Landini — and yet when I saw her a few moments ago — '

Dudley Ward paused in his task of refilling the glasses. 'A few moments ago?' he repeated.

'Yes. I drove up from Reno to the Tavern, and dropped in there for a chat with my friend, Jim Dinsdale, the manager. When I came into the lobby I thought it was deserted, but presently I saw a woman's green scarf lying on a table. Then I looked over to the fire and saw her — the woman — sitting there. I went closer — the light was poor — but even before my eyes told me, I knew that it was Ellen. I had known she was in Reno, of course, but I hadn't wanted particularly to see her. When we parted years ago — well, I needn't go into that. Anyhow, I've been avoiding her. Yet now we were meeting again — the stage all set, as though she'd arranged it, alone together in the dim-lighted lobby of a practically deserted hotel. She jumped up. 'Fred,' she cried — '

Romano came close, his face glowing with excitement. 'How was she looking, Signor? Not too much flesh? Her voice — how did her voice seem to you — '

Swan laughed. 'Why — why, she seemed all right to me. In fact — and this is the point of

25

what I started out to say — after all she'd done to me, I felt in that moment the old spell, the old enchantment. She seemed charming, as always. She held out both her hands — '

'She would,' snarled Ryder. 'May I have another drink?'

'She was lovely,' Swan went on. 'Just at that moment Dinsdale came in, and with him a young fellow named Beaton — '

'Hugh Beaton,' Romano cried. 'The infant she has snatched from the cradle. The callow child she would exchange for me across the counters of Reno. Bah! I, too, must drink again.'

'Yes, it turned out that way,' Swan admitted. 'He was her latest flame. She introduced him as such, with all her old arrogance. Also his sister, quite a pretty girl. The romance was rather gone from our meeting.'

'What was Landini doing at the Tavern?' Ward inquired.

'I gathered she was a friend of Dinsdale, and had just driven over for dinner. She's not stopping there, of course — she's served four weeks of her cure at Reno, and she's not staying out of the state more than a few hours. Naturally, I didn't linger. I hurried away.' He looked about the group. 'But pardon me. I didn't mean to monopolize the conversation.'

'It was Ellen who was doing that,' smiled Dudley Ward, 'not you. Up to her old tricks again. Dinner, gentlemen, is at seven. In the meantime, Sing will show you to your various rooms, though I'm afraid you'll have to sort out your own baggage in the upper hall. Doctor Swan, I've assigned you a room, even though, to my regret, you're not staying the night. Ah Sing — where is the old rascal?'

The servant appeared, and led the procession above.

Ward laid a hand on Charlie Chan's arm. 'At a quarter to seven, in my study up-stairs at the front of the house,' he said softly. 'For just a few minutes.'

Chan nodded.

'One more thing, gentlemen,' Ward called. 'No one need dress. This is strictly stag, of course.'

He stood and watched them disappear, an ironical smile on his face.

Presently Charlie entered a warm and pleasant bedroom, meekly following Ah Sing. The old man turned on the lights, set down Chan's bags, then looked up at his compatriot from Honolulu. His face was lean and the color of a lemon that has withered, his shoulders were hunched and bent. His eyes alone betrayed his race; and in them Chan detected an authentic gleam of humor.

'P'liceman?' said Ah Sing.

Charlie admitted it, with a smile.

'Some people say plitty wise man?' continued Sing. 'Maybe.'

'Maybe,' agreed Charlie.

Sing nodded sagely, and went out.

Charlie stepped to the window, and looked down an aisle of tall pines at snow-covered hills and a bit of wintry sky. The novelty of this scene so engrossed him that he was three minutes late for his appointment with his host in the study.

'That's all right,' Dudley Ward said, when Chan apologized. 'I'm not going over the whole business here — I'll have to do it anyhow at the table. I just want to say I'm glad you've come, and I hope you'll be able to help me.'

'I shall extend myself to utmost,' Charlie assured him.

'It's rather a small matter for a man of your talents,' Ward went on. He was sitting behind a broad desk, over which an alabaster lamp cast its glow. 'But I can assure you it's important to me. I got you in here just to make sure you know why I invited these three men up here tonight — but now I've done it, I realize I must be insulting your intelligence.'

Chan smiled. 'On second thoughts, you changed original plan?'

'Yes. I thought when I wrote you, I'd just get in touch with them by letter. But that's a terribly unsatisfactory way of dealing with things — at least, I've always thought so. I like to see a man's face when I'm asking him questions. Then I heard this Romano was in San Francisco, and broke — I knew money would bring him here. Swan was already in Reno, and Ryder — well, he and I've been friends from boyhood, and the fact that he was Ellen's second husband never made any difference between us. So I resolved to bring them all together here to-night.'

Charlie nodded. 'A bright plan,' he agreed.

'I'll ask all the questions,' Ward continued. 'What sort of replies I'll get, I don't know. None of them loves Landini any too much, I imagine, but because of one reason or another — perhaps in view of promises made long ago — the information we are after may be difficult to get. I rely on you to watch each one carefully, and to sense it if any one of them fails to tell the truth. You've had plenty of experience along that line, I fancy.'

'I fear you over-estimate my poor ability,' Charlie protested.

'Nonsense,' cried Ward. 'We're bound to get a clue somewhere. We may even get all we're after. But whether we do or not, I want you to feel that you are here not just as an investigator, but as my guest, and an honored one.' Before him on the desk stood twin boxes; one of bright yellow, the other a deep crimson. He opened the nearer one, and pushed it toward Chan. 'Will you have a cigarette before dinner?' he invited. Charlie declined, and taking one himself, Ward rose and lighted it. 'Cozy little room, this,' he suggested.

'The reply is obvious,' Chan nodded. He glanced about, reflecting that some woman must have had a hand here. Gay cretonnes hung at the windows, the shades of the several lamps about the room were of delicate silk; the rug was deep and soft.

'Please use it as your own,' his host said. 'Any work you have to do — letters and the like — come in here. We'll be getting on down-stairs now, eh?' Charlie noted for the first time that the man's hands trembled, and that a faint perspiration shone on his forehead. 'A damned important dinner for me,' Ward added, and his voice broke suddenly in the middle of the sentence.

But when they reached the group down-stairs before the fire, the host was again his debonair self, assured and smiling. He led his four guests through a brief passageway to the dining-room, and assigned them to their places.

That great oak-paneled room, that table gleaming with silver, spoke eloquently of the prestige of the family of Ward. Ever since the days of Virginia City and the Comstock Lode, the name had been known and honored in this western country. No boat around the Horn for the first Dudley Ward, he had trekked in with the gold rush, a member of that gallant band of whom it has been well said: 'The cowards never started, and the weaklings died on the way.' Now this famous family had dwindled to the polished, gray-haired gentleman at the head of the table, and Charlie, thinking of his own eleven children at home in Honolulu, glanced around the board and sighed over the futility of such a situation.

In its earlier stages, the dinner seemed a trifle strained, despite the urbane chatter of the host. Charlie alone knew why he was there; the others seemed inclined to silent speculation. Evidently Ward was not yet ready to enlighten them. As Ah Sing moved along with the main course, Charlie said a few words to him in Cantonese, and got a brief answer in the same dialect.

'Pardon, please,' Chan bowed to his host. 'I take the liberty of asking Ah Sing his age. His reply is not altogether clear.'

Ward smiled. 'I don't suppose the old boy really knows. In the late seventies, I fancy — a long life, and most of it spent in our service. I know it's not the thing to talk about one's servants — but Ah Sing years ago passed out of that category. He's been one of the family for as long as I can remember.'

'I have heard, my heart bursting with pride,' Chan said, 'of the loyalty and devotion of old Chinese servants in this state.'

Ryder spoke suddenly. 'Everything you have heard is true,' he said. He turned to Ward. 'I remember when we were kids, Dudley. Great Scott, how good Sing was to us in those days. The stuff he used to cook for us — grumbling all the time. Huge bowls of rice with meat gravy — I dream of them yet. He'd been with you ages then, hadn't he?'

'My grandfather picked him up in Nevada,' Ward replied. 'He came to our house when I was just three years old. I remember, because I had a birthday party that day on the lawn, and Sing was serving — his first day. There were a lot of bees down in the meadow and I imagine they were attracted by Sing's cooking, just as we kids were. Anyhow, I remember Sing — a young man then — marching toward us proudly bearing the cake,

32

when a bee suddenly stung him on the leg. He dropped the cake, let out a yell and looked at my mother accusingly. 'Melican buttahfly too damn hot,' he complained. If I were to write my memoirs, I think I should have to begin with that — my first conscious recollection.'

'I guess I missed that party,' Ryder said. 'It came a couple of years too soon for me. But I remember many a later one, in Sing's kitchen. Always a friend in need to us boys, Sing was.'

Ward's face was serious. 'They're dying out,' he remarked. 'The ones like Sing. Somebody ought to put up a statue in Golden Gate Park — or at least a tablet somewhere on one of the famous trails — to the best friends Californians ever had.'

Sing came in at that moment, and the subject was dropped. A long silence ensued. Romano and Swan seemed to be getting rather impatient over the long delay in reaching the real business of the evening. Since the discussion that had broken out on their first entrance, Ellen Landini had not been so much as mentioned. Romano's cheeks were flushed, his white hands fluttered nervously over his plate, he fidgeted in his chair. Swan also showed various signs of restlessness.

Coffee was finally brought, and then a tray

of cut-glass decanters was set before Dudley Ward.

'I have here, gentlemen,' he remarked, 'some Benedictine, creme de menthe, peach brandy. Also, some port wine. All pre-prohibition — you break no law in my house. What will you have? Just a moment — Sing! Where the devil is that boy?' He rang the bell, and the old Chinese hurriedly returned. 'Sing — take the gentlemen's orders — and fill them. And now — '

He paused, and they all looked at him expectantly. 'Now, gentlemen, you are wondering why you are here. You are wondering why Inspector Chan, of the Honolulu Police, is here. I have kept you waiting an intolerably long time, I know, but the truth is, I am loath to bring this matter up. To introduce it properly I shall have to go into a subject that I had hoped was for ever dead and forgotten — my life with Ellen Landini.'

He pushed his chair back from the table, and crossed his legs. 'Sing — you haven't overlooked the cigars? Ah, yes — gentlemen, help yourselves. I — I married Ellen Landini nearly twenty years ago, in San Francisco. She had just come to town from the islands, a young girl of eighteen, with a voice — even then it was magical. But she had more than the voice, she had a freshness, a vivacity, a

34

beauty — however, I needn't go into her charm, surely not in this company. She gave a little concert, I saw her, heard her sing. The courtship was brief. We were married, and went to Paris on our honeymoon.

'That year in Paris — I shall never forget it. I want to be fair. She was wonderful — then. She studied with the best teacher in Europe, and what he told her about her voice made her supremely happy. It made me happy, too — for a time.

'Only gradually did I come to see that this wonderful year had wrecked my dreams — my hopes for a home, for children. Domestic life was now impossible for us. She was determined to become a professional singer. I saw myself, the prima donna's husband, carrying a dog about Europe, waiting at stage doors, enduring for ever an artistic temperament. The career did not appeal to me. I said so.

'Perhaps I was unreasonable. I want, as I have said, to be fair to her. Men were not so complacent about careers for their wives in those days. At any rate, there began a series of endless quarrels. I brought her home from Paris, to San Francisco, and thence, since it was spring, up to this house. I could see she would never be reconciled to the life I wanted.'

He was silent for a moment. 'I apologize humbly,' he went on, 'for dragging you into affairs that should be private. I must add, however, that our quarrels became daily more bitter, that we began to say unforgivable things, to hate each other. I could see her hate in her eyes when she looked at me. One June day — in this very room — matters came to a climax and she left the house. She never returned.

'I refused to divorce her, but when, nearly a year later, she applied for a divorce in some middle-western state, on a false charge of desertion, I did not contest the suit. I still loved her — or rather, the girl I thought I had married — but I realized she was lost to me for ever. I balanced the account and closed the books.'

He turned to the doctor. 'Doctor Swan — won't you try that brandy again? Just help yourself, please. So far, gentlemen, you can see no reason for my story. But there is something more — and only within the past ten days have I come upon the trail of it.

'I have been told, by some one who ought to know, that when Ellen Landini left my house she carried with her a secret which she had not seen fit to divulge to me. I have heard, from a source I believe reliable, that less than seven months after she left this

36

place, she gave birth to a child, in a New York hospital. A son. Her son — and mine.'

He did not go on for a moment. All the men about the table were looking at him, some with pity, some with amazement.

'I have said,' Ward went on, 'that Ellen hated me. Perhaps with reason — oh, I want to be just. She hated me so much, evidently, that she was determined I must never have the satisfaction of knowing about — my boy. Perhaps she feared it would start the old argument all over again. Perhaps it was just — hate. I — I think it was rather cruel.'

'She was always cruel,' said Ryder harshly. He laid a sympathetic hand on Dudley Ward's arm.

'At any rate,' Ward went on, 'she gave this child for adoption to some wealthy friends of hers. It wasn't legal adoption, of course. But she agreed to give him up for ever, to let him be known by another name, never to try to see him. She could do that. Her career was everything.

'That, gentlemen, ends my story. You can see my position. I am not — not so young as I was. My brother and sister are both dead, childless. Somewhere in this world, if the story is true, and the boy lived, I have a son, now nearly eighteen. All this — is his. I intend to find him.' His voice grew louder. 'By heaven, I will find him. As far as Landini is concerned, bygones are bygones. I have no more hatred. But I want my boy.

'That is why,' he continued in a lower tone, 'I have sent for Inspector Chan. I shall back him to the limit in this search. I've had only ten days — I've only started — '

'Who told you all this?' Ryder inquired.

'Ah — that's rather interesting,' Ward replied. 'It was Ellen's return to this part of the world that, indirectly, brought it out. It seems that about eight years ago, when Ellen came to Nevada to divorce — er — Doctor Swan, she was, at the moment, interested in — you will pardon me, Doctor — '

Swan smiled. 'Oh, that's perfectly all right. We've all been victims — we can speak freely here. She wanted to divorce me because she had fallen in love — or thought she had — with her chauffeur, a handsome boy named Michael Ireland. I came out to fight the divorce — but she got it anyhow. She didn't, however, get Michael. It was one of her few defeats in that line. The day before her divorce, young Michael eloped with Ellen's maid, a French girl named Cecile. The maid just took him away from her. It was rather amusing. Michael and his wife are still living in Reno, and the former is a pilot for a passenger airplane company over there.'

'Precisely,' nodded Ward. 'When I first came up here two weeks ago I sent to Reno for a couple of servants — a cook and an up-stairs maid — and the latter happened to be Michael's wife. It seems they're not very prosperous, and she'd decided to go into service temporarily. She knew, of course, my connection with Ellen Landini when she came here, but for a time she said nothing. Naturally, I had never seen or heard of the woman before. But it appears that Ellen is doing a great deal of flying during her stay in Reno, and her favorite pilot is Michael Ireland. Cecile is wildly jealous, and that is no doubt what led her to come to me with the story about my son. She claims she went with Ellen as personal maid shortly before the baby was born, and that she had been sworn to eternal secrecy in the matter.'

Ryder shook his head. 'The story of a jealous woman,' he remarked. 'I'm sorry, Dudley, but aren't you building a bit too much on that? Not the best evidence, you know.'

Ward nodded. 'I know. Still, I can't well ignore a thing as important as this. And as the woman told it, I must admit it had the ring of truth. Also, I recalled certain little things that had happened, things that Ellen had said during her last mad weeks in this house — it

39

is quite possible the story is true. And I mean to find out whether it's true or not.'

'Have you questioned Landini?' asked Doctor Swan.

'I have not,' replied Ward. 'In the first excitement of the moment, I called her hotel in Reno, but before I got the connection, I had sense enough to ring off. Inspector Chan may have an interview with her later, if he sees fit, but I would expect nothing to come of it. I know her of old.

'No, gentlemen, it is to you three that, at the beginning of this hunt, I have seen fit to pin my hopes. You have all, like myself, been married to Landini. I do not believe that she would ever have deliberately told any of you about this child, but even so — these things sometimes come out. A telegram opened by mistake, a telephone call in some strange city, a chance meeting — by one or another of these methods, one of you may have come upon her secret. I am not asking you to be disloyal in any way. But I do contend that if Ellen deceived me in this matter, it was a piece of unwarranted cruelty, and as man to man I ask you, if you can, to relieve me of this horrible suspense. Nothing shall happen to Landini, or to the boy, save to his advantage. But — you can see — I am in hell over this — and I must know — I must know.'

His voice rose to an almost hysterical pitch as he looked appealingly about the table. John Ryder spoke first.

'Dudley,' he said, 'no one would be happier to help you now than I would be — if I could. God knows I have no wish to spare the feelings of Ellen Landini. But as you know, my life with her was of the briefest — and that was the only lucky break I ever got where she was concerned. So brief and so hectic that I never heard of this matter you have brought up to-night — never dreamed of it. I — I'm sorry.'

Ward nodded. 'I was afraid of that.' He looked toward Swan and Romano, and his expression changed. 'Before we go any further, I may add that I am willing to pay handsomely — and I mean no offense — for any information that may be of help. Doctor Swan — you were married to Landini for several years — '

Swan's eyelids narrowed. He toyed with his coffee cup, took out his eye-glasses, put them on, restored them to his pocket.

'Don't misunderstand me,' he said slowly. 'Landini means nothing to me, despite what I said earlier about her charm when I saw her again at the Tavern. It isn't very pleasant to be thrown over for a chauffeur.' Across his usually pleasant face shot a look of

41

malevolence that was startling and unexpected. 'No,' he added harshly, 'I have no wish to protect the woman — but I'm sorry to say that this is — well, it's all news to me.'

Ward's face was gray and tired as he turned to Romano. The opera conductor shot his cuffs and spoke.

'The figures — er — the figures of the amount you wish to pay, Mr. Ward — I leave them entirely to you. I rely on your reputation as a gentleman.'

'I think you may safely do so,' replied Ward grimly.

'Landini — she is still my wife — but what does she mean to me? In New York were drawn up terms of settlement by which I was to release her for this new divorce. Has she made the initial payment? She has not. I must live — is it not so? Once I had a career of my own — I was aimed high for success — all gone now. She has done that to me. She has wrecked my life — and now she casts me off.' He clenched his fist that lay on the table, and a sudden fire gleamed in his dark eyes.

'You were going to tell me — ' suggested Ward.

'There was, sir, a telegram opened by mistake. I opened it. It held some news of that son of hers. She told me little, but enough. There was a son. That much I can say. I have, of course, no recollection of the signature on the telegram.'

'But — the town from which it was sent?' Ward cried.

Romano looked at him — the sly anxious look of a man who needs money — needs it badly enough to lie for it, perhaps.

'The town I do not now remember,' Romano said. 'But I will think — I will think hard — and it will come to me, I am sure.'

Ward looked hopelessly at Charlie Chan. He sighed. At that instant, from the big room beyond the passage came the slamming of a door, and then, sharp and clear, the bark of a dog.

The four guests of Dudley Ward looked up in amazement, as though they found something sinister and disquieting in that bark. Sing came shuffling in and, leaning over the chair of the host, spoke in a low tone. Ward nodded, and gave a direction. Then, an ironical smile on his face, he rose to his feet.

'Gentlemen,' he said, 'I hope you will not be too much annoyed by my peculiar sense of humor. I have acted on impulse — and I may have been wrong. But it came to me when Doctor Swan spoke of his encounter at the Tavern — there was just one person lacking to make our party complete. And since she was so near — '

'Landini,' cried Ryder. 'You have invited Landini here?'

'For a very brief call — I have.'

'I won't see her,' Ryder protested. 'I swore years ago I'd never see her again — '

'Oh, come on, John,' Ward said. 'Be modern. Landini will regard it as a lark — I didn't tell her you were all here, but I know she won't care. Doctor Swan has already seen her. Mr. Romano has no objections — '

'Me?' cried Romano. 'I want to talk to her!'

'Precisely. I am willing to forget the past. Come on, John.'

Ryder's eyes were on the table. 'All right,' he agreed.

Dudley Ward smiled. 'Gentlemen,' he said, 'shall we join the lady?'

# 3

## The Fallen Flower

But when they stepped through the passage into the living-room the lady was not there. Two men were warming themselves before the fire: one, a round, cheery, red-faced little man, the other a pale youth with black curly hair and a weak but handsome face. The older of the two stepped forward.

'Hello, Dudley,' he said. 'This is like old times, isn't it? Ellen back at the old house again and — er — ah — and all that.'

'Hello, Jim,' Ward replied. He introduced his guests to Jim, who was, it appeared, Mr. Dinsdale, manager of the Tavern. When he had finished, the hotel man turned to the boy who accompanied him.

'This is Mr. Hugh Beaton,' he announced. 'Ellen and Mr. Beaton's sister have gone up-stairs to leave their wraps, and — '

Mr. Romano had leaped to the boy's side and was shaking his hand. 'Ah, Mr. Beaton,' he cried, 'I have wanted to see you. There is so much I must say.'

'Y-yes,' replied the boy with a startled air.

'Indeed — yes. You are taking over a very great responsibility. You, a musician, need not be told that. The talent — the genius — of Ellen Landini — it is something to guard, to watch over, to encourage. That is your duty in the name of Art. How does she behave with the pastries?'

'The — the what?' stammered the boy.

'The pastries? She has a wild passion for them. And it must be curbed. It is no easy matter, but she must be held back with a strong hand. Otherwise she will — she will expand — she will grow gross. And cigarettes. How many cigarettes do you permit her each day?'

'I permit her?' Beaton stared at Romano as at a madman. 'Why — that's no affair of mine.'

Romano looked toward high heaven.

'Ah — it is as I feared. You are too young to understand. Too young for this huge task. No affair of yours? My dear sir, in that case she is lost. She will smoke her voice into eternal silence. She will wreck her great career for ever — '

He was interrupted by a commotion at the head of the stairs, and Ellen Landini began to descend. The long stairway against one side of the room afforded her an excellent entrance. Of this she was not unaware;

46

indeed, she had just sent her companion back on a trivial errand in order that she might have the stage to herself. Which of itself was a good description of Ellen Landini, once young and lovely and innocent, but now a bit too plump, a bit too blonde, and a bit too wise in the tricks of the trade.

She had decided on a dramatic entrance, and such was the one she made, holding in her arms a small Boston terrier who looked world-weary and old. Dudley Ward awaited her at the foot of the stairs; she saw him and him alone.

'Welcome home, Ellen,' he said.

'Dudley,' she cried. 'Dear old Dudley, after all these years. But' — she held aloft the dog — 'but poor Trouble — '

'Trouble?' repeated Ward, puzzled.

'Yes — that's his name — but you don't know. You wouldn't. From the baby in Madame Butterfly. My baby — my sweet poor baby — he's having a chill. I knew I shouldn't bring him — it's bitter cold on the lake — it always was on this lake. Where's Sing? Call Sing at once.' The old man appeared on the stairs behind her. 'Oh, Sing — take Trouble to the kitchen and give him some hot milk. Make him drink it.'

'My take 'um,' replied Sing with a bored look.

Landini followed him with many admonitions. A young girl in a smart dinner gown had come unostentatiously down the stairs, and Ward was greeting her. He turned to the others.

'This is Miss Leslie Beaton,' he said. 'I'm sure we're all happy to have her here — '

But Landini was back in the room, overflowing personality and energy and charm. 'Darling old Sing,' she cried. 'The same as ever. I've thought of him so often. He was always — ' She stopped suddenly as her eyes moved unbelievingly about the little group.

Dudley Ward permitted himself a delighted smile. 'I think, Ellen,' he said, 'you already know these Gentlemen.'

She wanted a moment, obviously, to get her breath and she found it when her glance fell on Charlie Chan. 'Not — not all of them,' she said.

'Oh, yes — pardon me,' Ward answered. 'May I present Inspector Charlie Chan, of the Honolulu Police? On vacation, I should add.'

Charlie stepped forward and bowed low over her hand. 'Overcome,' he murmured.

'Inspector Chan,' she said. 'I've heard of you.'

'It would be tarnishing the lily with gilt,' Charlie assured her, 'to remark I have heard of you. Speaking further on the subject, I once, with great difficulty, heard you sing.'

'With — great difficulty?'

'Yes — you may recall. The night you stopped over for a concert in your home city, Honolulu. At the Royal Hawaiian Opera House — and they had but recently applied to it the new tin roof — '

The great Landini clapped her hands and laughed. 'And it rained!' she cried. 'I should say I do remember! It was my only night — the boat was leaving at twelve — and so I sang — and sang. There in that boiler-factory — or so it seemed — with the downpour on the tin above. What a concert! But that was — some years — ago.'

'I was impressed at the time by your extreme youthfulness,' Charlie remarked.

She gave him a ravishing smile. 'I shall sing again for you some day,' she said. 'And it will not be raining then.'

Her poise regained, sure of herself now, she turned to the odd party into which Dudley Ward had brought her. 'What fun,' she cried. 'What wonderful fun! All my dear ones gathered together. John — looking as stern as ever — Frederic — I miss the reflector on your forehead. I always think of you wearing that. And Luis — you here — of all people — '

Mr. Romano stepped forward with his usual promptness. 'Yes, you may bet I am here,' he replied, his eyes flashing. 'I, of all people, and of all people I will be present at a good many places to which you travel in the future — unless your memory speedily improves. Must I recall to you an arrangement made in New York — '

'Luis — not here!' She stamped her foot.

'No, perhaps not here. But somewhere — soon — depend on that. Look at your shoes!'

'What is wrong with my shoes?'

'Wet! Soaking wet!' He turned hotly on young Beaton. 'Are there, then, no rubbers in the world? Is the supply of arctics exhausted? I told you — you do not understand your job. You let her walk about in the snow in her evening slippers. What sort of husband is that for Ellen Landini — '

'Oh, do be quiet, Luis,' Landini cried. 'You were always so tiresome — a nurse. Do you think I want a nurse? I do not — and that is what I like about Hugh.' She stepped toward the boy, who appeared to draw back a bit. 'Hugh is more interested in romance than in arctics — aren't you, my dear?'

She ran her fingers affectionately through the young man's black hair, a theatrical gesture that was a bit upsetting to all who saw it. Dudley Ward, looking hastily away, caught on the face of Hugh Beaton's sister an expression of such bitter disgust that he sought to divert the girl's attention.

'Your first visit west, Miss Beaton?' he inquired.

'My very first,' she answered. 'I love it, too. All except — '

'Reno.'

'Naturally — I don't like that. The place sort of puts a blight on one's outlook — don't you think? What price romance — after seeing Reno?'

'Pity you feel that way,' Ward said. He looked at her admiringly. Hugh Beaton's sister was even prettier than he was. But there was a worried look about her brown eyes — the lips that should be always laughing were drawn and tired.

'Dudley — it's marvelous to be back here.' Landini was drawing him again into the general conversation. 'It's just as well you invited me, because I was coming anyway. Several times I've been on the point of descending on you.'

'I should have been charmed,' Ward replied.

'And surprised,' she laughed, 'because I mean that literally — descending on you. You see, I've flown over you often, and seen that flying field you've had cleared behind the house.'

'Oh, yes' Ward nodded. 'So many of my friends have planes — and I like to fly a bit myself.'

'My pilot told me he'd land any time,' Landini continued. 'But somehow — the hour never seemed right — too late — too early — or we had to hurry back.'

'You enjoy flying, I hear?' It was Doctor Swan who spoke, and there was an expression on his face that mingled malice and contempt.

'Oh — I adore it! It's the biggest thrill in the world. It's living — at last. Especially here, above the snow-capped mountains, and these marvelous lakes. And I've found such a wonder of a pilot — '

'So I've been told,' Swan answered. 'But as I recall, you found him some years ago — '

Landini walked quickly to where John Ryder was standing, as far apart from the others as he could get.

'John,' she said, 'I'm so happy to see you again. You're looking well.'

'Unfortunately,' Ryder said, 'I'm looking better than I feel. Dudley, I'm afraid I shall have to be excused. Good night.' He bowed to the room in general, and went hastily up the stairs.

Ellen Landini shrugged her generous shoulders and laughed. 'Poor John,' she said. 'Always he took life so seriously. What is to be gained by that? But we are what we are — we can not change — '

'Ellen,' said Dudley Ward, 'you enjoy seeing the old place again?'

'I adore it,' she sparkled. 'I'm simply wild with joy.'

He looked at her in amazement — still sparkling, after all these years. Not since she came in had she let down for a minute. He thought back to the days of their marriage. It had been one of the things that had driven him mad. 'Every day is Christmas with Landini,' he had once complained to himself.

'Then perhaps you'd like to take a tour about,' Ward continued. 'There are a few changes — I'd like to show them to you. If my guests will be so very good as to excuse me.'

There was a polite murmur, and Dinsdale raised his glass. 'These highballs of yours, Dudley, excuse anything,' he laughed.

'Good,' smiled Ward. 'Ellen, I want you to see the old study, I've just had it done over by a decorator. Probably all wrong. And as we can't afford any scandal, I'm taking along a chaperon. Inspector Chan — will you join us?'

'With great pleasure,' smiled Charlie. 'Everybody knows policeman always on hand when least needed.'

Ellen Landini laughed with the others, but there was a deeply puzzled look in her blue eyes. Dinsdale came forward, looking at his watch.

'Just to remind you, Ellen,' he said. 'You'll have to be starting soon if you're to be back in Reno by midnight.'

'What time is it, Jim?'

'It's twenty-five minutes to ten.'

'I'm starting at ten, and I'll be back in Reno before eleven.'

He shook his head. 'Not to-night — over these roads,' he said.

'To-night,' she laughed. 'But not over these roads. Not for little Ellen.'

Hugh Beaton looked up. 'Ellen — what are you talking about?' he asked.

She gave him a loving glance. 'Now, be a good boy. You and Leslie go back by car from the Tavern. It's a nasty old car, and you're liable to have a few blowouts just as we did coming over, but that won't matter to you. However, I must make better time. I had an inspiration when Dudley here called up and invited me to drop in on him. I telephoned to Reno for my favorite plane and pilot, and they'll be here at ten. Won't it be glorious?

54

There's a gorgeous moon — I'm simply thrilled to death.' She turned to Ward. 'Michael told me you have lights on the field?'

Ward nodded. 'Yes. I'll turn them on presently. Everything's in order — that's a grand idea of yours. But then — your ideas always were.'

Romano, who had been talking violently with Hugh Beaton in a corner, rose quickly. 'I will go to my room,' he announced, 'and I will make for you a list. The things she must do, and the things she must not do. It will be useful — '

'Oh, please don't trouble,' Beaton protested.

'It is my duty,' Romano said sternly.

Ward stood aside, and let his guests precede him up the stairs. Romano walked close to Landini's side, and as they came into the upper hall, he swung on her. 'Where is my money?' he demanded.

'Luis — I don't know — oh, hasn't it been sent?'

'You know very well it has not been sent. How am I to live — '

'But, Luis — there has been trouble — my investments — oh, please, please don't bother me now.'

'I suggest, Mr. Romano,' Ward said, 'that

you comply with Madame Landini's wishes. This, I believe, is the door of your room.'

'As you say,' shrugged Romano. 'But, Ellen, I have not finished. There must be an understanding before we part.'

He disappeared, and the three others went into the study in front. Ward flashed on the floor lamps, and Landini dropped into the chair beside the desk. Both men saw that her face was suddenly drawn and haggard, all the vivacity gone. Then she did let down at times. It was not always Christmas; it was sometimes the morning after.

'Oh, the little beast,' she cried. 'I hate him. Dudley, you can see what my life has been — lived in a whirlwind, excitement, madness, filled all the time with noisy nothings. I'm so tired — so deathly tired. If only I could find peace — '

Charlie Chan saw that Ward's face was filled with genuine tenderness and pity. 'I know, my dear,' said the host, as he closed the door. 'But peace was never for you — we knew that in the old days. It had to be the limelit highway — the bright parade. Come — pull yourself together.' He offered her one of the colored boxes on the desk. 'Have a cigarette. Or perhaps you prefer this other brand.' He reached for the companion box.

She took one from the latter, and lighted it.

'Dudley,' she said, 'coming here has taken me back to my girlhood. It has touched me deeply — ' She looked toward Charlie Chan.

A sudden harshness came into Ward's eyes. 'Sorry,' he said. 'Mr. Chan stays. I was wondering why you accepted my invitation to-night. I see now — it was to pull this airplane stunt. The spectacular thing — the thing you would do. Has it occurred to you to wonder — why I invited you?'

'Why — I thought, of course — after all, you did love me once. I thought you would like to see me again. But when I saw John, and Frederic, and Luis — I was puzzled — '

'Naturally. I invited you, Ellen, because I wanted you to realize that I am in touch with your various husbands. I wanted you, also, to meet Inspector Charlie Chan who, as you know, is a detective. Inspector Chan and I have begun to-night an investigation which may take us many weeks — or which may end here and now. You have it in your power to end it. Ellen, I have no bitterness, no ill will for you at this late day. I have thought it over so long — perhaps I was wrong from the first. But I have brought you to Pineview to ask you, simply — where is my son?'

Charlie Chan, watching, reflected that here was either a great actress or a much maligned woman. Her expression did not change.

'What son?' she asked.

Ward shrugged his shoulders. 'Very well,' he said. 'We won't go any further with it.'

'Oh, yes, we will,' said Ellen Landini. 'Dudley — don't be a fool. Some one has told you a lie, evidently. Don't you know they've been lying about me for years? I've got so I don't mind — but if you've heard something that's made you unhappy — that's sending you off on a wild-goose chase — well, I'd like to stop that, if I can. If you'll only tell me — '

'No matter,' said Ward. 'What's the use?'

'If you take that tone,' she replied, 'it's hopeless.' She was surprisingly cool and calm. 'By the way — hadn't you better turn on the lights on the field? And I should like a small blanket for Trouble — he'll need it, in addition to the robes in the plane. I'll send it back to you. He'll go with me, of course. He loves it.'

'Very well,' nodded Ward. 'I'll see about it, and then I'll get down to those lights.' He went to the door. 'Cecile,' he called. 'Oh, Sing — send Cecile to me, please.'

He stepped back into the room. 'Cecile?' said Ellen Landini.

'Yes,' Ward said. 'An old servant of yours, I believe. The wife of your wonder pilot. You didn't know she was here?'

Landini lighted another cigarette. 'I did

not. But I might have guessed it these last few minutes. A liar Dudley, always, with a temper like the devil. She stole from me, too, but naturally, one expects that. But the truth was not in her. I don't know what cock-and-bull story she has told you, but whatever it is — '

'What makes you think it was she who told me?'

'I have discovered that a lie has been told in this house, Dudley, and now I discover Cecile is here. It's effect and cause, my dear.'

'You wanted me, sir?' The Frenchwoman at the door was about thirty, with lovely eyes, but an unhappy and discontented face. For a long moment she stared at Landini. 'Ah, Madame,' she murmured.

'How are you, Cecile?' the singer asked.

'I am well, thank you.' She turned to Ward, inquiringly.

'Cecile,' said her employer, 'please go and get Madame Landini a small blanket of some sort — something suitable to wrap about a dog.'

'A dog?' The eyes of the Frenchwoman narrowed. There was a moment's silence, and in the quiet they all heard, suddenly, a far-off but unmistakable sound — the droning of an airplane. Ward flung open the French windows that led on to a balcony, which was in reality the roof of the front veranda. The

59

others crowded about him, and in the moonlit sky, far out over the lake, they saw the approaching plane.

'Ah, yes,' cried Cecile, 'I understand. Madame returns to Reno by air.'

'Is that any affair of yours?' Landini asked coldly.

'It happens to be, Madame,' the woman answered.

'Will you get that blanket?' Ward demanded.

Without a word, the Frenchwoman went out. Ward looked at his watch.

'Your pilot's ahead of time,' he said. 'I must hurry out to those lights — '

'Dudley — would you do something — ' Landini cried.

'Too late. When the plane has landed — '

He hastened out. The singer turned to Charlie.

'Tell me,' she said. 'Do you know which is Mr. Ryder's room?'

Charlie bowed. 'I think I do.'

'Then please go to him. Send him here at once. Tell him I must see him — he must come — don't take no for an answer! Tell him — it's life and death!'

She fairly pushed the detective from the room. He hurried down the hall and knocked on the door of the room into which he had seen Ryder ushered before dinner. Without awaiting an answer, he opened it and entered. Ryder was seated reading a book beside a floor lamp.

'So sorry,' Charlie remarked. 'The intrusion is objectionable, I realize. But Madame Landini — '

'What about Madame Landini?' asked Ryder grimly.

'She must see you at once — in the study at the front. She demands this wildly. It is, she tells me life and death.'

Ryder shrugged. 'Rot! There is nothing to be said between us. She knows that.'

'But — '

'Yes — life and death — I know. Don't be fooled by her theatrics. She was always that way. Kindly tell her I refuse to see her.'

Chan hesitated. Ryder got up and led him to the door. 'Tell her that under no circumstances will I ever see her again.'

Charlie found himself in the hall, with Ryder's door closed behind him. When he got back to the study Landini was seated at the desk, writing madly.

'I am so sorry — ' the detective began.

She looked up. 'He won't see me? I expected it. No matter, Mr. Chan. I have thought of another way. Thanks.'

Chan turned, and went down the hall toward the head of the stairs. As he passed the open door of Romano's room, he saw the conductor walking anxiously up and down. Ryder's door remained closed. The noise of the plane was momentarily growing louder.

In the living-room Dinsdale and Hugh Beaton were alone, evidently vastly uninterested in the spectacular approach of Landini's pilot. Charlie was not so callous and stepping out the front door, he crossed the porch and walked a short distance down the path to the pier. He was staring up at the lights of the plane, when some one approached from the direction of the water. It was Doctor Swan.

'Went out on the pier to see it better,' Swan said. 'A beautiful sight, on a night like this. Wish I could go back in it myself.' The aviator was turning in toward the house.

'Shall we find the landing field?' Charlie suggested.

'Not for me,' Swan shivered. 'It's somewhere at the back, God knows where. I'm going to get my things — I want to start for the Tavern as soon as Ellen has made her grand exit.' He ran up the steps to the house.

Michael Ireland, it appeared, was planning a few stunts. Despite the tallness of the pines, he swept down on the house, dangerously near. Hurrying through the snow to the rear, Charlie was conscious that the plane was circling about above the roof

62

of Pineview. Aviators never could resist the spectacular. Presently Chan came upon a cleared place, flooded with lights, and there, when the pilot had completed his exhibition, he finally brought the plane down, in a skillful landing.

'Pretty work,' cried a voice at Chan's elbow. It was Dudley Ward. 'By gad, that lad knows how to drive his old two-seater.'

He hurried out to meet Ireland on the field, and led him back to where Charlie stood. All three went up the narrow path to the back door, and entered a long passage that led to the front of the house. As they passed the open door of the kitchen Chan saw a large woman, evidently the cook. With her was Landini's dog, whining and still shivering from its chill. Ward led on to the living-room.

'Nice night for it,' he was saying to Ireland, a husky red-cheeked man of thirty or so. 'I envy you — the way you brought her down.' Dinsdale and Beaton rose to greet them, and the aviator, pulling off a huge glove, shook hands all round. 'Sit down a minute,' Ward continued. 'You'll want a drink before you start back.'

'Thank you, sir,' Ireland replied. 'And maybe I'd better be havin' a word with my wife — '

Ward nodded. 'I fancy you had,' he smiled. 'I'll arrange that. But first of all — what will it be? A highball?'

'Sounds good to me,' Ireland answered. He looked a bit apprehensive and ill at ease. 'Not too much, Mr. Ward, please — '

Ryder appeared on the stairs, lighting a cigarette. Halfway down, he paused. 'Has Landini gone?' he inquired.

'Come along, John,' Ward said genially. 'Just in time for another little drink. Is that right for you, Ireland?'

'Just, thank you,' the aviator replied.

From somewhere up-stairs came a sharp report that sounded unpleasantly like the firing of a pistol.

'What was that?' asked Ryder, now at the foot of the stairs.

Ward set down the bottle he was holding and looked toward Charlie Chan. 'I wonder,' he said.

Charlie did not pause to wonder. Pushing Ryder aside, he ran up the stairs. He was conscious of figures in the upper hall as he passed, figures he did not pause to identify. Chinese, he had always contended, were psychic people, but he did not have to be particularly psychic on this occasion to know which door to seek. It was closed. He pushed it open.

The lights in the study were out, but for a first glance the moonlight sufficed. Landini was lying just inside the French windows that led on to the balcony. Charlie leaped across her and peered out the open window. He saw no one.

Black shapes crowded the doorway. 'Turn on the lights,' Charlie said. 'And do not come too close, please.'

The lights flashed on, and Dudley Ward pushed forward. 'Ellen!' he cried. 'What's happened here — '

Chan intercepted him and laid his hand on the host's arm. Beyond Ward he saw frightened faces — Romano, Swan, Beaton, Dinsdale, Ireland, Cecile. 'You are psychic, Mr. Ward,' Charlie said gravely. 'All same Chinese race. Three days before the crime, you summon detective.'

'Crime!' repeated Ward. He sought to kneel beside the singer, but again Chan restrained him.

'Permit me, please,' the Chinese continued. 'For you, it means pain. For me, alas, a customary duty.' With some difficulty, he knelt upon the floor, and placed his fingers gently on Landini's wrist.

'Doctor Swan is here,' Ward said. 'Perhaps — can nothing be done?'

Chan struggled back to his feet. 'Can the

fallen flower return to the branch again?' he asked softly.

Ward turned quickly away, and there was silence in the room. Charlie stood for a moment, staring down at the body. Landini lay on her back, those evening shoes whose dampness had so distressed Romano were but a few inches away from the threshold of the open windows. In her dead hands was loosely held a chiffon scarf, bright pink in color, contrasting oddly with her green gown. And just inside the windows, close to her feet, lay a dainty, snub-nosed revolver.

Charlie removed his handkerchief from his pocket and stooping over, picked up the weapon. It was still warm, he noted through the handkerchief. One cartridge had been fired. He carried it over and deposited it on the desk.

There for a long moment he stood staring, behind him the murmur of many voices. He appeared to be lost in thought, and indeed he was. For an odd thing had suddenly occurred to him. When he had last seen Landini sitting at this desk, the two boxes containing cigarettes had been close at her elbow, both open. Now they had been restored to their places, farther back on the desk. But on the crimson box rested the yellow lid — and on the yellow box, the crimson.

# 4

## Upward No Road

As Charlie stood, silently regarding those boxes whose lids had become so strangely confused, he was conscious that some newcomer had pushed his way into the room. He swung around and beheld the shrunken figure of Ah Sing. The old Chinese held a blue bundle under his arm, which he now proffered to the room at large.

'Blanket,' he announced, his high shrill voice sounding oddly out of place at that moment. 'Blanket fo' lil dog.'

Chan watched him closely as his beady eyes fell on the silent figure by the window. 'Wha's mallah heah?' the old man inquired. His expression did not change.

'You can see what's the matter,' Charlie replied sharply. 'Madame Landini has been murdered.'

The dim old eyes turned to Chan with what was almost a look of insolence. 'P'liceman him come,' he muttered complainingly. 'Then woik fo' p'liceman him come plitty soon too.' He glanced at Ward accusingly. 'What my tell you, Boss? You crazy invite p'liceman heah. Mebbe some day you lissen to Ah Sing.'

Somewhat nettled, Chan pointed to the blanket. 'What are you doing with that? Who asked you to bring it?'

'Missie ask me,' the old man nodded toward the figure on the floor. 'Missie say she send Cecile fo' blanket, no catch 'um. She say, Sing, you catch 'um like goo' boy.'

'When was this?'

'Mebbe half past nine, between ten.'

'Where was the airplane at that time? Over the house?'

'Not ovah house no moah. Mebbe on field.'

'I see,' Chan nodded. 'The blanket is no longer required. Take it away.'

'Allight, p'liceman,' nodded the old man, and did so.

Charlie turned back and addressed Dinsdale. 'I have really no authority in this place,' he remarked. 'Those who are out of office should not meddle with the government. There is, I presume, a sheriff?'

'Bygad, yes,' Dinsdale said. 'Young Don Holt — this will be a whale of a job for him. He was elected less than a year ago. His dad, old Sam Holt, has been sheriff of this county for fifty years but he went blind a while back, and as a sort of tribute to him, they put up young Don. He'll be a puzzled kid over this. Horses are his specialty.'

'Does it chance that he lives near by?' Charlie inquired.

'He lives down at the county-seat,' Dinsdale answered, 'but he has charge of the riding stables at the Tavern during the summer, and it happens he's over there to-night. I'll get him on the telephone, and he can reach here inside of twenty minutes by boat.'

'If you will be so good,' Charlie said, and Dinsdale went quickly out.

For a moment Charlie stared at the varied group gathered in that little room. How unfortunate, he reflected, that he could not have announced this killing to them suddenly, and watched their faces at the news. But alas, they had come upon him in the dark, they had known of the tragedy almost as soon as he, and whatever their reception of this knowledge, he was never to learn it now.

Nevertheless, their faces were an interesting study. That of Romano, the emotional, was pale and drawn, and there were tears in his brown eyes. Doctor Swan's was taut and excited. Dudley Ward had dropped into a chair beside the fire, and was shading his eyes with his hand. Beaton and his sister stood as far from the body as possible, the girl was crying, and the young man comforted her. The look on the face of Cecile was a mixture of fright and sullenness, while Michael's expression was dazed and puzzled, bespeaking an honest but somewhat stupid simplicity. As for John Ryder, his blue eyes were cold as usual, and they looked at the woman who had once been his wife with no sign of pity or regret.

'I think it much better,' Chan said, 'if you all returned to the living-room below. You understand, naturally, sad state of affairs which makes it necessary you do not take departure now.'

'But I've got to get back to Reno,' Swan cried.

Charlie shrugged. 'You must not place blame on me. Place it on guilty shoulders of one who fired this recent shot.'

Dinsdale returned. 'I got hold of the sheriff,' he announced. 'He's on his way.'

'Thank you so much,' Charlie said. 'Mr. Dinsdale, you will remain here with Mr. Ward and myself, but I am inviting the others down-stairs. Before you go,' he added, as they started to file out, 'I must inquire — though there is no stern necessity to answer, for I am stranger here myself — has any one of you seen this before?' He lifted the snub-nosed revolver from the desk, and

70

held it high in the handkerchief.

'I have,' said Dinsdale promptly. 'I saw it once before, only to-night.'

'Where was that?' Charlie asked.

'At the Tavern,' the hotel man continued. 'Ellen Landini and I were engaged in a small financial transaction, and that revolver fell from her bag when she opened it. I picked it up, and handed it back — '

'Quite true,' nodded Luis Romano, coming close and staring at the weapon. 'It is Ellen's property. Some years ago there was an attempt to hold her up in a hotel room and always since she has insisted on carrying that with her. I pleaded with her — I did not approve — and now she has been killed with her own revolver.'

'Others, then, must have known she carried it,' mused Chan. 'Mr. Beaton?'

The young man nodded. 'Yes — I've seen it many times. It's hers, all right.'

Suddenly, Charlie swung on the girl at Beaton's side. 'And you, Miss Beaton?'

She shrank away from him as he held the weapon close. 'Yes — yes — I've seen it too.'

'You have known it was always in Madame Landini's bag?'

'I have known it — yes.'

'For how long?'

'Ever since I met her — a week ago.'

Chan's voice softened to its customary tone. 'What a pity,' he said. 'You are trembling. It is too cold for you here, with these windows open.' He restored the revolver to the desk. 'You should have a scarf,' he continued. 'A pretty pink scarf to match that gown of yours.'

'I — I have,' she said. She was on her way toward the door.

'This one, perhaps,' Charlie cried. He stepped to the side of the dead woman and lifted one corner of the chiffon scarf that lay in her lifeless hands. 'This, perhaps, belongs to you,' he continued. The girl's eyes had followed him, fascinated, and now her scream rang out sharply in the room. Her brother put his arm about her.

'My scarf,' she cried. 'What is it doing — there?'

Chan's eyebrows rose. 'You had not noticed it before?'

'No — no, I hadn't. It was dark when I came in here — and after the lights went on — I never really looked in this direction.'

'You never really looked,' Chan went on thoughtfully. He dropped the corner of the scarf and rose. His eyes strayed to the boxes on the table. 'I am so sorry — I can not return your property just at this moment. Later, perhaps — when the sheriff of the

72

county has beheld it — in a dead woman's hands. You will all go now — thank you so much.'

When the last one had left, he closed the door and turned to Dinsdale and Ward. The latter had risen, and was anxiously pacing the floor.

'Confound it, Inspector,' he cried. 'That young woman is my guest. You don't for a moment think — ' He paused.

'I think,' said Chan slowly, 'that one of your guests has to-night stooped to murder.'

'Evidently. But a woman — a charming girl — '

Chan shrugged. 'There is no such poison in the green snake's mouth as in a woman's heart.'

'I don't know who said that first,' Ward replied, 'but I don't agree with him. No — not even after all that has — that I've been through.' He stood for a moment, staring down at the dead woman on the floor. 'Poor Ellen — she deserved better than this. I'll never forgive myself for inviting her over here. But I thought we might induce her to tell — ' He stopped. 'By heaven — I hadn't thought of it until now. Shall we ever find the truth about my boy — after this? Ellen was our best chance — perhaps, in the final analysis, our only one.' He stared hopelessly at Charlie.

'Do not despair.' Charlie patted his shoulder pityingly. 'We will persevere — and we will succeed, I am sure. This event may really speed our search — for among the papers and effects of this lady we may find our answer. However, matter of even fiercer importance now intrudes itself. Who killed Ellen Landini?'

'What's your guess, Mr. Chan?' Dinsdale inquired.

Charlie smiled. 'Guessing is cheap, but wrong guess expensive. I can not afford it, myself.'

'Well, I'm a spendthrift. Sleuth all you like, but I can tell you now — Romano killed her.'

'You have evidence, perhaps — '

'The evidence of my eyes — I noticed he was sore at her about something. Money, I imagine. He's Latin, excitable — '

Charlie shook his head. 'Ah, yes. But Latins do not become so excitable they forget where financial advantage lies. Landini alive was worth money to him, but with Landini dead — unless — unless — '

'Unless what?'

'No matter. We will look into that later. There is long tortuous path to climb, and the wise man starts slowly, conserving his strength for a swift finish. By the way, you spoke of moment at Tavern to-night when

Landini opened bag to pay you money?'

'Yes, so I did,' Dinsdale replied. 'I meant to explain it. Last week I called on Ellen in Reno to invite her over to the Tavern for dinner. While I was there, a C. O. D. package arrived — there was the usual wild hunt for cash, which ended in her borrowing twenty dollars from me. To-night she insisted on repaying it — and that was when the revolver dropped out of her bag.'

'She did repay it?'

'Yes, with a brand-new bill which she peeled from a great roll of them in her purse.'

'Odd,' Charlie said. 'There are no bills in her purse now.'

'Good lord,' cried Ward. 'Not only a murderer but a petty thief. I'm afraid I've carried hospitality too far.'

'What did I tell you?' the hotel man said. 'Romano.'

Charlie rose. 'When I came to mainland,' he remarked, 'I was engaged deep in puzzling case. Remnant of that effort, I have in my baggage lamp-black and camel's-hair brush. Same are useful in matter of finger-prints, and while we await the sheriff, I may as well obtain them.'

He went to his room. While he searched his luggage for the tools of his trade, he heard the sound of footsteps ascending the stairs.

75

Presently he found what he was looking for, and returned to the study. A tall, black-haired young westerner in riding boots, breeches and leather coat was standing in the center of the room.

'Inspector Chan,' said Dinsdale, 'meet Don Holt.'

'Hello, Inspector,' the young man cried, and seized the hand of the Chinese in a grip that almost lifted him from the floor. 'Pleased to meet you — and I'm telling you I never meant that so heartfelt before in all my born days.'

'You have grasped situation?' inquired Charlie. He set down his burden and caressed his right hand with his left, seeking to restore the circulation.

'Well — in a way — at least I've gathered there, is a situation. Coroner lives over to the county-seat, so he won't be able to see this lady till to-morrow. But I got a Tahoe doctor on the way to make a preliminary examination, and after that I guess we can move her down to town — what town there is. So far — am I right?'

'So far you appear to act with most commendable speed,' Chan assured him.

'I know, but this is my first case of this — this sort of thing, and I can assure you, Inspector, I'm trembling all over like a roped yearling. Mr. Ward was just telling me you was here, on a visit to him. He says he's got a little job for you, but it can wait while you give the county and me a helping hand. How's that sound to you?'

Charlie looked at Ward. 'We are, of course, very lucky to be able to enlist the inspector's services,' his host remarked. 'My affair can wait.'

'In which case,' Charlie said, 'my very slight talents are yours to command, Mr. Holt.'

'Fine,' Holt answered. 'I could speak a couple of volumes on the way that makes me feel, but action, not words, is my specialty. Let's get down to brass tacks. What happened here to-night, anyhow? Who was all them people downstairs? Where do we start, and how soon?'

They all looked at Charlie, and patiently he went over the events of the evening, up to the firing of the shot and the discovery of Landini's dead body. The young man nodded.

'I get you. At the time the shot was fired, who was unaccounted for?'

'Quite a number,' Charlie told him. 'Of the guests, Miss Leslie Beaton, whose scarf, oddly enough, is clutched in dead woman's hands. Also, Dr. Frederic Swan and Mr. Luis

77

Romano. Of the servants, Cecile and — er — Ah Sing.'

'Five of 'em,' commented the sheriff. 'Well, it could have been worse. It really is only four because I've known Ah Sing since I was ten inches tall, and he wouldn't — '

'Pardon,' said Chan.

Mr. Holt laughed. 'I know,' he said. 'That's no way for a sheriff to act. Getting ideas all set in advance — anything can happen, at that. Well, that's lesson number one. Just deal 'em out to me as we go. And now, Inspector, you just go ahead and solve this case, and don't pay any attention to me.'

'Ah, but I must pay attention to you. You are constituted authority in this place, and everything I do must be done with your approval and permission.'

'Granted in advance,' nodded Holt. 'What I want is results, and I guess you can get 'em. You see, I got a sort of family reputation to uphold — '

Chan nodded. 'Yes — I have heard of your honorable father. Maybe we also call him in. It has well been said — in time of severe illness summon three doctors. One might be good.'

'Dad was good,' the young man replied softly. 'But he's blind now.'

'A terrible pity,' Charlie said. 'But even a

blind man, if he has been over the road before, may point out the way. Just now, however, you and I are in charge. You have spoken of lesson number one. May I, with all humility, now proffer the second lesson?'

'Shoot,' said Holt.

'It has been my good fortune to know famous detectives, some from Scotland Yard. All these say, in case of homicide, first duty of detective is to examine position of body as it fell. What does that examination suggest to you?'

The boy considered. 'I should say — well, she may have been shot from the balcony. Or at least by some one standing in the window.'

'Precisely. The body is well arranged to present that effect. Let us now examine the room. Kindly come and view this desk. You observe upon it fine particles of — what?'

'Tobacco,' Holt answered.

'Correct. Very fine tobacco, such as is contained in cigarettes. Observe these two boxes, in which cigarettes of two brands are kept. What strikes you?'

'Somebody got twisted and put the wrong lids on them.'

'So it would seem,' Chan nodded. 'Somebody was in very great hurry, no doubt. The time for escape was brief, for the shot was heard instantly below. We will open boxes.' He did so, using his handkerchief, which he pulled from under the weapon. 'Behold. Cigarettes are not piled in neat order, but are in unsettled state. They were tossed back hurriedly. What shall we say to that? Was there a struggle at this desk? When last I saw Madame Landini she was seated here. Was the struggle here, and was she then dragged to window in hope to make it appear killing was done from balcony? Why else should there be this frantic effort to tidy desk? The time was brief, but there was just enough, perhaps — though great haste was needed, so great that wrong lids got on to boxes. The killer could have so performed, then fled through open window and escaped into another room that opens on balcony. I should have examined those rooms at once — it may be killer lurked there until all were crowded into this study, then moved away — perhaps crowded into study himself. You will perceive that your new assistant has sinking spells of stupidity.'

'Ain't we all?' grinned Holt. 'What you say's mighty interesting. I take it you think, then, that the lady was shot by some one who was with her in this room, and not from the balcony?'

Chan shrugged. 'I am merely putting facts on parade. I find it wise not to draw conclusion too rapidly. We get answer too quick, we may be wrong, like my children who labor with algebra. I leave it open for present. Lady may, in spite of all I say, have been shot from balcony. She may even have been shot on balcony, and taken step back into room before falling. Perhaps doctor can tell us that. We will now travel to balcony, if you please.'

All four stepped through the windows, past the dead Landini, and came into the bracing night air. The lake lay calm and chill under the full moon, the stars here were dim and remote, Chan noted, lacking the friendliness of those in the Hawaiian sky. Charlie took a deep breath.

'I regret there is no snow here,' he said to Ward.

'Unfortunately, no,' his host replied. 'I had this balcony cleared off when we first came, and Sing has kept it swept and garnished ever since. Otherwise the snow piles against the windows and chills the rooms.'

Charlie shrugged. 'After many years I encounter snow, and the clue of the footstep is denied me. Such, I presume, is life.' He examined the scene. 'Two other rooms, I perceive, open on this veranda. This one is —'

'That,' said Ward slowly, 'is the room

Landini used to have as a sitting-room. I have kept it — just as she left it.'

Charlie tried the window. 'Locked from the inside, of course. Naturally, if killer went that way, he — or she — would attend to that. We will study threshold in the morning.' He led the way to the windows on the opposite side of the study. 'And this room?' he inquired.

'It's my bedroom,' Ward told him. 'I believe Sing showed the ladies here with their wraps.' He peered through the window into the room, where a dim light was burning. 'Yes — there are coats on the bed — '

'And a woman's scarf,' added Chan, at his side. 'A green scarf. The one Landini should have been clutching in her hands. Her own.'

Ward nodded. 'I suppose so.' Chan tried this window with the same result as before, and they returned to the study.

'Next step,' said Chan to the sheriff, 'finger-prints. Matter about which we hear so much, and from which we get so little.'

'Oh, lord, I suppose so,' the young man answered. 'I've got a homicide squad, but he's sick in bed. Fingerprints are in his department — I wonder if he knows it. My Dad never took a finger-print in his life.'

'Ah, but we are more unfortunate — we live in age of science,' Charlie smiled. 'Great marvels happen all times, and world gets less

82

human by minute. Sorry to say I possess utensils to get scientific here and now. I will proceed to examine fatal pistol and discover not a print on it. The suspense will be terrible. Humbly suggest you ease your mind by careful study of room.'

He sat down at the desk and busied himself with his lampblack and brush. Don Holt began a careful survey of the room, as suggested. Dudley Ward picked up a log, and was about to place it on the fire, when a cry from Chan startled him.

'Please,' Charlie called, 'just a moment, if you will be so good.'

'Why — er — what — ' Ward was puzzled.

'The log, pardon me. Not just now,' Chan explained.

Ward nodded and put the log back in the basket. Presently Charlie stood up.

'Suspense now over,' he announced. 'No print on pistol anywhere. Gloves, held in handkerchief, wiped clean — take your honorable choice. Something more suggestive, though — there are also no marks on lids of pretty colored boxes. I think we may go below — '

Holt approached him, holding out his great hand. In it Chan beheld a cheap little gold pin, with semi-precious stones.

'Ah — you make discovery,' Charlie said.

'Bedded deep in the carpet,' the sheriff

explained. 'Somebody stepped on it, I guess.'

'Plenty ladies around here,' Charlie remarked. 'That was not Landini's — we know that much. It has not the rich look of prima-donna jewelry. Let us carry it below — and I suggest that you now remove pink scarf, so we may take that also. But one thing remains to be done here. Gentlemen — if you will do me the favor to await me one moment — '

He went briskly out, and walked part way down the stairs to a point where he had a clear view of the room below. The silent little party seated there looked up at him with interest. The detective's eye lighted on one who sat far from the others. 'Mr. Ryder,' he said.

For a moment there was no reply. 'Yes?' said Ryder finally.

'If you please — will you be so good as to return to the study?'

With annoying slowness, Ryder got to his feet. Chan waited patiently. When finally the bearded man reached him on the stairs, the Chinese bowed low. 'You are quite right,' he said. 'He who hurries can not walk with a stately step. Precede me, I beg of you.'

They came again into the room where Landini lay. 'I don't quite know,' Ryder said, 'why I should have the honor of a separate inquisition.'

'You will yet learn,' Chan assured him. 'Have you met Mr. Don Holt, sheriff of this county?'

'I've not had the pleasure,' Ryder replied, shaking hands.

'Mr. Ryder,' Charlie began, 'it is not my purpose to keep you here for long time. Before tragic passing of this lady, I visited your room with urgent message from her to you. A message which you belittled. You hurried me out, closing door almost against my back. And then — '

'Then — what?'

'Kindly detail your acts from that moment until lady's murder.'

'A simple matter,' Ryder said easily. 'I sat down and resumed my reading. Shortly afterward I heard the airplane approaching. I went on reading. Then I heard it over the house.'

'You went on reading?'

'Precisely. After a time I thought the airplane must have landed. Ellen Landini, I decided, was leaving by plane. So — I went on reading.'

'An interesting book,' Charlie nodded. 'But sooner or later — you put it down.'

'Yes — I went to the door, opened it and listened. Everything was rather quiet — I couldn't hear Landini's voice — so I decided she must have gone out on the field. I went to the stairs — '

'One moment, please. From the time I left you, until I saw you again on the stairs, you did not visit any other part of house? This room, for example?'

'I did not.'

'You are certain on that point?'

'Of course I am.'

'Mr. Holt,' said Chan, stepping to the fireplace, 'will you come here, please?' The sheriff did so. 'Permit that I point out to you certain matters,' Charlie continued. 'We have here' — he took up the poker — 'the completely consumed ashes of a letter, written, I may tell you, on paper similar to that on desk. And over here, in far corner, we have partly consumed envelope, burned but slightly at top. Will you be so kind as to rescue same?' Holt took it up in his fingers. 'What would be address on envelope, Mr. Sheriff?'

The young man examined it. 'Why — it says: 'Mr. John Ryder. Urgent. Private.' In a big bold hand — but it doesn't look like a man's writing, at that.'

'Mr. Ryder will tell you whose writing it is,' Chan suggested.

Ryder glanced at it. 'It is the writing,' he said, 'of Ellen Landini.'

86

'Correct,' cried Chan. 'It was addressed to you as private and urgent. It was sealed. It was torn open, and the letter removed. Who would do that, Mr. Ryder?'

'I'm sure I don't know,' Ryder answered.

'Not many in this house,' Chan continued. 'No gentleman, surely — no lady. Such would not tear open the letter of another, marked private. No, it appears to me, Mr. Ryder, there is only one person who could have opened that letter. Yourself.'

Ryder stared at him coldly. 'A natural inference, Mr. Chan,' he replied. 'However, even if you were correct — and I can tell you at once that you're not — what of it? Surely you haven't forgotten that at the moment Landini was killed, I was standing at the foot of the stairs, in the living-room below.'

Charlie turned to the sheriff. 'You and I — we have long journey to take together,' he remarked. 'Often it will seem matter of upward, no road, downward, no door. But the man with a tongue in his head can always find the way. Let us go down-stairs and exercise our tongues.'

# 5

## Downward No Door

The five men descended to the living-room at once. A glance at the formidable company that awaited them there caused Charlie's heart to sink. He looked toward the sheriff. The young man nervously cleared his throat.

'This is sure too bad,' he began. 'It's going to be pretty unpleasant for all of us, I guess. I'm Don Holt, sheriff of the county, and I don't aim to cause no innocent person any unnecessary trouble. But I got to get to the bottom of this business, and the shorter the route, the better for all of us — well, most of us, anyhow. I've asked Inspector Chan, who's had more experience in this line than I have, to give me a hand here, an' I want to say right now, that when he asks, you answer. That's all, I reckon.'

A diversion at the door interrupted the proceedings. Sing admitted a small gray-haired man with a black satchel, who proved to be the doctor from Tahoe Holt had mentioned. The young man took him aside for a brief talk, and then called to Sing, who led the newcomer upstairs.

'I guess we can get goin' now,' said Holt, looking helplessly at Charlie.

Charlie nodded. 'We begin with least important of the gathering,' he announced. 'When fatal shot was fired, terminating brilliant career of one who was much beloved, six men were present in this room. One of these, Mr. Ryder, has already made statement. I would learn from remaining five all actions just before they met here, their conduct and locations, and when they last saw Landini. In this way, some light might be thrown. Since hour of the clock is uncertain, we can perhaps fix times by location of airplane overhead. I myself was one of these five. Answering my questions without asking same, I last saw Landini above in study while airplane was still over lake. She had requested I summon to her side Mr. Ryder, and I reported back to her he refused to accede. She was then writing hurriedly at desk. I left her, came down here, and went outside, where I eventually met Mr. Ward and Mr. Ireland at edge of field.' He turned to the aviator. 'Mr. Ireland, we can pass over you completely. You can scarcely be involved in this, or have any information of any sort.'

The big Irishman nodded. 'All I know is, Landini called me up to come and get her.

And I came.' He looked up, and his eyes met those of his wife. 'I had to,' he added. 'That's my job. I'm workin' for others.'

'Exactly,' said Charlie. 'Mr. Ward — you last saw Landini — '

'You were with me, Inspector,' Ward replied. 'You remember I left the study to turn on the lights at the field, as soon as we saw the plane over the lake. The lights are worked from a small shed in back of the hangar. We keep it closed and locked. I had to get the keys, and the lock stuck — a bit rusty, I fancy. It was a hurry-up job, but I got them on in time.'

Chan turned to Ireland. 'When did lights blaze on?' he asked.

'It was while I was circling over the house, I think,' the aviator said. 'Thanks a lot,' he added to Ward. 'But it wouldn't have mattered if you hadn't made it — the moon was good enough.'

'Leaving two of the five,' Charlie persisted. 'Mr. Dinsdale and Mr. Beaton. It is my impression that neither left this room during the evening, until after the shot was fired. Am I correct?'

'In my case, yes,' Dinsdale said. 'A good fire and a good drink — all the airplanes in the world landing in the back yard couldn't rout me out. Yes — I sat here, right from the time I came until we heard the shot and ran upstairs.'

'And Mr. Beaton was with you?'

'Well — not all the time — '

'No — no, I wasn't, that's true.' Young Beaton stood up, fragile and pale and evidently very nervous. 'You see — I went outside. You remember you went through the room, Mr. Chan, and then we heard you talking with some one out there, and in a minute Doctor Swan came in. He said the airplane was a beautiful sight, or something like that, so I said I guessed I'd have a look at it too. I went out — it was just coming in from over the lake then. I stepped down on to the path, and suddenly I heard a voice up above me.'

'Ah — you heard a voice,' repeated Charlie with sudden interest.

'Yes — it — it was Ellen — I couldn't mistake that, of course. And I heard her say — she was calling to somebody, really — I heard her call: 'Oh, it's you, is it? I'm freezing — get me my scarf. It's on the bed in the next room. The green one.''

Chan smiled with sudden understanding. 'Ah — most interesting. You heard Miss Landini ask for her scarf?'

'Yes, yes,' cried the boy eagerly. His manner was almost pathetically ingenuous. 'It's true,

Mr. Chan. It really is. I know it sounds — '

'Let us not trouble how it sounds. Continue, please.'

'I went a little farther along the path, and I saw Landini standing alone on the balcony just over the front door. She was looking up and waving her handkerchief. Then the airplane came down terribly close, and began to circle around the house. I started to cough and realized I didn't have my hat or overcoat — so I hurried inside. Anyhow — the picture sort of sickened me — Ellen standing there and waving like a mad woman — '

'That's O.K., Inspector,' Dinsdale said. 'He was out there only a few minutes.'

'But long enough,' shrugged Chan, 'to hear Landini demand a scarf. Her green scarf. How much better, Mr. Beaton, if you had not added that last.'

The boy's face contorted. 'But it's the truth,' he cried. 'I'm telling it to you just as it happened. Somebody came into that room, and she asked for her scarf. And — and — '

'And the person, intending murder and wishing to incriminate innocent girl, returned with your sister's scarf. You are asking me to believe that?'

'I'm not asking you to believe anything,' the boy almost screamed. 'I'm just telling you what happened. I'm just trying to help you

— and you won't believe me — you won't believe me — '

'Never mind, Hughie.' His sister got up and patted him on the back. 'Please don't get so upset.'

'It happened, I tell you.'

'I know. I know.'

'Thank you, my boy,' Charlie said gently. 'I have not said I do not believe you. As a matter of fact — ' He paused, his eyes on the sheriff. Mr. Holt was staring at Leslie Beaton with the most unsheriff-like look Chan ever remembered having seen in his long career. He sighed. A new complication, perhaps.

'As a matter of fact,' Charlie continued, 'this brings you, Mr. Ireland, unexpectedly back into limelight. Though you had not yet arrived on the place, it must be that you, none the less, were one of the last people to see Landini alive.'

Ireland shifted in his chair. 'Maybe I was,' he remarked. 'It didn't strike me before. When I turned in over the house, I looked down and seen some dame waving to me from the balcony. I dropped down to see who it was — '

'You knew well enough who it was,' flashed his wife.

'How could I, dearie? I thought maybe it was you. So I got down as near as I dared,

93

and I seen it was Landini — '

'So then you stunted around, risking your neck to give her a thrill — '

'Now, dearie, I just circled round a few times, to get my bearings and locate the field — '

'Did you, then, think the field was on the roof?' Cecile sneered.

Her husband shrugged. 'I knew where it was, and I knew what I was doing. I don't need no back-seat drivers — '

'Pardon,' Chan said. 'How many times did you circle the house?'

'Three times.'

'And three times you beheld Landini on that balcony.'

'No — only the first. The last two times she'd gone inside.'

'And could you see — were the windows open?'

'Well — I couldn't be sure of that.'

'Thank you so much.' Charlie walked off to a corner of the room with the sheriff. 'Which concludes all those who were in this room when shot was fired,' he said in a low tone. 'Now we advance to more important sector of our attack.'

'But say,' demanded Holt. 'Oughtn't we to be writing all this down in a book?'

Chan shook his head. 'Not my method.

Sight of paper and pencil sometimes has deleterious effect on speaker. I keep all this in mind, and at early opportunity, I make slight notes of it.'

'My gosh — can you do that?' Holt answered. 'I've forgot it already.'

Charlie smiled. 'Large empty place makes good storehouse,' he remarked, tapping his forehead. 'Now we proceed.'

'Just a minute,' Holt laid his hand on the detective's arm. 'Who's that girl in the pink dress?'

'Owner of the pink scarf,' Chan answered. 'And I would humbly recall to you for the next few minutes the stern realities of lesson number one.'

They went back to the other end of the room, and Chan again faced the assembly. 'We come now,' he said, 'to members of this party who were not in view when death came to unfortunate lady above. One of these has already made at least partial statement. Sing, here, was probably last person to see Landini alive, having been dispatched for blanket, he says, after airplane landed. What you do, Sing, up to that time?'

'My don' know,' shrugged Sing.

'You must know,' replied Chan sternly.

'Mebbe my min' own business,' suggested Sing slyly.

Charlie glared at him. He was finding his own compatriot a bit trying. 'Listen to me,' he said. 'This is murder case, understand — murder case. You answer my question, or maybe the sheriff here lock you up in big jail.'

Sing stared at the young man. 'Who — him?' he asked, incredulous.

'That's right, Sing,' Holt said. 'You answer. Understand?'

'Allight,' agreed Sing. 'Why you no say so light away? My jes' go aloun' tendin' to own business.'

'What was your business? What did you do?' Chan continued patiently.

'Boss see me in has, say you catch 'um Cecile. My catch 'um. Then my go down-stair. Go out back step watch landing field. Boss come out, say to me, 'Sing, Landini want something, you catch 'um.''

'Just a minute.' Chan turned to Dudley Ward.

'That's right,' Ward said. 'I'd just passed Cecile on the back stairs and I gathered she had no intention of getting that blanket. I was in too much of a hurry about the lights to argue, so I just sent Sing to attend to it.'

'My go in house,' Sing continued when urged. 'Heah lil dog bark in kitchen. Stop lissen. Plitty soon go up-stair, membah Missie. Go to room, say, 'What you want,

96

Missie? She say, 'Sing, you catch 'um blanket like go' boy, covah up dog.' Dog, dog, dog all time when she 'lound. My go out — '

'The airplane had now landed on the field?' Charlie inquired.

'Yes.'

'How you know that?'

'Damn noise quiet now. My go my loom — '

'On the third floor?'

'Yes. My catch 'um blanket. Plitty soon heah noise. Mebbe pistol. So my come down with blanket — '

'Very slowly, I judge,' remarked Chan.

'Wha's th' mallah?' inquired Sing. 'Plenty time. Plitty soon see Missie gits shot. Too bad,' he added, without emotion.

'Thank you so much,' said Chan, with obvious relief. 'That will do, for the present.' He glanced at Holt. 'Probably the last person to see Landini alive. I'll talk with him later, alone.' He turned to the conductor. 'Mr. Romano, so sorry to say I have somewhat warm interest in your actions for half-hour preceding this sad event.'

'Me?' Romano gazed at him with innocent eyes.

'You, indeed. When I last saw you, airplane was still over lake, and you walked about room with panther tread. What next?'

'Ah, I recall,' said the musician slowly. 'I was engaged in making a list of rules for this young man — a list which, alas, will not now be required. I was no doubt at that moment seeking to determine whether or not I had fully covered the ground. I saw you pass my door on your way down-stairs — '

'And continued with the list, maybe?'

'No,' Romano answered, 'not at all. It comes to me — now Landini must be alone. I hasten to the study, she is writing letter, she puts it in envelope, seals the flap. Now, I say, is come the time to talk about that settlement. I am — what you say — broke. I am — am I right? — flat. Landini addresses the envelope. 'I am so sorry,' she say, 'but, Luis, I am in financial difficulty too. My investments do not pay proper dividends.'

'Then I say, impassioned, 'Ellen, you can not afford a new husband at this time. Why not cling to the old? I am still fond of you' — but, Mr. Chan' — his old voice broke — 'need I discuss that scene?'

'Not at all,' Chan answered, 'except to tell me her reply.'

'It was,' Romano bowed his head, 'it was not flattering to me. Imagine, if you can — after all I had done for her — cared for her like a bambino. The airplane was now approaching the house. She leaped to her feet, flung wide the windows. 'Come and see me in Reno,' she cried. 'I will do what I can.' And she ran on to the balcony.'

'And you, Mr. Romano?'

'Me — I was broken-hearted. I stared at her there on the balcony — it was to be my last sight of her alive — though of course I did not know that. Then I returned to my room, closed my door. I sat by the window, staring out at the snow, the dark trees, the sad night. Flung off, like an old coat, I sorrowed. But I was indignant, too. I remembered all I had done — '

'Ah, yes. And you sat there, brooding, until you heard the shot.'

'It is true. I heard the shot, and for a time, I wondered. Then, I hear footsteps, voices, and I follow you in here to your sad discovery.'

'Tell me this.' Chan studied him keenly. 'You were still the husband of Ellen Landini — at the least for two weeks more. As such, will you inherit any property she may leave?'

Romano shook his head. 'Alas, no. At the time the settlement was drawn up — the one which she so cruelly ignored — she told me she was making a will, leaving everything she had to her future husband — to Mr. Hugh Beaton here.'

Surprised, Chan turned to the young man.

'Did you know of this, Mr. Beaton?'

Beaton looked up wearily. 'Yes — she told me about it. Naturally, I didn't want her to do it.'

'Do you know whether the will was made or not?'

'She told me one day it had been drawn up. Signed, too, I suppose. I didn't ask any questions. I hated the whole idea.'

Charlie looked at Miss Beaton. 'You, too, had heard of the affair?'

'I had,' said the girl softly. 'But I paid no attention. It didn't matter.'

Chan turned back to Romano. 'What a sad position for you. Wife, money, everything lost. Do you, may I ask, happen to have that list you drew up for Mr. Beaton?'

'It is in my — ' Suddenly he stopped. 'It is in my room. I will get it for you.'

'So sorry.' Chan's eyes narrowed. 'You were about to say, I think, that it is in your pocket.'

'You are mistaken,' Romano said, but his pale face had suddenly grown paler than ever. 'What does it matter, at any rate?'

'It matters so much,' Chan continued gently, 'that unless you empty pockets here and now, I must reluctantly do same for you. Believe me, such a barbarous action would bring me pain.'

Romano stood for a moment, considering.

'The story,' he said finally, 'of my interview with my wife was not quite complete. I — a man does not willingly speak of such things — but — ' He reached into a trousers pocket and took out a roll of crisp new twenty-dollar bills which he handed to Chan. 'Just before Ellen rushed on to the balcony she removed these from her bag, flung them on the desk. I — I accepted them. My case — was — desperate.' He dropped into a chair and covered his face with his hands. Chan looked down on him with real pity.

'I am so glad,' the detective said, 'that you saw way clear to amending own story. Unfortunately, these must remain with sheriff at present as evidence. But in meantime — we will see — way will be found — do not worry, Mr. Romano.' He turned with sudden grim determination on Doctor Swan. 'And now, Doctor, your turn arrives. Where did you go after you left me in path before house?'

'I haven't much to tell,' said Swan. 'I came in here, had a word or two with Dinsdale and Beaton, and then went upstairs — to the room that had been assigned me before dinner. I was planning to leave at the earliest possible moment.'

'Ah — and you had left something in that room you wished to obtain?'

'No — I had nothing up there. My coat and hat were in the closet down here. I had no luggage — it was not my intention to spend the night.'

'You had nothing up there — then why did you go?'

Swan hesitated. 'The windows of that room faced the back. I figured I could see the plane land — and — '

Charlie and the sheriff exchanged a look.

'Well, I'll be frank with you,' Swan went on. 'As a matter of fact, it occurred to me that after Ireland had landed his plane, he'd probably come inside for a moment. I didn't care to meet him. He knows what I think of him.'

'And you know what I think of you,' said Ireland sneeringly.

'No man,' continued Swan, 'can look forward to a social meeting with a greasy chauffeur who once made love to his wife behind his back — '

Ireland was on his feet. 'Is that so — '

'Sit down,' said Don Holt. 'Now this is getting to be a case that I can handle. Sit down, Ireland, and shut up.'

Big as he was, the aviator was not inclined to argue with the sheriff. He sat down, and Holt looked somewhat disappointed.

'Let us continue,' said Chan, 'peacefully.

You went upstairs to avoid Mr. Ireland, Doctor Swan?'

'Yes. I went into that room and closed the door. It was not my intention to come out of there until Ellen and the plane had gone. I watched it land, and I was standing by the window waiting to see it depart before returning down-stairs. That is where I was when the shot was fired. It's not much of an alibi, I know, but — '

'I'll say it's not much of an alibi,' growled Ireland. 'A fat chance you've got putting that over. Especially when they find out you've been blackmailing poor Landini for seven years — '

'That's a lie,' cried Swan, trembling with fury.

'Blackmailing,' remarked Chan. He looked at Dudley Ward.

'Yeah — blackmailing,' Ireland repeated. 'She told me all about it. Two hundred and fifty a month for seven years, and the other day she told me she couldn't pay any more. I advised her to order this buzzard to scram. Did she tell you, Doctor? I guess she did — from the looks of to-night.'

'You'd better be careful,' said Swan through his teeth. 'You're not out of the woods yet yourself.'

'Me?' Ireland said. 'Why — I was flying

around in the sky, innocent as a bird. I had nothing to do with this — '

'But — your wife?' cried Swan. 'How about your wife — or don't you care what happens to her? Poor Cecile — wandering about up-stairs almost insane with jealousy — and with good reason, too, I imagine. Where was Cecile when that shot was fired — that's what I want to know.'

'The proper authorities,' Chan put in, 'will resume the inquiry into this case — if you have no objection, Doctor Swan. Cecile — pardon, Mrs. Ireland — we come now, with the doctor's kind assistance, to you. Courtesy has not ruled us, you will observe. It appears to be a matter of ladies last.'

'I — I know nothing,' the woman said.

'As I feared. But let us push questions, none the less. When last I saw you, you had been sent to obtain blanket for dog. You did not busy yourself with such task?'

Her eyes flashed. 'I did not. I had no intention of doing so.'

'Hot anger was in your heart?'

'Why not? I had just seen Michael's plane — I knew that woman had sent for him to take her home in the moonlight. And he, like a fool — '

'It was my job, I tell you,' Ireland persisted sullenly.

'And how you hated it, eh? No matter. I thought, 'Let her find her own blanket for that accursed dog.' I was on my way down the back stairs, when Mr. Ward hurried down after me. He asked about the blanket — I told him frankly I would not get it. 'I wonder where Sing is,' he said, and hastened past.'

'And you — '

'Me — I went to the kitchen, where the cook was. I heard Michael risking his life above the house. I waited — I would have a word with him, I thought. The plane landed — and Michael came into the passageway, as I expected. But he was not alone — Mr. Ward and Mr. Chan were with him. I was too unhappy — 'I will have no scene here,' I said, so I let him pass. Then I started up the back stairs again — my place was above — and I figured how I would send Sing to bring Michael to me there. But on the stairs — '

'Ah, yes — on the stairs,' nodded Charlie.

'I — I paused to weep, Monsieur. I was so very unhappy. I had known from the sound how close Michael had come to the house — reckless, a fool — to impress that woman, with whom he was always infatuated — '

'Bologny,' interrupted her husband.

'You were — you know it. But I will say no more of the dead. I wept quietly for a moment, then I dried my eyes and started again up the stairs. It was then I heard the shot — loud, unexpected, clear. That — that is all.'

Chan turned to Holt. 'The little object, please, which you found embedded in study carpet.'

'Oh — oh, yes.' The sheriff found it and turned it over. Charlie held it out to the woman. 'Have you, by any chance, ever seen this pin before?' he inquired.

She glanced at it. 'Never, Monsieur.'

Chan showed it to her husband, closely studying his face as he did so. 'You — Mr. Ireland. Have you seen it before?'

'Me? No. Why should I?'

Charlie put it in his pocket. 'Long routine business,' he remarked. 'But it comes shortly now to a finish. One person alone remains — '

'I know.' Leslie Beaton got up and stood, facing him. Tall, slender and appealing, she seemed at first glance quite helpless and lost. But — thought Chan — a competent look in those deep eyes of hers. Not for nothing had she cared for a spineless, artistic brother; she had learned, meanwhile, to take care of herself.

'I'm awful sorry about this,' Don Holt said. And looked it.

'Don't worry,' the girl replied. She flashed

him a friendly smile. 'These things will happen, I imagine, even to the kindest-looking of sheriffs. You will want to know of my actions here to-night, Mr. Chan. I'll be as brief as I can — '

'But you needn't stand,' Holt protested. He picked up a large chair in one hand, and tossed it casually into position for her.

'Thank you,' she remarked. 'Well, Mr. Chan — when we heard the airplane over the lake, I was the first out of this room. I got my brother's overcoat, put it on and ran out to the pier. I went to the end and watched the plane approaching. It was a lovely thing — if I hadn't been — well, like Cecile — a bit unhappy, I could have been terribly thrilled. Doctor Swan appeared presently, and we watched it together. We had — a little chat, and then he went back to the house. I believe he met you just outside. I — I stayed where I was.'

'Ah, yes,' Chan nodded. 'For how long?'

'I watched the airplane circle over the house — '

'You saw Landini on the balcony, perhaps?'

'No — the trees came together there — I couldn't see the study windows. But I saw Mr. Ireland circling, and then I saw him come down somewhere in the rear. By that time I was thoroughly chilled, so I ran back to the living room. Hugh and Mr. Dinsdale were here together. I imagined we would be starting back to the Tavern as soon as Ellen had gone, so I ran up the stairs to the bedroom where our wraps were.'

'One of the rooms next to the study where Landini died?' Chan suggested.

She shivered slightly, but went on. 'Yes — of course. I sat down at the dressing-table to powder my nose — rearrange my hair — when suddenly, in that next room, I heard a shot — '

'One moment,' Chan cut in, 'pardon so much. But you heard first — what? A struggle?'

'No — nothing.'

'But voices, perhaps?'

'Nothing at all, Mr. Chan. You see, there is no door connecting the rooms.'

'Ah, I see,' Chan replied. 'Continue, please.'

'Well — I just heard this shot. And — I sat there. I couldn't quite comprehend what had happened. Then I heard people running along the hall, crowding into the study. And I followed them. That's — that's all.'

'Alas,' Charlie answered. 'I wish very much that it were. But — Mr. Holt — that pink scarf — one end of which I see hanging from your pocket — '

'Say — I'm sorry,' Holt said. 'I'm afraid I've mussed this up something terrible. You know — when I tucked it in there — I hadn't seen you — '

'It's all right, I'm sure,' the girl replied.

'It is not all right — pardon me,' cried Chan sternly taking the scarf. 'Excuse that I call attention to the fact, but we are not enjoying social hour of tea. This is your scarf, Miss Beaton?'

'As I told you, up-stairs.'

'It was found in dead hands of Ellen Landini? How do you account for same?'

'I can not account for it, Mr. Chan.'

He took the pin from his pocket. 'Have you seen this before?'

'It is mine.'

'It is yours. It was found by the dead woman's side.'

'It's a little old pin I used to fasten my scarf. When I left the scarf on that bed up-stairs, I just carelessly stuck the pin in it. That's all.'

'You are alone in room next to one in which murder occurs. Your scarf and your pin are in dead person's presence. And you can not explain — '

'Perhaps, as my brother said — '

'Your brother made gallant effort to think up explanation. It is not enough, Miss

Beaton. I have long experience in these matters, and never before have I encountered evidence so damaging — '

'But — ' Suddenly the girl's face was stricken with fear. 'Surely you don't think that I — that I could — kill Landini? What motive — '

'What motive?' cried Doctor Swan. 'What motive indeed?'

With one accord, they turned and looked at the doctor.

'I'm sorry, Miss Beaton,' he said. 'It's rather painful — such a charming girl, too. But under the circumstances, I should be shirking my duty shamefully if I did not recall our little conversation on the pier — what you said — '

'Very well,' said the girl in a low voice. 'What did I say?'

'Our little conversation about Landini,' the doctor continued suavely. 'Your last words to me, as I recall, were: 'I hate her! I hate her! I wish she were dead!''

# 6

## Three O'Clock in the Morning

A tense silence followed in that big bright room, broken at last by the collapse of a burning log, which fell into a hundred pieces, sending sparks and embers in all directions. Sing moved forward to attend to it, and at that moment young Hugh Beaton faced Doctor Swan. He was livid with rage; an utterly unexpected transformation seemed to have taken place in the boy.

'You contemptible lair!' he cried hoarsely.

'Just a minute,' Swan replied coolly. 'It so happens I am telling the truth. Am I not, Miss Beaton?'

The girl's eyes were on the handkerchief which she twisted nervously in her hands. 'You are,' she said softly.

'So sorry,' Charlie began. 'But, Miss Beaton, it now becomes necessary for us to know — '

'Yeah — I suppose it does,' said the sheriff. 'But look here, there's no need of any more of this inquisition in front of everybody. Mr. Ward — is there another room — '

Ward rose. 'Yes,' he answered. 'You may use the dining-room, if you wish. If you'll come with me — '

'That's the idea,' Holt approved. 'The rest of you stick right here — understand? Now, Miss Beaton — yes, your brother too — and Doctor Swan — you come along with me and the inspector.' As they followed Ward, he added to the girl: 'I don't aim to make any public show of you. Some things is private.'

'You're very kind to me,' the girl said.

Ward ushered them into the dining-room, closed the door and disappeared. Doctor Swan was looking rather sheepish.

'Miss Beaton, believe me — I am very sorry that I was faced with such an unpleasant duty,' he remarked. 'Still — you understand my position — '

'Oh, we understand it, all right,' her brother cried hotly. 'Try to pin this terrible thing on some one else if you can. Your own situation is pretty shaky. Looking out the window when the shot was fired — enjoying the beautiful snow! Did you carry my sister's scarf into the study? Was it you Landini asked to — '

'Hughie,' interrupted his sister, 'please be quiet.'

'Most admirable suggestion,' Chan smiled. 'It is Miss Beaton who should be talking now.

112

So sorry, my dear young lady — but why did you cry out that you wished Landini dead?'

The girl sat down in the chair which Don Holt had placed for her near the fire.

'It's quite true,' she began. 'I did say that. I said I hated too. I did hate her. To explain I have to go back — a long way back — and even then — I doubt if you will quite understand. You don't know what it is to be poor — horribly poor — and to have some one in the family with a great gift, a gift you believe in — to slave and struggle and fight for that person's training and education. That's — that's what happened to us.'

'Must you tell all this?' her brother protested.

'I have to, Hughie. You see, we knew very early that Hugh had a voice — and from then on, everything went for that. My father wearing the same old overcoat year after year — my mother going without, scrimping, saving — neither having any fun, any joy in life — just to pay for Hugh's education. New York — and then, Paris — and finally, after years of that sort of thing — Hugh giving a concert here and there, making a little money at last — seemingly on the threshold of a great career. The moment we'd always dreamed about. And then this woman, pouncing on him, threatening to ruin everything — '

'You're wronging her, my dear,' said the boy.

'Wronging her! She was fifteen years older than you. Had she any interest in your career? Would she have helped you to success — of course not. We all knew that. You knew it yourself. You said, only the other day — '

'Never mind. She's dead now.'

'I know,' the girl nodded. 'I don't want to say anything — I just want to make clear my feeling about her.' She turned to Chan and the sheriff. 'It just seemed I couldn't let this marriage happen,' she explained. 'I mustn't. I came out here to try to stop it if I could. I talked with her — she laughed at me. I became desperate — I wanted to save Hugh from this terrible mistake. He was just a passing fancy with her, I felt. I was furious when she began going around with this Ireland person — '

'Stop it,' put in the boy. 'There was nothing in that. It was — Ellen's way.' He was very white.

'It was not much of a way,' the girl replied. 'It sickened me. To-night when she called him up, and left us to go home alone — I was furious. Hughie might weakly stand for that sort of thing — '

'Go on,' the boy said. 'Tell 'em I'm weak — no good — spineless. Tell 'em I always have

114

been. That you've always had to care for me — mother me — '

'Have I said so?' the girl answered gently. 'Don't be angry, Hughie. I'm only trying to explain the mood I was in when I went out on that pier. Soon Doctor Swan came out. I'd met him before in Reno. We got to talking about Landini, and I — I went a little wild, I guess. I told him what I thought about her marrying my brother — and as the plane came nearer, I burst into tears, and I — I said I hated her and I wished she was dead. And I did — I did — but I didn't kill her.' She was weeping now. 'I — I know it looks terrible,' she went on. 'I was in the next room. My scarf was in her hands, and my pin beside her. Why — how? I don't understand. I can't explain it. Some one — put them there. Some one who must have known how I felt toward her. For what other reason?'

She stopped suddenly, staring at Doctor Swan. Charlie and the sheriff were also looking at the doctor. Landini's third husband felt of his collar nervously, and his face flushed slightly.

'Yeah,' nodded Don Holt. 'Might be something in that theory, Miss Beaton, Well, we won't detain you in here any longer. I want to say right now, I understand exactly how — '

'Quite true, quite true,' Charlie put in. 'Yes, Miss Beaton, you may return to other room. But I would falsify facts if I hid from you you are for present moment in dangerous position. Later discoveries may clear same up. With deep sincerity I may say, I hope so.' He smiled. 'You see, I like the sheriff.'

Holt stared at him. 'What's that got to do with it?' he wanted to know.

'Another mystery which time, I trust, will solve,' Charlie said. 'Mr. Sheriff, will you be good enough to remain in this room with me for one moment?'

After the others had gone, Charlie sat down and motioned Holt to a chair near by.

'Well?' said Holt rather gloomily.

'Feel somewhat same way myself,' nodded Chan. 'Well! A moment's summing up in order now. By this time we have questioned all those who were not present in my vision when the shot was heard. What have we got?'

'Not much, if you ask me,' sighed Holt. 'Swan and Romano were shut up in their rooms, looking out the windows. Oh, yeah? Cecile was climbing the back stairs, Sing was foraging for a blanket in his room, and Miss Beaton was right next door to the study, powdering her nose. Doggone it, I wish she'd been somewhere else. But anyhow, she was there when the shot was fired. And that accounts for the five. What's the answer?'

'Somebody is lying,' Chan remarked.

'Sure — somebody is certainly lying. But which one? Romano?'

Charlie considered. 'Romano had the money from her purse. Did she, then, give it to him? Or did he slip in to protest matter of settlement, lose temper, kill her, and himself remove money? Possible. No alibi.'

'That fellow Swan,' mused Holt. 'I don't like him.'

Charlie shook his head, 'Again — please maintain neutral attitude. But — Swan — I can not say I admire his looks myself. Did he kill the lady? Possible. No alibi.'

'Cecile had a mighty good motive,' the sheriff reflected.

'So far — absolutely nothing connects Cecile with murder,' Charlie reminded him. 'And yet, she is quite possible selection. She has no — ' He paused, and a slow smile spread over his face. 'Note the peculiar situation,' he added. 'Perhaps not so strange to you, but to me, with my experience, up to this minute unheard of. Five people not accounted for at time of shooting, and of the five not one has even offered alibi. I wonder — '

'What?' inquired Holt eagerly.

Chan shrugged. 'No matter. It lightens

work — we have no alibis to investigate. But it also adds heaviness — we have, alas, five healthy suspects. I have kept you here to remind you of one thing — we are near state line. It is your duty to see that no one of five departs across that line to-night.'

'I know. I suppose there'll be an argument. Perhaps we could put some of them up at the Tavern.'

'It is very late,' Chan replied. 'Romano, Cecile and Sing remain here naturally. You must persuade the good doctor and Miss Beaton to do the same — for to-night at least. There are plenty rooms. I will be responsible.'

'Suppose one of them slips out in the night,' suggested Holt.

'Only the thief oils his wheelbarrow,' Chan said, as they rose. 'And only the guilty flee. It would be a happy solution. I shall be sitting just inside my door all night. I shall try not to take nap — but I can not guarantee. For I now realize suddenly that I have been napping all evening.'

'How so?' Holt inquired.

'There were six, not five, unaccounted for at time of shot.'

'Six?' Holt cried. 'Good lord — another one. Who?'

'I forgot the cook,' Chan explained. 'Most impolite of me — for she is a very good

118

cook. Perhaps very good witness, too. If you will arrange matter of overnight stay, I will visit kitchen. You might join me there, when able.'

'Sure,' said Holt. He paused. 'I suppose I may as well let Ireland go back to Reno?'

'Why not?' Chan shrugged. 'He could have had nothing to do with killing. Yes, Ireland, Dinsdale and young Beaton, if he wishes — these may go.'

Separating from Holt, he followed the passageway toward the rear until he came to the kitchen door. Looking in, a homey scene greeted him. Beside an old-fashioned kitchen range, in a large easy chair, sat the ample figure of the cook, sound asleep. At her feet, on a bit of old carpet, lay Trouble, the dog, also mercifully slumbering. Chan smiled and moved on to the back steps.

For a time he walked about outside, using a flashlight he had obtained from his luggage when he went for the fingerprint paraphernalia. He studied the path which led to the hangar, but the snow on that was packed hard, and no clear footprints were discernible. The lights on the field were still blazing, and Michael Ireland's plane stood like an actor in a spotlight.

The examination yielded him nothing, and he paused for a moment, staring at the clear beauty of the distant mountains, then went inside. Holt was standing beside the kitchen door.

'Sleeping, eh?' he said, nodding toward the cook.

'The slumber of innocence,' Chan smiled. 'Matters are now arranged for the night?'

Holt nodded. 'All set. Swan put up a battle — got to get back to Reno — lot of appointments early in the morning. But he's staying all right — that bird's not putting anything over on me. I don't like — oh, yes, lesson number one. Anyhow, I hate the sight of him. Miss Beaton is staying — Cecile's fixing her up with the necessary feminine doodads. Her brother has decided to put up here for the night, too.'

'We shall be a large party,' Chan answered.

The cook was stirring in her chair, and the two stepped into the kitchen.

'So sorry to disturb you,' Charlie apologized.

'Sure, I should be in me bed,' the woman answered. 'Why am I here — oh, yes — the poor lady. I was after forgettin' — '

'Let me explain, Mrs. — ' Holt began.

'O'Ferrell,' she added.

'Mrs. O'Ferrell. I am Don Holt, sheriff of the county.'

'God have mercy on us,' she cried.

120

'And this is Inspector Chan, of the Honolulu Police.'

'Honolulu, eh? Sure, he got here quick.'

Charlie smiled. 'Honored, if I may say so. Earlier this evening I had great pleasure to sample your cooking, and I bow to you in humble congratulation.'

'You talk very nice,' she responded, pleased.

'But sterner topics now engage us,' he continued. 'You are evidently aware of what happened a short time ago?'

'Murder,' she said. 'I am. I don't hold with it.'

'We none of us hold with it,' he assured her. 'That is why we seek the murderer. It becomes necessary to ask a few questions, which I know you will answer gladly.'

'I will that. I'll not be at peace in this house, with a murderer havin' the run of it. But I'm afraid I can't help ye much. I been busy in this room all evenin', for a dinner like that is no joke, nor is washin' dishes after a picnic, ayether. I'm supposed to have the help of Sing, but like a will-o'-the-wisp he's been this night, now here, now gone.'

'He's been in and out occasionally, however?'

'In an' out is right.'

'Well, Mrs. O'Ferrell, let us take it from the

121

time you heard the airplane. Where was the plane when you first heard it?'

'I couldn't tell you that exactly, Mr. Chan, but it must have been some distance off, over the lake, ye might say. I heared it buzzin', an' I thinks, now what can that be, an' thin Cecile — no, wait a minute — thin Mr. Ward himself stops in that door, an' asks me have I seen Sing. I says I think Sing is on the back porch, an' Mr. Ward is hardly gone, whin Cecile comes in mad as a hornet, with somethin' about her husband, an' a blanket, an' this opera singer, an' what-not. An' thin the plane comes over th' house, an' from that minute I have me hands full, what with Cecile ravin' and this poor lamb at me feet' — she indicated the dog — 'scared near out of his wits be the noise.'

'Ah — Trouble was frightened by the plane?'

'He was that, sir, an' no mistake, cryin' an' whinin' an' carryin' on until I had to take him on me lap, an' comfort him, an' him tremblin' all over like gelatine.'

'And Cecile — '

'Cecile wint out in th' passage, like she was waitin' f'r some one. I see Mr. Ward an' you an' the leather man come in, but I didn't hear any talk from Cecile. I was too busy with th' dog to come to th' door. Look at him, th' poor little orphan, sleepin' there so peaceful an' not knowin' his loss.'

Chan smiled. 'We will leave him in your care for the present, Mrs. O'Ferrell, and I'm sure he could not be in kinder hands. That is all. I suggest you retire for the night.'

'Thank ye kindly, sir, but I'll not rest in me bed until this wild murderer is caught. Ye'll move as fast as ye can, I hope.'

Charlie shook his head. 'We must collect at leisure what we may use in haste,' he explained. 'The fool in a hurry drinks his tea with a fork.' He and Holt went into the passage. At the foot of the back stairs, Holt stopped. 'A lot we got out of that,' he remarked glumly.

'You think so?' Chan asked.

The sheriff looked at him suddenly. 'We didn't get anything, did we?'

Charlie shrugged. 'He who fishes in muddy waters can not tell the great catch from the small.'

'Yeah. I guess this is the back stairway, isn't it? I told that doctor to wait for me up-stairs — he'll think I've forgot him. Let's go up.'

They found the doctor in the study, his work evidently completed, his bag closed on the desk, and himself with professional calm seated by the fire. He rose as they entered.

'Well,' he said, when he had been

introduced to Chan, 'I've made the examination, although the coroner, of course, will want to make another in the morning. Poor Landini — I knew her as a young bride in this house, and she comes back to it to die. Um — er — that is, of course, beside the point. Nothing much to be said. The bullet entered about four inches below the shoulder, and pursued I believe, a downward course. Perhaps the person who fired it was standing over her, and she was on her knees.' He looked at Chan.

'Perhaps,' Chan said. He seemed very sleepy, and not overly keen. The doctor turned to Holt.

'We can tell more about that to-morrow,' he continued. 'The caliber of the gun — that must wait until tomorrow, also.'

Holt held out the small pearl-handled revolver. 'We've found this,' he said.

'One thing, Doctor,' Charlie remarked. 'Was death, in your opinion, instantaneous? Or could the lady have taken a step or two after the wound?'

The doctor considered. 'I can tell you better after we have probed for the bullet,' he said. 'At present, all I can say is — there is a chance that she did move after the shot. But you must understand — '

He was interrupted by the loud whirring of

an airplane engine, and then the steady drone of it moving off, evidently away from the house.

'It's Ireland,' said the sheriff to Charlie. 'I told him he could go.'

'Naturally,' nodded Chan. He stepped on to the balcony and watched the plane as it moved out over the sapphire lake. Much had happened, he reflected, since that machine had first been sighted in the still night sky.

'I'd like to be getting along,' the doctor was saying. 'I had a hard night last night.'

'Sure,' said Holt. 'We can take this poor lady with us, I guess. I phoned Gus Elkins to wait up for us. We'll need some blankets, won't we? I hope everybody's out of that room down-stairs — especially the women — '

Charlie took up his lampblack and brush from the desk. 'While you busy yourself with unhappy task,' he said, 'I will make superficial investigation of room next door — that old sitting-room of Ellen Landini's — through which her slayer must have left the scene. Kindly visit me there before taking departure for the night.'

'I'll do that,' Holt promised.

Some fifteen minutes later he pushed open the door of the room in question. Chan was standing in the center of it, all the lights, both on the walls and in the ceiling, were blazing. The atmosphere of the place was faintly out-of-date, for the furnishings were those of twenty years before, though probably this made no impression on Holt.

'What luck?' the young man inquired.

'A little,' Charlie shrugged.

Holt went over and examined the catch fastening the windows that opened on to the balcony. 'Any prints on this?' he asked.

'None whatever,' Chan answered. 'There are also no prints on door-knob, either side.'

'But there should be — shouldn't there?' Holt inquired. 'I mean — if everything was O.K.?'

'There should be dozens,' Charlie admitted. 'But alas — too many people read detective stories now — get fingerprint complex. All have been rubbed away.'

'Then Landini's murderer did come this way,' Holt mused. 'And probably went this way to reach her, too. Leaving the window unlocked so he could return through it.'

Chan nodded. 'You are learning fast. Pretty soon, your instructor must take lessons from you. Yes — the firing of that pistol must have been premeditated. Otherwise the killer could not have come through here without smashing glass in the window.'

'Anything else to make you think he — '

'Or she,' suggested Chan.

'Or she, escaped through this room?'

Chan pointed. There was a dressing-table against one wall of the room, and overturned on the floor in front of it was a heavy bench.

'Some one came, hurrying in the dark,' he said. 'Knee met sharp edge of plenty solid bench, which is turned on side. Maybe somebody have pretty sore knee.'

Holt nodded. 'I hope so. Even if a bad infection sets in, it will be all right with me. This room doesn't connect with any other, does it?'

'No — that is closet door over there,' Chan told him.

'Well, I'd better be getting along,' Holt said. 'I'll be up early in the morning, of course. Poor Landini is in my launch, and the doctor has already taken his boat and gone. He was a candidate for coroner himself last election, and lost out, so he's not very keen about this job.'

They went down-stairs, through the living-room, which was now deserted. Chan stepped outside, and walked toward the pier with his new-found friend.

'I'm certainly glad to have you on this job with me,' Holt remarked. 'It just looks hopeless. I can't see any light ahead.'

'Be cheerful,' urged Charlie. 'When the

127

melon is ripe, it will fall of itself. I have always found it so.'

'Have you got any clue?' asked the boy.

'Clue?' Chan smiled. 'I have so many clues, I would sell some very cheaply. Yes,' he mused, 'if I was complaining man, and were asked for complaint against this case, I would say, bitterly, too many clues. Pointing all ways at once.'

'I'll have to take your word for it,' Holt sighed.

'But long experience shows,' added Chan briskly. 'That in time clues fall into place, false ones fade and wither, true ones cluster together in one unerring signboard. I may say I am interested in this case. Unusual event has roused itself and occurred here to-night, and one unusual clue may point our final path. But I anticipate.' They had come to the pier. Charlie held out his hand. 'Good night. I enjoy knowing you, if you permit my saying so. I enjoy knowing cool fresh country like this. I am plenty happy.'

'Fine,' said Holt. 'Let's all be happy. See you tomorrow, Mr. Chan.'

'Just one matter.' Charlie laid a hand on his arm.

'What's that?'

'The bullet for which they probe in the morning — get it, and guard it well. It must on no account be lost.'

'I'll hang on to it,' Holt promised, and ran down the pier to his launch.

Charlie came back to the living-room to find Dudley Ward waiting there.

'Ah, Mr. Chan,' he said. 'I fancy you're the last of my guests to retire.'

'I will do so at once,' Charlie assured him. 'So sorry to delay your own rest.'

'Not at all,' Ward answered. He sank into a chair. 'But I am rather weary, at that. Poor Ellen — I shall never forgive myself for inviting her here. However, I was so anxious — about my boy.'

'How natural,' Chan said.

'I am more anxious than ever, now,' Ward continued. 'I hope, in the terrible excitement of to-night, you won't forget why you have come here, Inspector. You must, of course, find who killed Landini if you can — but you must also find my boy. He needs me more than ever — with Landini gone.'

'I am not forgetting same,' Chan nodded.

'You heard what Ireland said about Doctor Swan's having blackmailed poor Ellen,' Ward went on. 'Did it occur to you that he might have known about the boy, and been threatening to tell me of him?'

'It did,' Chan nodded gravely.

'Of course, he denied at dinner that he had

ever heard of the child — '

'He was lying,' Charlie said firmly.

'You thought so?' Ward inquired.

'I was certain of it. Just as I was sure Romano was lying when he said he had.'

'Well, I am glad to have such expert confirmation of my own opinion,' Ward went on. 'I went to Swan's room a moment ago to loan him some things — and I told him what I thought. I pleaded with him, if he knew anything of the boy, to tell me about him. He still denied any knowledge.'

'Still lying,' Chan suggested.

'I think so,' Ward agreed. 'Well, we must look elsewhere, perhaps. But as a last resort, we must not forget Doctor Swan.'

'I shall not forget him,' Chan promised. 'And now — if you don't mind — I will go to my room.'

'Ah, yes,' said Ward, rising. 'You know where it is. I have just remembered that I forgot to turn off the lights on the landing field. I must send Sing to attend to that — then perhaps I can retire for the night myself.'

Charlie had been in his room but a few minutes, when Ward knocked on his door. 'Just to say you must let Sing or me know if you want anything,' he remarked. 'Good night, Inspector.'

'Good night, Mr. Ward,' Chan said.

There was, he noted, plenty of wood in the basket beside his fireplace. That would come in handy, if he was to keep his promise to Don Holt and sit up through the night. A rather silly promise, he reflected, as he began to undress. No one of these people would be so foolish as to attempt escape.

Nevertheless, he changed to pajamas, dressing-gown and slippers, put another log on the fire, opened his door a few inches and sat down in a comfortable chair just inside it. He looked at his wrist-watch. One thirty. All was quiet in the hall outside, save for the sounds that afflict an ancient wooden house on a frosty night. Crackings, creakings, moanings. But the human company, Chan knew, were in their beds.

He settled more deeply into his uphol-stered chair, to think about this case upon which he was so unexpectedly engaged. Pictures flashed through his mind — the calm lake under the stars — Dudley Ward greeting his fellow husbands on the pier — Landini lively and vivacious on the stairs, holding aloft the dog, Trouble — Ireland circling the house in his plane — Landini lying on the study carpet — promised to sing for him some day — never would sing for him now — never —

Chan sat up with a start. He looked at his wristwatch. Ten minutes to three. Too comfortable, that chair. But what had startled him? — ah, now he knew. A groan — a faint groan from somewhere outside his door. Not the groan of an old house in the night, but of a human being in pain.

Charlie slipped out into the hall, which was in utter darkness. Feeling his way along the wall, still somewhat confused by sleep, he approached the head of the stairs His foot encountered some soft object on the floor.

Then at last he remembered his flash-light, and removed it from the pocket of his dressing-gown. Its glare fell on a supine figure at his feet — then on the face — the lined yellow face of Ah Sing.

The old man groaned again, and raising one thin hand, rubbed his even thinner jaw.

'No can do,' he protested feebly. 'No can do.'

# 7

## The Blind Man's Eyes

For a moment Chan stood looking down at the crumpled figure of Ah Sing, and a wave of pity for this loyal servant who had been with the house of Ward so many years swept through him. He bent over solicitously.

'What has happened here?' he asked. Gently he shook the old man. 'Who has done this thing to you?'

Sing opened his eyes, sighed and closed them again.

Rising, Charlie found the switch on the wall with his flash, and turned on the light in the upper hall. He surveyed the many doors. With the exception of his own, all were closed; they seemed blind, uninterested, secretive. He walked down the hall and knocked softly on the door of Dudley Ward's room.

Presently it opened and Ward appeared, a weary gray-haired man in pajamas, looking older than Chan had thought him.

'Mr. Chan!' he exclaimed. 'Is anything wrong?'

'There has been,' Chan explained, 'an accident.'

'An accident! Good lord! What now!' Ward ran into the hall and, seeing Sing, went with Charlie toward the recumbent figure.

'I find your servant unconscious from blow in face.'

'A blow! Who the devil — '

At sound of the familiar voice, the old man sat up. He looked his master over disapprovingly.

'What's mallah you?' he demanded. 'You crazy? You walk loun' heah no bathrobe, no slippahs, you catch 'um plenty col'. You mebbe die.'

'Never mind that,' Ward said. 'Who hit you, Sing?'

Sing shrugged. 'How my know? Plenty big man, mebbe. Plenty big fist. Jus' hide in dahk an' hit me. Tha's all.'

'You didn't see him?'

'How my do that?' He struggled to get to his feet, and Charlie helped him. 'No light nowheh.' With a groan he pushed Chan aside, and tottered unsteadily into Ward's room. In a moment he returned with bathrobe and slippers. 'Heah, Boss — you lissen to Sing. You go loun' like crazy man, you catch 'um all kin' col'.'

Ward sighed and submitted meekly to the

additions to his costume. 'Very well,' he said. 'But what were you doing down here, anyhow?'

'What my always do?' Sing queried in a complaining voice. 'Woik, woik, all time woik. Wake up, take look-see clock, think mebbe moah bettah my go down cellah fix fiah. People all ovah house, too many people, they wake up say too col'.' He viewed his master as one who had been meaning to speak of this matter for some time. 'Too much woik this house. Nevah no stop. Too much fo' me. No can do. No can do.'

'He's been talking like that for fifty years,' Ward explained to Chan, 'and I have to battle him tooth and nail to get another servant on to the place. God knows I don't want him to get up at three in the morning and fix the furnace. Well' — he turned to Sing — 'did you fix it?'

'My fix 'um,' nodded the old man. 'Put new logs down-steh, too. Then came up heah, fist come out f'om dahk, catch 'um my jaw. Tha's all.'

Charlie patted him on the back. 'You go to bed now,' he suggested. 'Too many people in this house — you have spoken truly there. Not very nice people, some of them. Aged men should not consort with ruffians. Eggs should not dance with stones.'

'Goo' night,' replied Sing, and departed.

Chan turned to his host. 'I note you are shivering,' he said. 'Kindly step into my room for a moment. I have maintained my fire, which you will find welcome, I think.' He led the way and indicated a chair. 'Who, I would ask, has perpetrated this latest outrage?'

Ward sat down, and stared into the fire. 'Don't ask me, please,' he said wearily. 'I'd like to get my hands on him, whoever he is. A harmless old man like Sing — but good lord — I'm all at sea.'

'I am inclined to wonder,' Chan mused. 'In a way, the sheriff left me in charge here to-night. Can it be that one of my birds has flown? With your permission, I intend to make a brief survey.'

'Maybe you'd better,' Ward nodded.

'The rooms of Romano, Ryder and Swan I know,' Charlie continued. 'I will also, I think, investigate that of young Hugh Beaton, if you will acquaint me with his door.'

Ward did so, and Chan went out. In less than ten minutes he returned.

'The loss of one night's sleep means ten days of discomfort,' he smiled. 'Happy to say none of the gentlemen we mentioned faces such a fate. I opened the door of each, flashed light on bed. One and all they appeared to slumber.'

'Well — that gets us nowhere,' Ward remarked.

'As far as I expected,' Charlie replied. 'Yes, they slumbered — and not one faced the door. The long arm of coincidence, I believe it is called. Speaking for myself, I was plenty glad to find them here at all, asleep or otherwise.'

Ward rose. 'I may as well go back to bed, I fancy. It is not easy for me to sleep to-night, Inspector. Ellen dead — in this old house where I had expected to spend a happy life with her. And to-morrow we must go over to Reno and look into her affairs.' He laid his hand on Chan's arm. 'I'm afraid,' he added.

'Afraid?' Chan asked.

'Yes. Suppose — I have a son. A boy who has never heard of me — never seen me. It came to me to-night — after I went to bed. What will I mean to him? Less than nothing. Love — affection — never, under those conditions. Too late, Mr. Chan. Always too late, for me.'

'Go back and seek for sleep, at least,' Charlie said gently. 'As for the future — when you have reached the river, then is the time to take off your shoes.'

After Ward had gone, Charlie put fresh logs on the fire and sat down — in front of it this time, but with his door open. He was thoroughly awake now, and four o'clock in the morning is an excellent time to think. What was behind this unprovoked attack on Sing? Or was it unprovoked? Did Sing know who it was that had struck him? If so — why should he hide it? Fear, no doubt, fear of the white man inspired in the old Chinese of mining-camp days by years of rough treatment and oppression.

A clue. Charlie eagerly searched his mind for a clue. 'No can do,' the old man had muttered, semiconscious on the floor. But that was probably just the refrain that ran through all his days: 'Too much woik this house. No can do.' The complaint under which he hid his real devotion.

Chan sighed. It was too early, he decided, to place this attack in the scheme of things, too early to come to any real decision regarding the murder of Landini. For the present, the mere marshaling of facts must suffice, and so he sat and marshaled them in that mind which he had called 'large, empty place that makes good storehouse.' He marshaled them while the chill dawn crept across the lake, and somewhere behind the snowcapped peaks a yellow sun was rising. Doors began to slam, the voice of Mrs. O'Ferrell was heard in the land, and from the distant kitchen came, faintly, the bark of a dog.

While Chan bathed and shaved, his mind was filled with Trouble. Trouble, the dog.

When finally Charlie was ready to go down-stairs, the sun was on the lake, and a prospect of breath-taking beauty was spread before him. He opened his window and leaned far out enjoying the cool, fresh, bracing mountain air. In the darkness of the night he had had his doubts, but now he felt he could conquer the world. Problems, puzzles — he welcomed them.

He walked, with his chest well out, through the chilly hall and down the stairs. The delicious odor of bacon and coffee floated about him. He knew he would enjoy his breakfast, even though, at the same table, sat the murderer of Ellen Landini.

Reaching that table, he found Ward, Ryder and Swan already there. They greeted him with varying degrees of cordiality. At Chan's heels came Romano, his sartorial elegance a bit cheapened by the clean light of day. Scarcely had he and Charlie sat down when Leslie Beaton appeared, and all the men rose.

'Ah, Miss Beaton,' said Ward. 'So happy to have you here. And looking, if I may say so, as fresh and beautiful as the morning.'

'I thought I'd have to appear in an evening gown,' she smiled. 'But Cecile saved the situation. She's really a brick.' She turned upon her heel for inspection. 'What do you think of it?'

She was referring to the morning frock in which she was garbed. Evidently it met with their approval.

'I think it's cute,' the girl went on. 'But why shouldn't it be? Cecile is French. Of course, there's not enough of me to fill it, quite. But I'm so hungry, I'm sure there will be — after breakfast.' When she was seated, she looked suddenly at Chan. 'I'll simply have to go over to Reno today and get my things — '

'That,' said Charlie, 'depends on the sheriff. Do not, I beg of you, squander such a charming smile on me.'

'Oh, I have others,' she assured him. 'Plenty for the sheriff, too.' For the first time, the shadow of the night before crossed her face. 'Must — must we really stay here?'

'Come, come,' said Ward with forced gaiety. 'That's not exactly complimentary to me. And I'm trying so hard to be the perfect host.'

'Succeeding, too,' the girl replied. 'But the conditions — they are unusual. One can't help feeling that underneath you may be — for all your kindness — an unwilling host.'

'Never — to you,' Ward murmured. And as Sing appeared at his elbow, he added: 'What

140

fruit will you have? We have all kinds — of oranges.'

'I'll have the nicest kind,' said the girl. 'Good morning, Sing. Why — the poor man! He's hurt his face.'

Chan had already noted that the left jaw of the servant was swollen and discolored. Sing shrugged his shoulders and departed.

'Sh,' said Ward. 'He's had an accident. We won't say anything about it — he's rather sensitive, you know.'

'He's limping, too,' the girl went on.

'It was rather a bad accident,' Ward explained. 'He fell on the stairs, you see.'

'Poor Sing's getting old,' Ryder remarked. 'I was noticing it last night. He doesn't see very well. Shouldn't he have glasses, Dudley?'

Ward grimaced. 'Of course he should — and has. Or had, rather. But he broke them about a month ago — and you know how stubborn he is. I've been pleading with him ever since to get them fixed — by George, I'll take them over to Reno with me this morning. An optician over there has his prescription.'

Hugh Beaton came in, glum and in the mood of genius at breakfast. The repast continued, to the accompaniment of a conversation that was surprisingly cheerful, all things considered.

But in this Charlie took no part. He had several new facts to marshal in the storehouse of his mind. So Sing was limping this morning? It seemed impossible he could have hurt his leg in the fall that resulted from an encounter with an unknown fist. He had given no indication of such an injury at the time. And — there was the overturned dressing-table bench in the old sitting-room next to the study upstairs.

And Sing needed glasses. Usually wore them, in fact. Well, that fitted in, too. The confusion of the box lids. For a moment Charlie's appetite lost some of its keenness. But no — too early yet, he decided. Get all the facts in mind. Wait until you reach the river before you start to unlace your shoes.

After breakfast, Charlie visited the kitchen for a brief call on Mrs. O'Ferrell and Trouble. He spoke enthusiastically of the former's coffee — so much so she never dreamed that he greatly preferred tea. The dog romped in a friendly fashion at his feet.

'Look at him — the little darlin',' Mrs. O'Ferrell remarked. 'Sure, I've only knowed him a few hours, an' he's like an old friend.'

Charlie picked up the dog and stroked it musingly. 'I have known him but a brief time myself,' he said, 'and yet I have for him a deep affection.'

'I been thinkin',' the cook continued. 'If no wan else wants him, couldn't you leave him here, Mr. Chan? What with the lady gone, an' no wan to take care iv him — '

'As to that,' Chan replied, 'I can not say. I can only tell you that at least once — Trouble must go back to Reno.' He put the dog on the floor, gave it a final pat and moved to the door. 'Yes,' he repeated firmly. 'Trouble must make that journey to Reno. And he must make it — by airplane.'

Leaving Mrs. O'Ferrell deeply mystified by this cryptic statement, he returned to the big living-room. Most of the guests were there, and in the center of the room stood Don Holt, the sheriff. Beside him was a man who would have been a figure of distinction in any company, tall, erect, with snow-white hair. Chan's heart was touched as he noted the sightless eyes.

'Morning, Mr. Chan,' cried Don Holt. 'Great day, ain't it? I brought my Dad along — want you to know him. Father — Inspector Chan, of Honolulu.'

Chan took the groping hand in his. 'To meet an old-time sheriff of the mining camps,' he said. 'An honor I have always longed for, but never dreamed should encounter.'

'Old-time is right, Inspector,' replied Sam

Holt, with a grim smile. 'And the old times — they don't come back. I sure am glad that you're on hand to give my boy a lift.'

'I am plenty happy, too,' Chan assured him.

'Well, we're all ready for business, I reckon,' Don Holt said. 'Miss Beaton here has just been telling me that she's got to go to Reno to get her tooth-brush — and — and — I said I guessed we'd better let you decide.'

Charlie smiled. 'A diplomatic reply. You put all the young lady's disfavor on me.'

'Then you don't think — '

'There were, you recall,' Chan continued, 'five — no, six — people not in view at a certain fatal moment last night. None of the six must cross state line — '

Swan pushed forward. 'What about me? I've got a dozen appointments to-day. And not so much as a clean collar on this side of the line.'

'What a pity,' Chan shrugged. 'Give us a list of what you desire from your residence — and the location of same. Also — if you so desire — the key.' Swan hesitated. 'We go there in any case,' Chan added meaningly.

'Oh, very well,' Swan agreed.

'Say — that's an idea,' young Holt said. 'Miss Beaton — if you'll give me a list — '

'Not quite the same,' she smiled.

'Well — ah — er — maybe not, come to think of it,' he admitted, suddenly embarrassed.

'We will take Miss Beaton's brother with us,' Chan suggested. 'He may be given the list.'

'That's a fine idea,' Holt cried. The girl shrugged and turned away. 'Now' — the young sheriff turned to Chan — 'before we go, I guess we better have a talk. Upstairs — what do you say?'

Ah Sing suddenly appeared from the dining-room. He stood for a moment, staring at Sam Holt, then hurried over and grasped the old man's hand.

'Hello, Shef,' he cried. 'Haply see you.'

'Hello, Sing,' Sam Holt answered. 'I'm happy to — er — to see you, too. But I ain't sheriff no more. Things change, boy. We're old men now.'

'You go on being shef fo' me,' Sing insisted. 'Always shef fo' me.'

On the handsome face of Sam Holt appeared an expression that was a mixture of regret and resignation. He patted his ancient friend on the back affectionately, then put his arm about the other's shoulder.

'Take me up-stairs, boy,' he said. 'I want to see that there study. Used to know my way about this house so well — I could travel it in

— in the dark. But now — I sort of forgit. Lead the way, Sing.'

With loving solicitude the servant helped him up the stairs, and his son and Charlie followed. When they all reached the study, Sam Holt turned to Sing.

'More better you run along now,' he remarked. 'I see you later. Wait a minute. You catch 'um Dudley Ward — tell him Sam Holt's up here.'

Sing departed, and the old man began to move slowly, feeling his way about the room. His son stepped forward to assist him. 'This is the desk, Dad,' he said. 'Where we found the loose tobacco — and the boxes with the jumbled cigarettes.' He added aside to Chan: 'I've been all over the case with him this morning.'

'An excellent course,' nodded Charlie heartily.

'And here,' the boy went on, 'these are the windows, Dad.'

'There used to be a balcony out there.'

'There still is. That was one of the last places Landini was seen alive. By the aviator, you know.'

'Oh, yes — by the aviator. But Sing — Sing saw her last?'

'Yes — when she sent him to bring the blanket.'

'Needn't go all over it again,' his father objected. 'My memory's as good as yours, I reckon. Give me a chair, son.' He sat down in a velvet-covered chair before the fire. 'Poor Ellen Landini. Mighty curious, Mr. Chan, that she had to come way back to this house to hand in her chips. Knew her, long ago. Beautiful. Beautiful girl. Somebody's comin' down the hall.'

Dudley Ward appeared in the doorway and greeted the old sheriff cordially.

'Jes' wanted to pay my respects, Dudley,' Sam Holt said. 'Tell you I'm sorry about — all this. Poor Ellen — I was jes' sayin'. Kyards always seemed stacked against her, somehow. You too, boy, you too.' He lowered his voice. 'Don was tellin' me that story — mebbe a son — a kid somewhere — '

'Maybe,' Ward said.

'Who knew about that, Dudley?' the old man continued. 'Of course, Mr. Chan — and that other three — Swan, Romano, Ryder? And Sing, I reckon. Of course, you'd tell Sing. But who else?'

'Why — nobody, Sam. Just this woman — this Cecile. The woman who told me the story first.'

'Nobody else, boy?'

'Not that I know of.'

'Well — 'taint important. Don tells me

147

you're all goin' off to Reno — you run along an' git ready. Don't let me keep you.'

When Ward had gone, Don Holt got up and shut the door. 'Anything happen last night?' he inquired of Charlie.

Quickly Chan reported the assault on Sing. Both men received the account with rising indignation. Charlie ended with the information that Sing was limping this morning.

'Oh, yes — that bench in the next room,' Don Holt said. 'Still — maybe that's not the tie-up. Might have cracked it when this guy hit him and he fell. No — Sing's got nothing to do with this — we can bank on that. I ain't going to waste any time on Sing.'

Sam Holt was idly plucking with his thin old hand at the arm of his chair. 'Ain't it about time Cash Shannon showed up, son?' he inquired.

'Ought to be,' the boy agreed. 'Cash is a cowboy down at the stables,' he explained to Charlie, 'and a deputy of mine. I'm havin' him up here to-day to keep an eye on things while we're all away. I'll go down an' see if he's got here yet.'

'Shet the door when you go out,' Sam Holt suggested. When he heard it close, he said: 'Mr. Chan, I'm sure glad you're with us on this case. I reckon, from what Don tells me about ye, you an' me would sort of think

148

along the same lines. I ain't never had no use for science — the world was gittin' along a whole lot better before science was discovered.'

Charlie smiled. 'You mean finger-prints, laboratory tests, blood analysis — all that. I agree, Mr. Holt. In my investigations of murder I have thought, always, of the human heart. What passions have been at work — hate, greed, envy, jealousy? I study always — people.'

'Always people — you said it, Mr. Chan. The human heart.'

'Yes — though even there, one meets difficulties. As a philosopher of my race has said: 'The fishes, though deep in the water, may be hooked; the birds, though high in the air, may be shot; but man's heart only is out of our reach.''

Sam Holt shook his head. 'Mighty purty language, that is, but man's heart ain't always out of our reach. If it was, you an' me wouldn't of made no record on our jobs, Mr. Chan.'

'Your statement has truth,' Chan nodded.

For a long time the former sheriff of the mining camps did not speak. His sightless eyes were turned toward the fire, but his hands were busy. He seemed to be gathering some invisible substance from the arm of his

149

chair with his right hand, and depositing it in his left.

'Mr. Chan,' he said suddenly, 'how close kin you git to the heart of Ah Sing?'

'It overwhelms me with sadness to admit it,' Charlie answered, 'for he is of my own origin, my own race, as you know. But when I look into his eyes I discover that a gulf like the heaving Pacific lies between us. Why? Because he, though among Caucasians many more years than I, still remains Chinese. As Chinese to-day as in the first moon of his existence. While I — I bear the brand — the label — Americanized.'

Holt nodded. 'You've stated the case. These old Chinese in this stretch of the state ain't never been anything else. Maybe they didn't admire the ways of the stranger — I dunno. Which I wouldn't of blamed 'em. But they was born Chinese, an' they stayed that way.'

Chan bowed his head. 'I traveled with the current,' he said softly. 'I was ambitious. I sought success. For what I have won, I paid the price. Am I an American? No. Am I, then, a Chinese? Not in the eyes of Ah Sing.' He paused for a moment, then continued: 'But I have chosen my path, and I must follow it. You are sitting there as one about to tell me something.'

'I'm sitting here wondering,' Sam Holt

replied. 'Can I make you understand what Ah Sing's been to me — a friend fer fifty years? I used to take the Ward boys an' him camping, up where it's really high. We used to lay out under the stars — why, I'd ruther cut out my tongue — than say a word — but duty's duty — an' this is my boy's first big case — ' He stopped, and held something out to Chan. 'Mr. Chan — what is this I been pulling from the arm of my chair?'

'It is light, airy fuzz,' Chan told him. 'Sort of fuzz readily yielded by wool blanket in contact with velvet.'

'And the color, man — the color?'

'It — it appears to be blue.'

'Blue. Landini sent Sing fer a blanket. He came back with it after you found the body. Came back with — a blue blanket. You sent him away with it. Yes, Don was tellin' me. He took it and went out — he never laid it down?'

'That is quite true,' said Chan gravely.

'He never laid it down — that time,' the old sheriff continued, his voice trembling, 'but — God help me — that blanket had been in this room before.'

Neither spoke. Chan regarded the old man with silent admiration.

Sam Holt rose, and began to stumble about the room. He found an unobstructed path, and started to pace it.

'It's all clear. Mr. Chan. He was sent fer that blanket — he came back with it — Landini was here alone — he threw the blanket over that chair — he shot Landini with her own revolver. Then he snatched up the blanket, tidied up that desk, went through the room next door — open because he'd planned it all — and when the stage was clear, walked calm-like on to the scene with the blanket he'd been sent fer. As simple as that. And do I have to tell you why he killed her, Mr. Chan?'

Charlie had listened to this with growing conviction. Now his eyes narrowed. 'I was wondering why you asked Dudley Ward whether or not Sing knew about the child. You did it most adroitly.'

'The kid,' said old Sam Holt. 'The kid — there's our answer.' He offered Charlie the collection of fuzz. 'Put it in an envelope, please. We'll compare it with that blanket later — but it ain't really necessary. Yes, Mr. Chan — that lost boy of Dudley Ward's was the first thing I thought of when Don told me the story of the murder.' He stumbled back to his chair and dropped into it.

'You see, sir, I knew the way of these old Chinese servants with the boys of the family. They love 'em. Year after year I seen old Sing cookin' an' slavin' fer Dudley Ward an' his brother — takin' care of 'em since they left the cradle — lovin' an' scoldin' 'em an' treatin' 'em always like babies. An' I knew what it must have meant to Sing that they was no little boys in this house, or in the big house down in 'Frisco. Jes' loneliness in the kitchen, no kids beggin' fer rice an' gravy. An' then he hears that there was a kid — only Landini kept it dark — never let its father know — never brought it out here where it belonged. He hears that, Mr. Chan, en' whet happens? He sees red. He hates. He hates Ellen Landini — an' I kain't say I blame him.

'Even Dudley Ward doesn't suspect what's in the old man's heart. He invites Landini over here. An' Sing gits his chance. Yes, Mr. Chan — it was Sing who came into this room last night an' killed Landini — an' I would ruther be hung myself than say it.'

'I have somewhat similar feeling,' Charlie admitted.

'But you reckon I'm right.'

Chan glanced toward the envelope into which he had put the wool from the blue blanket. 'I very much fear you are.'

The door opened, and Don Holt entered. 'Come along,' he said. 'Cash is here, an' we're off to Reno. Why — what you two looking so solemn about?'

'Shet the door, son,' said Sam Holt. He rose and moved toward his boy. 'You know what I said to you this morning — about Sing?'

'Oh, but you're all wrong, Dad,' the boy assured him.

'Jest a minute. You know how Sing appeared in this room right after the murder, with a blue blanket under his arm?'

'Sure I do.'

'Well — if I was to tell you I found blue fuzz from a blanket on the arm of that thar chair over there — what would you say? You'd say the blanket had been in this room before Sing appeared with it, wouldn't you?'

Don Holt considered. 'I might,' he admitted. 'And then again — I might say that it had come back here later — after the murder.'

'What do you mean by that?' his father asked.

'Why, when we carried Landini out of the house last night, we wrapped her in blankets. Sing brought them to us here. Blue blankets they were, too. And while I don't exactly recall, we may have laid 'em across that chair before we used 'em.'

A delighted smile spread over Sam Holt's face. 'Boy,' he said, 'I ain't never been so proud of you before. Mr. Chan, I reckon I've gone and wandered into the wrong pew. What do you think?'

'The wrong pew, perhaps,' Charlie replied politely, 'but maybe correct church. Who can say?'

# 8

## The Streets of Reno

When they came down-stairs, Doctor Swan was waiting for them beside the fire. He handed the sheriff an envelope and also a folded sheet of paper.

'A letter to my landlady,' he explained. 'And a list of things I'll need — you'll find a bag in the closet to put them in. I hope to heaven I'll be able to get home pretty quickly — what do you think?'

'I hope so, too, Doctor,' the sheriff replied.

'You — have no clue, I suppose?'

'None at all,' responded the young man. 'Except that some one, who knew all about how Miss Beaton felt toward Landini, planted that pink scarf and the pin. We're investigatin' that.'

The doctor gave him an unpleasant look and turned away.

Romano came up, looking rather forlorn. 'Pleasant journey,' he remarked.

'Sorry you ain't goin' anywhere,' smiled Don Holt.

Romano shrugged. 'Me — I have no place

to go — and no money to take me there, if I had.'

'Does it chance,' Chan inquired, 'that there exists some errand we could perform for you in Reno?'

'None,' Romano answered. 'But' — he came closer, and lowered his voice — 'would you be kind enough to inquire of Miss Meecher as to whether or not poor Ellen ever signed that new will?'

'Miss Meecher?'

'Yes — an estimable woman — Ellen's secretary. Estimable, but alas — so — what you call close-mouthed.'

Charlie nodded. 'Do not fret, I beg of you. That is one of the things we visit Reno to discover.'

'Good,' cried Romano. 'Splendid news. Excellent.'

Leslie Beaton and her brother appeared, the latter going at once for his hat and coat. Don Holt had stepped to the door leading to the kitchen, and he now returned with a youth whose costume suggested that a rodeo was impending. Bright blue corduroys were tucked into high-heeled boots, his shirt was yellow silk embroidered with pink roses, around his neck was a crimson scarf, and he carried a two-gallon hat in his hand.

'Folks,' said Holt, 'this here is Cash

157

Shannon, my deputy. You'll be seein' more of him — if your eyes can stand it.'

'Pleased to meet you,' remarked Mr. Shannon cordially.

'Miss Beaton — I hope you won't mind him — much,' Holt went on.

'Not at all,' the girl smiled. 'He's to keep an eye on me, I presume?'

'Lady,' said Cash in a deep emotional voice, 'the softest snap of my life. Easy to look at — that's what you are.'

Holt laughed. 'Don't pay any attention to him. He's such a fast worker he gets all tangled up. A lady's man — jes' born that way.'

'Better that than a woman-hater, like you,' Cash averred.

'A woman-hater,' cried the girl. 'You mean Mr. Holt?'

'Lady — you said it. These divorcees we git round here has jes' naturally soured him on the sex. Takes a herd of 'em out on a picnic, an' comes back ravin' about their war-paint an' their cigarettes, an' how women ain't what they used to be — an' probably never was.'

'Some women,' Holt corrected. 'I never said all.'

'I ain't deaf,' Cash returned. 'All women, you always said.' He squinted his eyes. 'Ain't never heard you make no exception — until now.'

'Well, let's get going,' said Holt hastily.

Dudley Ward appeared, ready for the journey. Miss Beaton went with them to the veranda, pronounced the morning gorgeous and moved on with the little group to the pier. Chan and Don Holt walked with the old sheriff, but he seemed perfectly able to keep a straight course down the path. Cash Shannon came up behind them.

'Say, listen, Don,' he remarked in a loud whisper, 'you're crazy. If that dame done murder, I'm Al Capone.'

'Get the girl off your mind,' Holt smiled. 'Remember, you're here to watch a lot of people. Sing, and the doctor, and Romano — that little Italian guy. Cecile, too. How do you know they ain't all goin' out the back door right now?'

'I get you,' nodded Cash. 'Mebbe I better go back.'

'Mebbe you had. An' when it comes to this girl, jes' keep one thing in mind. You ain't the sheriff. You're jes' the deputy.'

'Yes, sir,' responded Cash, and returned reluctantly to the house.

As they were about to step into the sheriff's launch the front door banged, and Sing ran like a rabbit down the path. He was waving wildly.

'Hey, Boss,' he panted when he reached

159

them. 'Heah — you catch 'um umbrella.'

'Umbrella,' Ward protested. 'The sun's shining.'

'Sun him shine now,' Sing announced, portentously. 'Plitty soon lain him fall. Sing know. You lissen to Sing.'

'Oh, all right,' Ward grinned. 'Give it to me.' Sing handed it to him, and retired up the path. 'Let's get off quick,' Ward continued. 'He's forgot to make me put on my arctics. Poor chap — I'm afraid he is getting old, after all.'

They guided Sam Holt into the launch, then Ward, Beaton and Chan followed. Don Holt turned to the girl.

'Look out for that Cash,' he warned. 'He's got a Romeo complex. I'll be back on the job myself by sundown.'

'Fine,' she smiled. 'I'll feel much safer then.'

The launch put-putted and they swept off over the sunlit lake. As they turned toward Tahoe, they could see the girl waving to them from the pier. A shrill cry from the house caused them to look back. Sing was standing on the steps, waving an arctic in each hand.

They all laughed, and Dudley Ward said, above the noise of the motor, 'Great! Two victories over Sing in one morning. I slipped into his room and got his broken glasses.' He held up a spectacles case. 'Mr. Chan —

160

please don't let me forget them while we're in town.'

Charlie nodded, but did not reply. The loveliness of the scene, so foreign to anything he had ever encountered before, enchanted him. The vista of snow-clad mountains, of deep blue water, of dark green pines, might indeed have thrilled one far less sensitive to beauty. And the air — he pitied all those who could not breathe such air this morning. Those of the cities, who awoke to the same old scent of gasoline — even those of his own Honolulu, who awoke to an air likely to send them, mentally at least, back to slumber. He was grateful to the fate that had brought him to this spot.

All too soon they reached the Tavern pier. As he walked with Sam Holt along the unsteady planks, solicitous lest the old sheriff's cane become caught in one of the many cracks, he sought to express some of his admiration for the Sierra Nevada country.

'Yes — it's a good place, I reckon,' Holt said. 'I was born here seventy-eight years ago, and I've stuck close. Read about them Alps in Switzerland. Used to think I'd like to see 'em. Kain't see my own mountains — no more. Are we alone, Mr. Chan?'

'We are,' said Charlie. 'The others are now far in advance.'

'I reckon you an' me — we're goin' to accept Don's explanation about the fuzz on that chair?'

'With the greatest of pleasure,' smiled Chan. 'On the part of both.'

Sam Holt smiled, too. 'I reckon so. But that don't mean we don't have to push ahead an' solve this case, Inspector.'

'I am keenly aware of the fact,' Charlie assured him.

'Nothing else against Sing — except that bench which got kicked over. You kain't prove anything by that. Ain't nothin' else, is they?'

'Not — not much,' Chan answered. 'Be very careful, please. The next plank is of a faulty nature.'

'I remember it,' Sam Holt replied. 'What was Dudley Ward sayin' about Sing's glasses? They got broke? When was that?'

'A long time ago — so I understand.'

'He wasn't wearin' 'em when you come last evenin'?'

'No — his sight was his own.'

Holt hesitated. 'Mr. Chan — the person who mixed them box lids last night wasn't seein' any too well.'

'I am forced to agree,' Charlie replied.

'Has it jes' happened to occur to you that the story told by that Beaton boy may have been correct? That Ellen Landini may have sent some person for her green scarf?'

'It has occurred to me,' Chan admitted.

'And the person came back with a pink one. Mr. Chan — that person wasn't seein' any too well, either.'

'I understand,' Chan replied.

Holt shook his head. 'If that boy Sing don't stop poppin' back into this thing like he was the killer, he'll jes' plumb break my heart,' he said.

'Cease to worry,' Charlie replied sympathetically. 'Maybe pretty quick we eliminate him.'

'Or else — '

'In any case, Mr. Holt,' Chan continued, 'please be so good as to accept my advice, so humbly offered. Cease to worry.'

Don Holt was waiting for them at the pier's end. 'Mr. Chan — the car's ready for us up in the drive. Dad, what are you going to do to-day?'

'Never mind, son. I kin take care of myself. I'm havin' lunch with Jim Dinsdale, an' other times I'll jes' loll round an' mebbe do a little thinkin'.'

'Well, you be careful,' the young sheriff said. 'Better keep inside — you don't want any cold — at your age. And whatever you do, watch your step — '

'Run along,' cut in Sam Holt. 'My God

— anybody would think I was a baby in the cradle to hear you. Mr. Chan — you got sons, I suppose?'

'Abundantly,' Charlie answered.

'They treat you this way?'

Chan took his hand. 'Princes have censors,' he remarked, 'and fathers have sons. A happy day to you — and once again — so proud to meet you.'

On the way to the drive in front of the garage, Chan encountered Dudley Ward. 'Now we are on our way,' the detective said, 'to important discoveries, I hope. May I venture the wish that such stirring morning does not find you — as you said last night — '

'Afraid?' Ward finished. 'No, Mr. Chan. A man is likely to feel a little low at four in the morning. If I have a boy somewhere, it will be happy news for me. I'm starting late, but by heaven, I'll win his respect and affection if it's the last act of my life. It will give me what I've lacked and needed for many years — an incentive — something to live for.'

Hugh Beaton joined them from behind. A silent young man, Charlie reflected. He had scarcely spoken all morning; his face was pale and drawn. No doubt the events of the night before were a bit hard on the artistic temperament.

Don Holt herded them into a big closed car, which he said belonged to Dinsdale, and they were off. Down through the scattered village, then on to Truckee, a bit more cheery in the bright morning. There they came on to the main highway, almost clear of snow, and the sheriff stepped on the gas.

They entered Reno through quiet pleasant streets that in no way suggested anything but the average western town. Charlie looked eagerly about him; here was no hint of night clubs, faro games, bars and merry prospective widows. The main street, Virginia, seemed the usual one, save for a preponderance of lawyers' offices and beauty parlors.

'Just a moment, Sheriff,' Ward said. 'Here's that optician's. I'll drop these glasses now — it will take some time to fix them. If you don't mind.'

'Sure, I don't,' resumed Holt amiably. He waited while a car slipped out of a parking place, and then moved in. Ward left them.

'Well, Mr. Chan,' Holt remarked, 'what do you think of the biggest little city in the world?'

'So far,' Charlie told him, 'it refuses to sustain its reputation.'

'You got to get it gradually,' the sheriff explained. 'For instance — them black chiffon nightgowns in that window. Not for

165

the western trade, Mr. Chan. An' all these beauty parlors — women have gone dippy over warpaint, but the local girls couldn't support so many. And that nurse in the funny dress — with them cute kids — goin' to have a brand-new papa, the poor little devils. Gradually it soaks in. The best people from the East come here — and raise hell with the West.'

But at this end of the street, Chan reflected, the West still ruled. Cowboys whose costumes were a faded imitation of the Cash Shannon splendor, cattle men and ranchers — and here an Indian woman with a papoose strapped to her back. It was not until Ward returned and they crossed the bridge over the yellow, tumbling Truckee River, that they began to mingle with the best people from the East. Holt parked in front of the new hotel, sliding in beside a long, low, foreign car, over which a glowering chauffeur, also foreign, stood guard. At the left was the dignified white court-house, the heart of the community. They entered the busy lobby of the hotel, and although Charlie never guessed it, he beheld a Patou hat and a Chanel ensemble for the first time in his life.

'I wonder,' Hugh Beaton said timidly, 'may I go up to my — to our — rooms now?'

He looked so pale and helpless that the

sheriff gave him a kindly pat. 'You gather up all the stuff you and your sister will need, and — '

'Need — for how long?' Beaton asked.

'How the heck should I know? Jes' gather up some stuff, an' meet us here in this lobby — say, at three o'clock. Run along, kid — an' cheer up.' He turned to Charlie. 'Why are you lookin' at me like that, Inspector?'

Chan smiled. 'Ah — I am just thinking. Is that the method of a good detective? Such a one would enter those rooms simultaneously — he would search — he would investigate correspondence.'

Holt shrugged his broad shoulders. 'I ain't no detective, good or otherwise. Thank the lord. I'm only a sheriff.'

The sleek young man at the desk looked at them suspiciously when Holt asked to be shown to Landini's apartment. 'Miss Meecher is up there alone,' he said. 'She's had a frightful morning. The reporters have been so rude.'

'Well, we're not reporters,' said Holt, He flashed his badge. 'I'm the sheriff from over the line, this is Mr. Dudley Ward, of Tahoe and San Francisco, and this is Mr. Charlie Chan, of Honolulu.'

Don Holt had a carrying voice, and it was not surprising that three young men at once leaped forward from behind near-by potted palms. They represented various press associations and the local paper, it appeared. The passing of Landini was news all over the world. The method of her passing was better still. After a struggle which reached major proportions, the sheriff and his companions got away, and started upstairs, where Miss Meecher awaited them. As the elevator ascended, Chan thought of Henry Lee, the steward, with a wry smile. 'I shall watch newspapers,' Mr. Lee had said.

Miss Meecher greeted them at the door, a repressed, middle-aged woman dressed in black. Very proper-looking, rather grim, but breathing efficiency.

'Come in, gentlemen,' she said. She met even Chan without a change of expression — a remarkable woman indeed, he thought. 'A terrible thing, this is. No one, evidently, thought to telephone me the news.'

'So sorry,' Chan remarked, 'but up to this morning, no one in authority knew of your existence. The others — Miss Beaton and her brother — were perhaps too overcome.'

'Perhaps,' she answered. Her voice was as crisp and cool as the mountain air. She added: 'I am glad you are here, Mr. Ward. Some one will have to attend to — to the services.'

Ward bowed his head. 'I'd already thought of it. I shall take full charge — it seems to be my duty. No one else appears to be interested — outside, of course, yourself.'

She nodded. 'Thank you. Then that is settled.' Efficient. No time for emotion. Just — what's the next thing to be done? Well — do it — and move on.

'Might I ask?' Ward continued, 'how long you have been with Madame Landini?'

'Over seven years,' Miss Meecher replied. 'I came first as secretary — lately I have more or less combined that post with the one of — maid. Times have not been so good — with any of us.'

Dudley Ward leaned suddenly forward. 'I'm sorry,' he said, and his voice trembled. 'I do not wish to seem abrupt. But there is one question I must ask you — and I can not hold it back — I can not wait. I have heard it rumored — that my wife had a son — my son — about whom she never told me. You can understand my feeling in this matter, I'm sure. I want to ask you — I want you to tell me — was there any truth in this rumor?'

Miss Meecher stared at him. The same expressionless face. 'I can not tell you,' she said. 'I do not know. Madame never mentioned the matter to me.'

Ward turned away, and sat looking out the window at his right, across an open space toward the white courthouse which had figured so largely in the life of Ellen Landini. Finally Chan broke the silence.

'Miss Meecher — the sheriff here will tell you that he authorizes me to speak for him — '

'That's right,' Holt nodded.

'Had you heard any word from Madame Landini, Miss Meecher, at any time, that might lead you to believe she considered her life in danger?'

'None at all. Of course, she carried a pistol, but that was from a fear of thugs, robbers. I'm sure she was not afraid of any of her intimates. She had no reason to be.'

'There are three or four men, Miss Meecher, about whose relations with Landini I wish to make inquiries.' The woman's expression finally changed — a little. 'Oh, most pleasant inquiries,' Chan assured her. 'Nothing of scandalous nature. I would mention John Ryder. Her second husband, you know.'

'I know.'

'She never heard from him? Had correspondence with him?'

'I don't imagine she thought of him, any more.'

'Have you the slightest idea why she separated from him? After many years, it would seem he still bears wound.'

'I can give you a notion,' Miss Meecher said. 'Madame's scrap-books of clippings from all over the world always traveled with us. In an early one, when I first came to her, I once read a certain item. Just a moment.' She rose briskly, went into the other room and reappeared with a worn old-fashioned book. Opening it, she handed it to Chan, and pointed.

Chan read slowly and carefully a newspaper clipping, now yellow with age:

ELLEN LANDINI SNOWED IN
Recently Divorced San Francisco
Singer in a Cabin 'Up the Ravine.'

SAN FRANCISCO, Feb. 9 — Ellen Landini, the singer, formerly the wife of Dudley Ward, of this city, but who was recently married to John Ryder, a mining man, is snowed in for the winter at Calico mine in Plumas County. After their marriage Mrs. Ryder gave up her career and took the trail with her husband over the Sierra Nevada Mountains to the Calico claim, of which he is manager. Heavy snow fell soon after the couple had established themselves in the superintendent's cabin up the ravine.

Some mining men who have come down from that country say snow is twenty-five feet deep on the level, and that it is one of the hardest winters northern California has known in many years. Twenty-five feet of snow means candle-light all day in the cabin and no fresh grub and little if any mail; snow on the ground until June and no chance to get out with comfort before summer.

Chan handed the book to the sheriff, and looked at Miss Meecher. 'It has aspect of romantic situation,' he remarked, 'rather than grounds for divorce.'

'That,' the woman replied, 'is what I remarked to Madame when I read it. I — I was somewhat younger at the time. Madame burst into loud laughter 'Romantic, Mary,' she cried. 'Ah, but life is not like that. Romantic to find yourself shut up in one room for eternity with the most colossal bore since the world began! A sullen egotist, with the conversational powers of a mummy. In a week I loathed him, in another I despised him, in a month I could have killed him. I was the first person out of that camp in the spring, and I thanked God it was only a few miles to Reno.' I am quoting Madame, you understand, Mr. Chan.'

Charlie smiled. 'Ah, yes — that would, I have no doubt, happen. It begins to explain Mr. Ryder. If you do not incline to object, I would remove this clipping.'

Miss Meecher looked startled at the idea, but then remembered. 'Oh, of course,' she said. 'It won't matter particularly now.'

Chan took the book from the sheriff, and carefully cut out the tale of Landini's second marriage. Meanwhile, Dudley Ward sat, still silent, by the window, apparently hearing none of this.

'We proceed,' Chan continued. 'And in the course of our proceedings we now arrive at Mr. Luis Romano.'

Miss Meecher so far forgot her stern aloofness as to permit herself a shrug of disgust.

'Romano,' she said, 'we haven't seen him in months. You don't mean to say that he is in this neighborhood?'

'He was at Mr. Ward's home last evening. I admired his attitude toward Madame Landini. What, if you please, was her attitude toward him?'

'Oh, she tolerated him. He was a harmless little idiot. Why she ever married him I'm sure I don't know — and I'm sure that Madame didn't either. She liked to be petted, pampered, looked after. But there is no real romance in that — and she finally sent him on his way.'

'Making a settlement — which she later ignored.'

'I'm afraid she did. She couldn't help herself. She owns a great deal of real estate — but ready cash has been very scarce.'

'Speaking of real estate — she drew up a will, leaving her property to her new attraction — Mr. Hugh Beaton. I am eager to know — was that will ever signed?'

Miss Meecher suddenly put her hand to her cheek. 'Good heavens — I never thought of that. It was — it was never signed.'

Even Dudley Ward looked up. 'Never signed, eh?' cried Don Holt.

'No. It came from her lawyers three weeks ago. There was something in it that wasn't quite right. She was going to have it fixed here — but she kept putting it off. She was always — putting things off.'

'Then Luis Romano inherits her estate?' Chan said thoughtfully.

'I'm afraid he does.'

'Do you think he knew this?'

'If he didn't, it wasn't his fault. He kept writing, trying to find out whether or not the will had been signed. He wrote to me, privately. But of course I didn't tell him. Perhaps — perhaps he wrote to her lawyers, in New York.'

Chan sat for a moment quietly, considering this startling possibility.

'We drop that for the present,' he said finally. 'I turn now to Michael Ireland, the aviator. Would you talk about him, please?'

'There's nothing to say,' Miss Meecher answered. 'I believe there was once a sort of love-affair between him and Madame. It was before my time. Since she came here, she's enjoyed riding about in his plane. But the affair was over — on her side, at least. I'm sure of that.'

'And on his side?'

'Well — I suppose I must tell everything. I did overhear him making love to her here one evening. But she only laughed at him.'

'So — she laughed at him, eh?' Again Chan considered.

'Yes — she told him to stick to his wife. She reminded him that when she first saw him, he had just come home from the war, and was in uniform. 'It was the uniform, Michael,' I heard her say. 'I loved every man who wore one!''

Chan's eyes narrowed. 'So Ireland served in the war? A steady hand. A clear eye. An expert — ' He saw Don Holt looking at him with amazement. 'What of it?' he added hastily. 'Miss Meecher, there is one I have saved to the last. I refer to Doctor Swan.'

'Contemptible,' spoke Miss Meecher, and her thin lips closed tightly.

'So I have gathered,' Charlie replied. 'Since you have come to Reno, he has visited Madame?'

'He has.'

'Ah, yes — he lied to us about that. But visits were necessary if he was to follow his trade.'

'You mean — as doctor?'

'Alas, no. I mean as blackmailer, Miss Meecher.'

The woman started. 'Who told you that?'

'No matter. We know it. We know that Madame had long paid him two hundred and fifty dollars a month. Why did she pay him this money?'

'I — I don't know,' the secretary said.

'Ah — I am so sorry to contradict a lady,' Charlie went on sadly. 'But you do know, Miss Meecher. You know quite well Landini paid him this money because he had somehow become aware of the birth of her child. She paid it to him because he threatened that, if she did not, he would acquaint Mr. Dudley Ward, the child's father, with the facts. Come — Miss Meecher — this is not the time for double dealing. I want the truth.'

Dudley Ward was on his feet. Perspiration gleamed on his forehead as he faced the woman. 'I — I want it too,' he cried.

Miss Meecher looked up at him. 'I'm sorry,' she said. 'When you first came in — I wasn't sure — I wanted a moment to think. I — I have thought. It doesn't really matter now, I suppose. You may as well know: Yes — Madame had a son. A lovely boy. I saw him once. Dudley — she called him. He would have been eighteen next January — if — '

'If — what?' Ward cried hoarsely.

'If he — had lived. He was killed in an automobile accident over three years ago. I'm so sorry, Mr. Ward.'

Ward had put his hands out, feebly, as though to fend off a blow. 'And I never saw him,' he said brokenly. 'I never saw him.' He turned, and walking to the window, leaned heavily against it.

# 9

## Trouble Takes Wing

The three other people in Landini's small sitting-room looked at one another, but did not speak. For a time Ward continued to stare out the window. At length he turned, he was pale, but self-controlled and calm. Blood, the young Sheriff thought to himself, will tell. The cowards never started on that rush of '49, and the weaklings died on the way, but Dudley Ward was descended from a man who had reached journey's end. His voice was steady as he said: 'Thank you so much for telling me.'

'I knew, of course, the child was dead,' Chan remarked, 'when you told us Romano was Landini's only heir. You have, perhaps, Miss Meecher, some documents regarding the boy's death?'

She rose. 'Yes. I have the telegram that was our first news of it, and the letter that followed from his foster-mother. Madame always kept them close to her.'

She opened a desk drawer, and producing these, handed them to Dudley Ward. They

178

waited while he read them. 'That is finished,' he said finally, and returned them.

'Madame read that letter over and over,' Miss Meecher told him. 'I want you to know, Mr. Ward, that she adored this boy. Though she rarely saw him, though he regarded himself as the son of — of others — he was always in her thoughts. You must — believe this.'

'Yes,' Ward said dully, and again turned to the window.

'Then it is true,' Charlie said to the woman in a subdued voice, 'that Doctor Swan was blackmailing her about this matter?'

'Yes — he was. She did not want Mr. Ward to hear about the boy — even after — the accident.'

'Recently she stopped the payments, and Doctor Swan — perhaps he threatened her?'

'He was very violent and abusive about it. I don't believe he had a successful practice, and it appeared that this money meant a lot to him. I don't know that he actually threatened her life, however. But he was a man capable of almost anything.'

Chan nodded toward the desk. 'I note there long strips of paper with printing. Am I correct in calling them proofs of book?'

Miss Meecher nodded. 'They are galley proofs of Madame's autobiography, which I have been helping her to write for the past few years. The book is to be published very soon.'

'Ah,' returned Charlie, a sudden eagerness in his voice, 'would you, perhaps, object if I took same with me and perused them? Some little detail, some chance remark — '

'By all means,' Miss Meecher replied. 'If you'll be kind enough to return them. As a matter of fact — I'd like to have you read them. I'm afraid you've got rather a — well, a mistaken idea of Madame. If you had really known her as I knew her — ' She stopped, and a terrible dry sob shook her thin shoulders. It passed in a moment. 'She was really the kindest person — the victim of a wrong impression fostered by her many marriages. She was just restless, unhappy, always seeking romance — and never finding it.'

'No doubt she has been misjudged,' Chan returned politely. 'Public opinion is often an envious dog barking at the heels of greatness. Ah, thank you — you needn't wrap the proofs. This large elastic will suffice. You shall have them back at very earliest moment. Now, I think, Mr. Ward, if you are willing, we will trouble this lady no longer.'

'Of course,' Ward answered. He looked at Miss Meecher. 'There were — photographs — I suppose?'

'Many. They belong to you now.' She started on her efficient way, but he laid a hand on her arm.

'Please,' he said, 'a little later. I — I couldn't bring myself — If you will be so kind, you might gather them up for me.'

'I will,' she promised.

'You have been so good, Miss Meecher,' Chan remarked, bowing low. 'Always I shall remember your frankness. It is of such great help.'

'There's just one thing,' the secretary returned, 'that you might do for me.'

'You have only to name it.'

'Trouble,' said the woman. 'Trouble, the dog. He and I had much in common — we both loved Madame. I should like to have him, if I might. I am certain Madame would wish it.'

'I will despatch him to you with the greatest speed,' Chan promised. 'Perhaps — by airplane.'

'Thank you so much. He — he will be company for me here.' And Charlie saw, as he took his leave, that at last there were tears in the eyes of the aloof Miss Meecher.

The three men rode down in the elevator, Chan and the sheriff both slightly uncomfortable at the feeling that there was something they should say to Ward and neither being

181

able to put it into words.

'There are a number of things I must attend to,' Ward remarked, when they reached the lobby. 'I fancy I'm not concerned in your further investigation here. I'll meet you again on this spot at three.'

'That'll be fine,' the sheriff said, and Chan nodded. Ward disappeared, and Holt added: 'Doggone it, I wanted to say something about the kid, but I jes' plumb couldn't.'

'There are times,' Charlie told him, 'when words, though meant in kindness, are but salt in the wound.'

'There sure are. Well, what do you say? I had breakfast at six, and it's nearly one. Let's eat, Inspector.'

Into the rather effete dining-room Don Holt brought a breath of the West. Women in smart Paris costumes looked up admiringly as he passed, and registered a startled interest at sight of the broad figure which followed meekly at his heels. Ignoring them all, the sheriff sat down and with difficulty selected a man-size lunch from the French items on the menu. When the waiter had departed — a friendly waiter who treated them like old pals — Charlie ventured a question.

'You propose to visit local police?'

Holt grinned. 'No — reckon I'll give them a bitter disappointment by passing them up.

Nothing to gain, that I can see. Say, won't they be sore! All this lovely publicity, an' they on the outside, lookin' in. But you're going to be all the help I'll need, Mr. Chan. I can see that, right now.'

'Sincerely trust you are not too optimistic,' Charlie answered. 'Can it be you glimpse light of solution ahead?'

'Me?' cried Holt. 'I ain't got the slightest idea what's goin' on. But some men — well, you jes' look at 'em, and you get confidence. You're one like that.'

Charlie smiled. 'I should gaze more often in mirror,' he replied. 'Myself, I am not so sure. This is hard case. However, Miss Meecher was mine of information.'

'Yeah — you got plenty out of her, didn't you?'

'Our success was gratifying. We learn — what? The background of Landini's second marriage — that to John Ryder. Snowed in with him up the ravine — the poor lady has, even at late day like this, my sincere condolences. We learn what may prove vastly important clue — new will was left unsigned, and Romano is happy heir. Did he know this? If he did, then case may end a very simple one. We learn that Swan's blackmail concerned the dead son of Landini, hear of the doctor's anger when payment at last was ended. Also, that Michael Ireland made love, and was repulsed. Is our motive hidden somewhere among these?'

'Also — though I can't see that it means anything — we hear that Ireland was in the war,' Holt remarked. 'I must say, Mr. Chan — you acted mighty mysterious right there. Last night you said some pretty queer things, too — but I want to assure you here an' now — I ain't going to ask any questions.'

'Thank you so much,' Charlie said. 'But as clues pop up in this case, I promise I will draw them to your attention. We work on the matter together.'

'Yeah — but with different brains,' grinned Holt. 'Well, here's once I guessed right. Filet mignon does mean steak — but not much of it.'

After lunch they visited Swan's lodgings. The landlady, who appeared to be waging a battle against age with the assistance of various drug-store preparations, was suspicious at first, but soon succumbed to Don Holt's charm. From then on, she was almost too solicitous. However, they managed a search of the rooms, with absolutely no result, and then proceeded to gather up the articles the doctor had listed.

'Well, I reckon we're jes' errand boys, after all,' remarked Holt, as he tossed an armful of gaudy shirts into the suitcase. 'And I wanted to get something on this bird, the worst way.'

'Ah,' nodded Chan, 'you still hold him responsible for awkward situation regarding Miss Beaton's scarf.'

'He put it there, of course. That's plain enough.'

'If he did,' Chan continued, 'then he also persuaded Landini to grasp it before he killed her. I am plenty sure of that.'

'Well, maybe he did,' said the sheriff.

They returned presently to the hotel. Ward and Beaton were sitting in the lobby, the latter with two large bags at his feet. A little later they were on their way down Virginia Street. Dudley Ward sat silent, and as they passed the optician's, Chan turned to him.

'You recalled the spectacles of Sing, Mr. Ward?'

Ward came to himself with a start. 'No — by George — I forgot all about them — '

'Permit that I go,' Charlie suggested. 'I need not climb out over luggage, you will perceive.'

'That's very kind of you,' Ward answered. 'Just charge them to me. I have an account there.'

Holt parked some distance down the street, and Chan got out. He walked back to the optician's, through a colorful western throng, and going in, made clear his errand. The optician remarked that Sing should have come himself — the frame should have been adjusted on him.

'Sing has but little interest in the affair,' Chan remarked. 'Which is a great pity, since his eyes are so very bad.'

'Who says his eyes are bad?' the man wanted to know.

'Why — I have always understood that he could see very little without these spectacles,' Chan returned.

The optician laughed. 'He's kidding you,' he said. 'He can see about as well without them as with them. Except when it comes to reading — and I don't guess Sing does a great deal of that.'

'Thank you so much,' Charlie responded. 'The charge is to be made on Mr. Dudley Ward, of Tahoe.'

He returned and handed the glasses to Ward. Holt started the car and in a few moments they were again out on the main road west, rolling along between the snowy hills.

Charlie was turning over in his mind this latest news. Sing was really not deprived of much when he broke his glasses. It was amusing how fate was constantly exonerating the old man. It had probably not been Sing who mixed the box lids.

No one seemed inclined to conversation, so Chan settled in his seat to meditate on the puzzle of those lids. They went over a bump. 'Excuse me, folks,' Don Holt said. The galley proofs of Ellen Landini's autobiography fell from Chan's lap to the floor of the car. He picked them up and carefully dusted them off. If he had been as psychic as he sometimes pretended to be, he would have known that the answer to this particular puzzle was at that moment in his hands.

Something more than an hour later, they drove up before the Tavern garage. As they alighted, all rather stiff from the ride, Don Holt looked up at the sky.

'Clouding a bit,' he commented. 'Sort of a dampness in the air, too. Perhaps Sing was right, Mr. Ward. Shouldn't be surprised if we had rain — or maybe snow.'

'Sing's always right,' Ward answered. 'That's why I took the umbrella. And I felt a little uncomfortable about the arctics, too.'

They stopped for a moment in the big lounge of the hotel, where a welcome fire was blazing. Charlie took Sam Holt by the arm, and led him to a far corner of the room.

'How was the fishin' down to Reno?' asked the former sheriff.

'A few minnows,' Chan answered. 'But as

you and I know, Mr. Holt, in our business, most innocent-looking minnow may suddenly enlarge to a whale.'

'True enough,' the old man answered.

'Being somewhat pressed for time,' Charlie continued, 'I will leave to your son the pleasure of detailed account. Suffice to say, once more our good friend Sing is clear of suspicion.' He related his conversation with the optician.

Holt slapped his leg with keen delight. 'By cricky, I ain't had so much fun bein' wrong since I played roulette on a crooked wheel, an' run the owner out of Angel's Flats. I sure got off on the wrong foot with this case. Which it served me right — fer I didn't have no business suspectin' that boy — the years I've knowed him. Well, that's out. He didn't mix them lids, nor bungle that scarf business. Who did?'

'At present,' Chan returned, 'only echo is on hand to answer.'

'You'll be answerin' fer yourself soon enough,' Holt nodded. 'I git more confidence in you every time I hear you speak.'

'It will remain one of the triumphs of my life,' Chan replied, 'that I stood in such high favor with honorable family of Holt. Should events not justify your esteem, I leave this lovely country in the night.'

Don Holt joined them. 'Hello, Dad,' he said. 'How about the coroner?'

'Jes' got here an hour ago,' his father answered. 'Slow, as usual. Down at the mortuary now.'

'Reckon we'll have to get his report later, Mr. Chan,' the young man said. 'By the way, I was talking to Dinsdale this mornin', an' he agreed to take a few of the suspects off Dudley Ward's hands. It'll be a load off your shoulders, too. Cash and me is both down here, en' between us we can handle 'em, I reckon. I thought maybe Swan, en' Romano, an' Hugh Beaton, an' — er — '

'Hugh Beaton would not come over here without his sister,' Charlie smiled.

The sheriff blushed. 'Well, we could fix her up, too,' he said. 'It ain't fair to Ward, all the trouble he's had, to load these strangers on him. And it's so near you could go on investigatin' as usual. Dinsdale's all tied up with painters an' decorators now, an' he tells me there's only one room ready tonight. It ain't a very good one — so I thought I'd bring Swan back with me en' put him in it.'

Charlie nodded. 'I yield him with great pleasure. It will, as you say, narrow my watching.'

'Well, we may as well get goin',' Don Holt remarked. 'It's comin' on dusk.'

Chan shook hands with Sam Holt. 'Until we meet again,' he said. 'Aloha.'

'Same fer you,' Holt replied. 'An' thanks fer that news about Sing. I'll sleep better to-night.'

Ward and Beaton joined them, and they went down to the sheriff's launch. The afterglow was fading on tan distant peaks as they swept over the darkening lake. Presently they tied up at Ward's pier. Dudley Ward and Beaton went on ahead. Charlie waited, and helped with the mooring ropes.

'I'll just leave Swan's bag in the boat,' Holt said. 'I needn't have brought it, in the first place. Not much of a thinker, I reckon.'

They were walking up the path. Suddenly Chan put his hand on the young man's arm. 'As resident of semitropic country,' he remarked, 'mostly sprinkled with palms, I have vast interest in these lofty pines. Could you give me name of variety?'

'Why — they're just pines,' said Holt. He sought to move on, but Chan still held him.

'We have a tree resembling the pine on our island of Oahu,' the detective went on. 'It is called the ironwood. At one time I knew the Latin name, but — a busy life — those things escape. It was — it was — no use, I can not recall.'

'Too bad,' Holt answered, squirming.

'Fine examples of the ironwood border the road to the Pali,' Charlie continued. 'The bark is much less sturdy, less thick, than that of your trees. Do not go, please.' He ran across the snow to pick up a large segment of bark that lay at the foot of a near-by tree. 'You behold how thick the bark of your trees is,' he added, and handed the piece to the sheriff. 'Shall we continue now to the house?'

At the foot of the steps, Holt suddenly stopped and stared at Chan. 'What'll I do with this?' he asked, indicating the bark.

Charlie grinned. 'Toss it away,' he said. 'It does not matter.'

Sing admitted them, and they found Leslie Beaton and the resplendent Cash seated before the fire. 'Back already?' Cash inquired. 'Well, this day sure has gone fast.'

'Not for Miss Beaton, I reckon,' Holt said.

'Oh, indeed it has,' the girl cried. 'Mr. Shannon has been telling me the most amazing things — '

'Yeah,' nodded Holt, 'I can imagine. He ought to write for the magazines, old Cash.'

'Never do that,' said Cash. 'I want my audience where I kin see it. I sure had one nice audience to-day.'

'Yeah,' agreed Holt. 'An' how about the rest of these people? Any of 'em still around the place?'

'Sure — they're all here — far as I know.'

'Anything happen?'

'Not a thing. That aviator — Ireland, I guess his name is — dropped in on us a while ago. I reckon he's in the kitchen now.'

Holt turned to Sing, who was fumbling about the fire. 'Look here — Sing — go catch Doctor Swan. Tell him I want to see him.' The old man went out. 'Well, Cash — much obliged. I guess I can carry on from this point.'

Cash frowned. 'Don't you think you ought to leave me right here, Chief?' he inquired. 'I'd keep my eyes open — '

'Yeah — I know you would,' Holt grinned, 'but Mr. Chan will do that — an' he'll look in the right direction. Say good night to this kind patient lady that must be nearly dead from the sound of your voice, an' go out to the boat. I'll be with you in a minute.'

As Cash reluctantly departed, Doctor Swan came downstairs. 'Ah, Sheriff,' he said, 'back safely, eh? Did you get my bag?'

'I got it. It's waiting for you out in the launch.'

'Waiting for me?' Swan looked slightly startled.

'Yes — we're moving a few people down to the Tavern, and you're the first to push off.'

'Of course — that's quite all right. I'll just

get my hat and coat, and say good-by to my host.'

Sing had appeared on the stairs. 'Boss — he sleep. Say, keep evahbody out. My tell 'um you say goo'-by. Hat an' coat light heah.' He removed the latter from a closet. 'Goo'-by, Doctah.'

With a somewhat dazed air, Swan got into his coat. Holt led him outside and, calling to Cash, turned the doctor over to him. When the sheriff returned to the living-room, he found Leslie Beaton alone.

'Why — where's Mr. Chan?' he asked.

'He just ran out the back way,' the girl explained. 'He told me to tell you to be sure to wait. And he asked me — as a favor to him — to keep you company.'

'Always thinking of others. Fine fellow,' the sheriff said.

Silence fell. 'Nice day,' said the sheriff.

'Lovely.'

'Not so nice to-night.'

'No?'

'Looks like rain.'

'Really?'

'Sure does.'

More silence.

'Wish I could talk like Cash,' the sheriff remarked.

'It's a gift,' smiled the girl.

193

'I know. I wasn't there when they passed it.'

'Don't you care.'

'I — I never did. Before.'

'Are you moving the rest of us to the Tavern?'

'Yes. There'll be a nice room for you to-morrow. Do you mind?'

'I think it's a grand idea.'

'Yeah. Cash'll be there.'

'Where will you be?'

'Oh — I'll be around, too.'

'I still think it's a grand idea.'

'That's — that's great,' said the sheriff.

In the meantime, Charlie Chan had hurried to the kitchen. Cecile was alone there, with Trouble. 'Your husband?' Charlie cried.

'He's just gone,' Cecile answered. 'Did you wish to see him?'

'I wanted him to do an errand for me,' Chan explained. 'I desired that he convey Trouble back to Miss Meecher, in Reno.'

'You can catch him, I think,' Cecile answered. She snatched up the startled dog, and thrust it into Chan's arms, 'Michael will be glad to do it, I'm sure.'

'Thank you so much,' Chan cried and rushed out the door. As he approached the field, the hum of a motor rose on the still evening air. At the first sound of the engine

Trouble leaped to life. He trembled with excitement, threw back his head, and time after time he barked a short happy bark. He was almost overcome with joyous anticipation.

As Charlie ran on to the field, he saw that the aviator was about to take off. Near the whirring propeller stood Dudley Ward's boatman. Chan shouted as loudly as he could and hastening to the side of the plane, he held up the dog and explained what he wanted.

'Sure, I'll take him,' Ireland answered. 'We're buddies, ain't we, Trouble? Crazy about flyin', this dog is.'

The detective handed over the excited little terrier, and fell back to a safe distance. He stood and watched the machine taxi across the snowy field, then rise against the green splendor of the pines, and finally melt away into the fast-darkening sky. Deep in thought, he turned and walked back to the house.

When Charlie entered the living-room, the sheriff looked up with an expression that was almost one of relief. 'Oh, there you are,' he cried, rising hastily. 'I was waitin' for you.'

'The wait, I trust, was not unpleasant,' Chan smiled.

'No — but, of course — I got to get back now. Well, Miss Beaton, I'll be seein' you. I hope your brother got all the things you wanted.'

'If he got half of them,' smiled the girl, 'I'll be in luck. Poor Hugh — he's so artistic.' She said good-by and ascended the stairs.

'I also will say good-by,' remarked Charlie, and walked with the sheriff out the door and across the veranda. When they reached the path, he added: 'Also, I desire to tell you that I just turned Trouble over to Michael Ireland. He is taking the little fellow back to Reno by plane.'

'A great idea,' said Holt heartily. 'Saves time.'

Chan lowered his voice. 'It was not to save time that I did it.'

'No?'

'No. I would like to call to your attention the fact that Trouble was wild with joy at sound of the motor. He was not afraid of the plane to-night.'

'Does that mean anything?' asked Don Holt.

'It might. I incline to think it does. In fact, I believe that in this case Trouble is what my old friend, Inspector Duff of Scotland Yard, would call the essential clue.'

# 10

## Romano's Lucky Break

The young sheriff stood for a moment, staring across the lake at the last flickering of white on Genoa Peak. He removed his two-gallon hat, as though to give his mind a better chance.

'Trouble,' he said, 'a clue? I ain't gettin' it, Inspector.'

Charlie shrugged. 'Nevertheless,' he replied, 'such statement is based on facts equally well known to you.'

Don Holt restored his hat. 'Ain't any use, I reckon,' he remarked. 'You jes' go your way, an' I'll go mine, an' when you get to the top of the hill, drop a rope for me. By the way, when the coroner finishes, maybe you'd like to have a talk with him?'

'Very much indeed.'

'Can you run a motor-boat?'

'Sometimes I have been permitted to drive the one belonging to my son, Henry — as a generous recognition of the fact that I paid for same.'

'Good. I may give you a ring to-night. I'll

send Cash up to spell you here.' The sheriff paused. 'I wish I had a good sensible deputy in this neighborhood,' he added sadly. 'A married man.'

Chan smiled. 'I could bring Miss Beaton to the Tavern with me. Pleasant spin over lake would do her vast good.'

'A great idea,' agreed the sheriff heartily. 'Keep it in mind. Well, good luck. I'm sorry I ain't any use to you.'

'Nonsense — you must not be discouraged. I remember well the first important case which came to me. Could I make distinguished progress? Can an ant shake a tree?'

'That's about the way I feel — like an ant.'

'But you are indispensable. These are, as my cousin Willie Chan, baseball player, would say, your home grounds. I am only stranger, passing through, and it has been well said, the traveling dragon can not crush the local snake.' They walked together toward the pier. 'Do not believe, however,' Chan continued, 'that I consider myself dragon. I lack, I fear, the figure.'

'And you don't breathe much fire,' Holt laughed. 'But I guess you'll get there, jes' the same.'

Cash and Doctor Swan were standing near the launch. The latter held out his hand to Charlie.

'Inspector,' he remarked, 'I fear we must separate for a time. But we shall meet again, no doubt.'

'Such is my hope,' the detective answered politely.

'I — I don't wish to seem overly curious — but was your visit to Reno successful?'

'In many ways — amazingly so.'

'Splendid! I realize it's none of my affair, but Romano has been speculating on the matter all day, so I am moved to ask — does it happen that Landini signed the will — the one leaving her property to Beaton?'

Charlie hesitated but a second. 'She did not sign it.'

'Ah,' nodded Swan. 'A lucky break for Romano. Good night, Inspector. I shall see you, no doubt, at the Tavern.'

'Good night,' Chan answered thoughtfully.

Cash was already in the launch, Swan followed, and Don Holt took his place at the wheel. In a moment they were off.

Charlie stood watching the little boat as it sped along the brief three miles of shore-line that separated Pineview from the Tavern. Swan, he reflected, would not be far away if he wanted him, and Swan was the sort of man who might be wanted at any moment.

Walking slowly up the path, Chan paused at the foot of the steps. There he stood for a moment, staring up into the branches of the lofty pines. His glance moved thoughtfully from the lowest branch of the tree nearest the house to the balcony outside the study. He retreated a few steps to obtain a better view of the study window. Suddenly a light flashed on inside. Sing appeared and drew the curtains.

Deep in meditation, Chan proceeded, not up the steps, but around to the rear of the house. There were various sheds and a good-sized garage between him and the hangar. From one of the sheds, a man emerged.

'Good evening,' said Chan. 'It was you, I believe, who brought us down in the launch last night?'

The man came closer. 'Oh — good evenin'. Yes — I'm Mr. Ward's boatman.'

'You do not live on the place?'

'No, not now. I'm here jes' July an' August. Other times, when Mr. Ward wants me, he telephones my home down t' Tahoe.'

'Ah, yes. You just now assisted Mr. Ireland in the starting of his plane. Did you by any chance do the same here last night?'

'Lord, no, mister. I wasn't here last night. Soon's I landed you all at the pier, I scurried back home. Mr. Ward said I wouldn't be needed no more, an' we was havin' the weekly meetin' of the contract bridge club at our house.'

Charlie smiled. 'Thank you. I will not detain you further.'

'Terrible thing, this murder,' the boatman ventured. 'Ain't had one o' them round here in years.'

'Terrible, indeed,' Chan nodded.

'Well — I guess I better be hurryin' back to supper. The wife ain't none too pleased with me to-day, anyhow. Say, mister — you don't happen to know anything about a psychic bid, do you?'

'Psychic?' Chan frowned. 'Ah, you refer to bridge. I don't play it.'

'Well, maybe you're right,' replied the boatman, and hastened round the house, evidently bound for the pier.

The door of the garage was open, and Chan stepped inside. Only a flivver there at present, he noted — perhaps a larger car could not as yet make its way up the road from the Tavern. For a while the detective explored the place as well as he could in that dim light. He had just come upon a long ladder lying at the rear, when one of the doors banged shut, and he had to hurry to make the opening in time. Sing stood just outside, about to adjust a padlock.

'Hello,' cried the old man, startled. 'Wha's

mallah you? You no b'long this place.'

'Merely taking look-see,' Chan explained.

'You look-see too much,' grumbled Sing. 'Some day, some place, you get in, no can get out. Why you no min' own business, hey?'

'So sorry,' Chan replied humbly. 'I go now and buy a fan to hide my face.'

'Allight. Plenty time you do,' Sing nodded.

Feeling decidedly embarrassed, Charlie walked toward the house. Always, he reflected, he seemed to be coming off second-best in encounters with Sing. He stamped the snow from his shoes, entered the rear door and heard at once the voice of Mrs. O'Ferrell.

'Take that out iv here,' she was saying in a loud voice. 'I won't have it in me kitchen.'

'It will not injure you.' It was Cecile who answered.

'That's as may be,' replied Mrs. O'Ferrell, 'but I've cooked f'r thirty year without — ah, Mr. Chan — is it you?' she added, as Charlie appeared in the doorway.

'Indubitably,' replied Charlie, 'and deeply sorry to interrupt.'

'Sure, 'tis nothing,' Mrs. O'Ferrell replied. 'I was just tellin' this Frinch girl that I've cooked f'r thirty year without guns in me kitchen, an' I ain't goin' to start now.'

Cecile produced a small revolver from the

folds of her skirt. 'I am so nervous,' she explained to Chan. 'All the time, since last night, I am so jumpy and nervous. So I ask Michael to bring me this — from Reno.'

'An' now we can all be nervous, an' with good reason, too,' the cook added.

'There is no cause for alarm,' Cecile assured her, 'Michael has taught me — ' she paused.

'Mr. Ireland taught you to use it,' Chan finished for her.

'Yes. He — he was in the war, you understand.'

'An aviator, it may be.'

'Ah — he wished so much to be an aviator. But no — that did not happen. He was sergeant of infantry.' Cecile started for the door. 'Do not fret, Mrs. O'Ferrell. I will take this to my room.'

'An' look which way ye point it, even there,' admonished Mrs. O'Ferrell. 'Thim walls on the third floor is none too thick.' She turned to Chan, as Cecile went out. 'I don't hold with guns,' she said. 'The way I see it, the fewer guns they is, the fewer people gets killed.'

'You are exponent of disarmament,' smiled Chan.

'I am that,' she replied firmly. 'An' it's a lonely thing to be — among the Irish.'

'Among any people, I fear,' Chan replied gravely. 'I have paused here, Mrs. O'Ferrell, to offer most humble apologies. It was not possible to retain the little dog at Pineview. It was not even possible, under the circumstances, that you should bid him farewell.'

The woman nodded. 'I know. Cecile was tellin' me. It's sorry I am to lose him — but if there was thim had a better claim — '

'There was one who had such claim,' Chan assured her. 'I am so very sorry. I trust I am forgiven.'

'Don't mention it,' said Mrs. O'Ferrell.

Charlie bowed. 'He who keeps the friendship of a prince,' he said, 'wins honors. But he who keeps that of a cook, wins food. My preference runs to the latter — when the cooking is as superlative as yours.'

'Ye have a nice way of talking, Mr. Chan. Thank ye so much.'

As he spoke with Mrs. O'Ferrell, Charlie had been conscious of music in the distant living-room. Walking down the passageway and pushing open the door, he saw that Romano was seated at the piano, and that Hugh Beaton stood beside him. Only a few lights were on in the big room; the reflection of firelight was on the paneled walls, the scene was one of peace and harmony. Romano played well, and Beaton's voice was surprisingly good as he sang, not very loudly, words in a language Chan did not recognize. The detective tiptoed toward the fire and dropped into a chair.

Presently the music stopped and Romano, leaping to his feet, began to pace the floor excitedly.

'Excellent,' he cried. 'You have a really excellent voice.'

'Do you think so?' Beaton asked eagerly.

'Ah — you lack confidence — you lack courage. You need the proper push — the proper management. Who has arranged your concerts?'

'Why — the Adolfi Musical Bureau — mostly.'

'Paughl Adolfi — what does he know! A business man — with the heart of a plumber! I — Luis Romano — I could manage you. I could make of you a huge success. Do I know the game? Signor — I invented it. From one end of the country to the other I would make you famous — in Europe, too. For a salary, of course — '

'I have no money,' the boy said.

'Ah — but you forget. You have Landini's money — and there is plenty believe me. I know. Plenty — though mostly now in real estate. Times will change — the real estate will sell. A house in Washington Square — an apartment building on Park Avenue — a summer place at Magnolia — '

'I don't want them,' Hugh Beaton said.

'But you should leap at the chance. I tell you, you need confidence. A voice like yours — all this money to exploit it — I will assist, gladly.'

'I gave a concert in New York,' the boy told him. 'The reviews weren't very good.'

'The reviews! Bah! Critics are sheep — they never lead. They follow. The path must be pointed out to them. I could arrange it. But first — you must believe in yourself. I tell you — you can sing.' Suddenly Romano walked over to the chair where Charlie was seated. 'Mr. Chan, will you kindly give this foolish boy your opinion of his voice?'

'To me,' Charlie answered, 'it sounded most beautiful.'

'You see?' Romano turned to Beaton, gesturing violently. 'What have I told you? A layman — an outsider — one who knows little of music — even he says so. Then will you believe me — Luis Romano — born with music in the very soul? I tell you that with Landini's money — '

'But I won't take Landini's money,' the boy repeated stubbornly.

Charlie rose. 'Do not worry,' he said. 'You will not be called upon to take it. It was not left to you.'

Romano leaped forward, his dark eyes glowing. 'Then the will was never signed?' he almost shouted.

'It was not signed,' Chan told him.

Romano turned to Beaton. 'I am sorry,' he said. 'I will not be able to accept the position you have so kindly offered me. I will be otherwise engaged. But I repeat — you have a wonderful organ. You must believe. Confidence, my boy, confidence. Mr. Chan, if Landini died intestate, her property is left — '

'To her son, perhaps,' Chan answered, keenly regarding the Italian.

Romano paled suddenly. 'You mean — she had a son?'

'You yourself said so, last night.'

'No, no — I had no real knowledge on that point. I was — '

'Lying?'

'I was desperate — I explained that. Any chance that offered — have you ever been hungry, Mr. Chan?'

'You were telling the truth, unconsciously, Mr. Romano. Landini had a son — but he died three years ago.'

'Ah — poor Landini! That was just before our marriage. I would not know.'

'So I fancy her property is yours, Mr. Romano.'

'Thank heaven for that,' remarked Hugh

Beaton, and started up the stairs.

Romano sat, staring into the fire. 'Ah, Landini,' he said softly, 'she would never listen to me. Time after time, I tell her — you must cease to procrastinate. You must not for ever put things off. You say, I will do this, I would tell her, and you never do it. Where will it finish? It has finished in fortune for me. She never took to heart what I said — and now that means fortune for me.'

For a time Charlie stood gazing down at this temperamental man whose sudden changes from one mood to another presented him with one of the greatest puzzles of his life.

'Yes,' he said slowly, 'the murder of Landini means fortune for you.'

Romano looked up suddenly. 'You will think I killed her,' he cried. 'For the love of God, don't think that! Landini — she was dear to me — I worshipped her — I adored her marvelous voice — do not think I would silence that — '

Chan shrugged. 'For the present, I do not think at all,' he answered, and turning, went up-stairs to his room.

His last words to Romano were not quite accurate. Seated in a chair before his fire, he thought very hard indeed. Could Romano have known that the will was unsigned? In that case, would he have made the determined effort to become the manager of Hugh Beaton? To acquire some portion of Landini's estate, by way of Beaton's pocket? No — hardly. And yet — ah, yes — his suggestion of the managership had been made with Charlie in the room, listening.

Might that not have been, then, a sly trick — for the man was undoubtedly sly. To make Chan think that he expected nothing, that he had resigned himself to the idea of Landini's money going to Beaton. When all the time, he knew only too well —

★  ★  ★

Charlie sighed ponderously. A problem, that was. And Cecile? Sending for a pistol — would a guilty person, who had already fired one pistol in that house, openly parade another? Probably not. But — might that not be a gesture of innocence, staged for his special benefit? Cecile was another sly one — her eyes betrayed her.

Leaning back in his chair, Chan considered the situation. About time, he reflected, that something definite, something a little less hazy and preposterous in the line of a clue, offered itself. Suddenly remembering, he rose and took the galley proofs of Landini's autobiography from the table where he had laid them a moment ago. Adjusting a floor lamp, he read the first three chapters of the woman's story. They were well written, he thought, with a touch of wistful nostalgia for the days of her youth that rather touched him. Especially since the scene of those days was his own beloved Honolulu.

A glance at the wrist-watch which his daughter Rose had given him on his latest birthday told him it was time to prepare for dinner. As he left his room, at a few minutes before seven, he saw Dudley Ward in the study at the front of the house. He went there at once.

'Ah, Mr. Ward,' he said as he entered. 'We are to have your company at dinner. You are brave man.'

'Sit down, Mr. Chan,' Ward answered. 'Yes — I'm coming to dinner. I have had many sorrows in my life, but I have never yet tried to share them with my guests.'

Chan bowed. 'A true definition of hospitality,' he replied. 'Mr. Ward — if I could find proper words — but such, alas, evade me.'

'I understand,' Ward said gently. 'You're very kind.'

'And speaking of kindness,' Charlie went on, 'I am telling myself that I must not impose upon yours. I was brought here for a certain task. That task, I am sorry to say, is now accomplished.'

'And you should have your check,' said Ward, reaching toward a drawer of his desk.

'Please,' cried Chan. 'That idea had not occurred to me. What I meant was that I should no longer impose upon you in the role of guest — '

'That idea,' Ward interrupted, 'had not occurred to me. My dear sir, the sheriff has asked you to stay. I demand that you stay — at least as long as you see a chance of solving this unhappy puzzle.'

'I had no doubt of your feeling. But have you thought of this — embarrassment might arise.'

Ward shook his head. 'How so?'

Charlie got up and closed the door. 'At moment of murder,' he remarked, 'five persons were wandering alone in house. In Swan, Romano, Miss Beaton and Cecile I presume you have no great personal interest. There was one other.'

'One other? Pardon me — but I have been so terribly upset.'

'The last person to see Landini alive.'

'Sing! You can't mean Sing?'

'Who else?'

For a long moment Ward was silent. On his face was an expression that Charlie had seen before. Where? Ah, yes, on the face of Sam Holt whenever the matter of Sing's possible guilt came up. The old Chinese, Chan thought, was a man who was much beloved.

'Surely you haven't found anything — ' Ward said at last.

'So far, nothing,' Charlie answered. 'We have been combing the hair of an iron donkey.'

'Just as I thought,' Ward nodded. 'Mr. Chan, I have known Sing since I was a child, and no kinder soul ever lived. I appreciate your speaking to me about the matter — but I'll take a chance on Sing.' He rose. 'Perhaps we'd better go down to dinner. I don't like to keep Mrs. O'Ferrell waiting — ' He stopped suddenly. 'Five persons, you said, unaccounted for.'

'I said five,' Charlie admitted.

'Six, Mr. Chan. Haven't you forgot Mrs. O'Ferrell?'

'Indubitably. But what interest could that lady have had in Landini?'

'None whatever, that I know of,' Ward replied. 'But accuracy, Mr. Chan — accuracy. I should have thought you would be a stickler for that.'

'It is true, I always have been,' Chan assured him. 'We will, in the future, call it six.'

He opened the door into the hall. Sing was standing very close to it.

'You hully up, Boss,' the old man cried, 'or mebbe bimeby you no catch 'um dinnah.'

'Coming right along,' Ward said. He insisted on Charlie's going first and they stepped into the hall. Sing went limping ahead of them and, still limping, disappeared in the direction of the back stairs.

# 11

## A Balcony in Stresa

The rest of the party awaited them in the living-room: Leslie Beaton, a charming picture in a blue gown by the fire, her silent brother, Romano, looking undeniably cheerful, and Ryder, grim and dour as always.

'Are we all here?' Ward asked. 'I don't see Doctor Swan.'

Evidently Sing had not kept his promise to pass on Swan's farewell. Chan explained the matter.

'Indeed,' Ward answered. 'Miss Beaton — may I have the honor? I trust I am not to lose any more of my guests — '

As they moved into the dining-room, the girl said something about leaving on the morrow, and Ward murmured his regrets. When they were all seated, their host remarked: 'Some one was singing down here this evening. Rather well, too.'

'I hope I didn't disturb you,' Hugh Beaton said.

'Disturb me? I enjoyed it. You have a remarkably fine voice.'

'What did I say to you, Mr. Beaton?' Romano cried. 'You would not believe me. Yet my opinion is highly regarded in some quarters. Even Mr. Chan agreed — '

'Ah, yes,' Charlie said. 'But I am glad to have the corroboration of Mr. Ward and yourself. For I am no expert. The croaking raven thinks the owl can sing. However, in this case, it was no owl I heard.'

Beaton smiled at last. 'Thanks, Mr. Chan,' he remarked.

'What is wrong with this brother of yours?' Romano demanded of the girl. 'He has a great gift, and does not trust himself.'

'The artistic temperament, I'm afraid,' Leslie Beaton remarked. 'Of late, Hugh has lost faith in himself. One of his reviews in New York was bad, and he can't seem to recover.'

'One of them!' Romano shrugged. 'Ah, he knows nothing of life. He needs a manager — a man of intelligence and musical taste — '

'Yourself,' smiled the girl.

'I would be ideal,' Romano admitted.

'You could at least teach him self-confidence.'

'That — yes. A bold front — it is vital to success in the modern world. And I could teach him more. At present, I do not believe I am available. But I would be glad to find a substitute.'

'That's good of you,' the Beaton girl replied.

Her brother stared morosely at his plate. A silence fell.

'I am so sorry you're leaving Pineview,' Ward said presently to the girl. 'But then, I realize there is little entertainment here.'

'It's a charming place,' she murmured, and in the silence that again fell upon the company, Charlie realized the strain it must be on the host to keep up the conversation. Modestly, he sought to help.

'There is vast entertainment here,' he said. 'Particularly for me. At home, I am amateur student of trees. I know the palms — the coconut, the royal, all of them. But I must confess myself shamefully ignorant of the coniferous trees.'

'The what?' asked Leslie Beaton.

'The coniferous trees. Those bearing cones, you understand.'

She smiled. 'I've learned something to-day.'

'That is good,' he told her. 'Learning which does not daily advance, daily decreases. Myself, I am fond admirer of study. He who listens to the chatter outside the window, and neglects his books, is but a donkey in clothes.'

'That sounds very sensible,' she assured him.

'I believe so. For that reason, I shall, if I

can find leisure, study the pines, the firs and the cedars. I am slightly familiar — in books — with the Scottish, the Corsican, the umbrella pine. The Austrian, too. Mr. Romano, when you fought so bravely on the northern front, you must have come in contact with Austrian pines.'

'With many things I came in contact,' Romano told him. 'Maybe an Austrian pine. Who shall say?'

'No doubt. I am at a loss to classify the local variety. Perhaps, Mr. Ryder, you can help me?'

'What should I know about it?' Ryder demanded.

'But you have been mining man in these parts. You have been snowed in among these very trees.' Ryder gave him a startled look. 'Is it too much to hope that you are interested in this subject?'

'It certainly is,' the other told him.

'Ah,' Chan shrugged, 'then perhaps I must pursue my studies alone. In a certain family of pine, the bark grows much thicker near the ground, and becomes more fragile as one ascends. Are these pines of that family? I must investigate. Alas — I have not much of the figure for tree climbing.' He gazed blandly about the table. 'I envy you all your delectable slenderness.'

Sing appeared at that moment with the main course, and as the conversation again lagged after his departure, Charlie deserted the pines, a subject which did not seem to interest his hearers to any extent, and launched into a little talk on the flora of the Hawaiian islands. Miss Beaton, at least, became an ardent listener. She asked many questions, and the dinner hour slipped by.

'I've always wanted to go to Hawaii,' she told him.

'Save it,' he advised, 'for honeymoon. Any husband seems possible under Waikiki sky. And the kind you will achieve — he will appear Greek god.'

The dinner presently ended, and they returned to the living-room, where Sing served coffee, and cordials from Dudley Ward's precious stock. For a time they sat and smoked, but before very long, Charlie arose.

'If you will pardon me,' he said, 'I go to my room.'

'More study?' asked the girl.

'Yes, Miss Beaton.' His eyes narrowed. 'I am reading very interesting work.'

'Would I enjoy it?'

'Not, perhaps, so much as I. Some day, we will allow you to decide.' He paused for a moment beside John Ryder's chair. 'Excuse, sir, that I intrude my business on this pleasant scene, but I would be greatly obliged if you would grant me an interview above.'

Ryder looked out from the cloud of cigar smoke that enveloped him — an unfriendly look. 'What about?'

'Need I tell you that?'

'If you wish me to come.'

Chan's usually kind face hardened. 'He who acts for the emperor, is the emperor,' he remarked. 'And he who acts for the sheriff — is the sheriff.'

'Even if he's a Chinaman?' sneered Ryder, but rose to go.

As Chan followed him up the stairs, hot anger burned in his heart. Many men had called him a Chinaman, but he had realized they did so from ignorance, and good-naturedly forgave them. With Ryder, however, he knew the case was otherwise, the man was a native of the West coast, he lived in San Francisco, and he understood only too well that this term applied to a Chinese gentleman was an insult. So, no doubt, he had intended it.

It was, therefore, in a mood far less amiable than was his wont, that the plump Chinese followed the long lean figure of Ryder into the latter's room. The door, as he closed it after him, might have almost been said to slam.

Ryder turned on him at once. 'So,' he remarked, 'judging from the conversation at dinner, you have been prying into my private affairs.'

'I have been asked by the sheriff of this county to assist in important case,' Charlie retorted. 'For that reason I must examine the past of Madame Landini. It is with no glow of self-congratulation, my dear sir, that I find you lurking there.'

'I lurked there, as you put it, very briefly.'

'One winter only?'

'Just about that long.'

'In a cabin — up the ravine.' Charlie removed a bit of paper from his pocket, and passed it to Ryder. 'I found this among Landini's clippings,' he explained.

Ryder took it and read it. 'Ah, yes — she would save that — among her souvenirs. To her, I suppose, it was a mere passing incident. To me, it was much more.' He handed back the clipping and Chan took it, staring silently at the mining man. 'What else do you want to know? Everything, I fancy. Good Lord — what a profession yours is! You may as well sit down.'

Charlie accepted this grudging invitation, and Ryder took a chair on the opposite side of the fire.

'I'd always admired Landini,' the latter

began, 'and when she split up with Dudley I followed her, after a decent interval, to New York. I found her in a rather discouraged mood. She said she'd marry me — give up her career — it was a case of whither thou goest — you know. A grand overpowering love. And it lasted — nearly a month.

'You see, I was bound for the mine, and she came along — a great lark, she thought it. Then it started to snow — and she couldn't get out. So she began to think. Night after night, with only the candles burning, she talked of Paris, New York, Berlin — what she'd given up for me. After a time, I talked of what I'd given up for her — my peace of mind, my freedom. And our hatred for each other grew.

'Toward the end of the winter, I fell ill — desperately ill — but she scarcely looked at me. She left me there in my bunk, at the mercy of a stupid old man who worked for us. When the first sled went out in the spring, she was on it, with scarcely a good-by to me. I told her to go — and be damned. She got a divorce in Reno — incompatibility — God knows I couldn't argue that.'

He was silent for a moment — staring into the fire. 'That's the whole story — a winter of hate — what a winter! There is no hate in the world such as comes to two people who are shut up together in a prison like that. Can you wonder that I have never forgotten — that I never wanted to see her again — that I did not want to see her last night, when Dudley foolishly invited her here? Can you wonder that I loathed the very mention of her name?'

'Mr. Ryder,' Chan said slowly, 'what was in that letter Landini wrote to you just before she died? The letter you tore open, read and then burned in the study fireplace?'

'I have told you,' the man replied, 'that I did not receive the letter. I couldn't, therefore, have opened it, read it or burned it.'

'That is your final statement?' Charlie asked gently.

'My only statement — and the truth. I did not go to the study. I remained in this room from the time you left me until you saw me again on the stairs.'

Chan got slowly to his feet, walked to one of the windows and stared out toward the empty flying field. 'One more question, only,' he continued. 'This morning, at breakfast, you remark to Mr. Ward that you have noticed Sing's eyes are bad — that he requires glasses. When did you notice that?'

'Last night, just after I came,' Ryder answered. 'You see, years ago, when I was a kid, I used to spend a lot of time at this house. One summer I taught Sing to read. English, I mean. I asked him, when we came in here last night, if he'd kept it up. I couldn't quite gather whether he had, or hadn't, so I picked up a book from the table and told him to read me the first paragraph. He held it very close to his eyes — couldn't seem to see very well. I made up my mind I'd mention the matter to Dudley.'

Chan bowed. 'It was most kind of you — to teach him the art of reading. But then — you are very fond of him?'

'Why shouldn't I be? A grand character, Sing. One of the real Chinese.'

The implication was not lost on Charlie, but he ignored it. 'I, too, have great admiration for Sing,' he replied amiably. He moved to the door. 'Thank you so much. You have been very helpful.'

Slowly he walked back along the hall to his own room, passing as he did so the spot where, only a few hours before, he had found Sing unconscious from a brutal blow to the face. So much had happened since, he had almost forgotten that incident. Among his many puzzles, he reflected, the assault on Sing was one of the most perplexing.

He entered his room, closed the door and took up again the galley proofs of Ellen

Landini's story. Seated in the chair beside the floor lamp, he read two more chapters. The spell of the woman's personality, as it crept from these inanimate sheets, began to take hold of his imagination. Warm, glowing, alive, she wrote gaily and with increasing charm. Her earliest marriage, those glorious days in Paris when first she was told that she was one of the gifted, would walk among the great. Her enthusiasm was contagious.

Chapter Six. As he stared at this caption, it came to him to wonder how many chapters there were in all. He turned to the final galley, and worked back from there to the beginning of the final chapter. Twenty-eight, it was. Well, in twenty-eight chapters, perhaps he could find something that would help him.

His eyes fell casually on the beginning of that last chapter. The names of foreign far-off places — always they intrigued and held him. Almost unconsciously he began to read:

'After my marvelously successful season in Berlin, I came for a rest to Stresa, on lovely Lago Maggiore. It is here, on a balcony of the Grand Hotel et des Îles Borromees that I write the concluding chapters of my book. Where could I have found a more beautiful setting? I gaze in turn at the aquamarine waters, the fierce blue sky, the snow-capped Alps. Not far away, I am enraptured by Isola

Bella, with its fantastic palace, its green terraces of orange and lemon trees rising a hundred feet above the lake. The thing that has always made life worth while for me — '

Charlie's small black eyes opened wide as he read on. His breath came faster; he uttered a little cry of satisfaction.

Twice he read the opening paragraph from start to finish, then rose and paced the floor, overwhelmed with an excitement he could not suppress. Finally he came back and lifted that particular galley from the company of its fellows. Galley one hundred and ten, he noticed. He folded it carefully, placed it safely in the inner pocket of his coat, and patted affectionately the spot where it reposed.

He must show this to the young sheriff. That was the fair thing to do — no clues should be concealed. And he had now, he thought exultantly, the clue he had been looking for, the clue that would ultimately lead them to success.

# 12

## 'So You're Going to Truckee?'

Charlie had sat down again and was plunging with renewed hope into the sixth chapter of Landini's story when Sing knocked on his door. Cash Shannon, the old Chinese announced, was below, and desired to speak with the detective at once. Recalling his conversation with the sheriff, Chan went immediately down-stairs. Ryder and Ward were smoking by the fire, Miss Beaton and her brother had evidently been reading, and Romano sat at the piano, his playing suspended for the moment. The resplendent Cash stood in the center of the room, smiling his confident smile.

'Hello, Mr. Chan,' he remarked. 'Don wants you to run down to the Tavern fer a while. He says to take his boat. I come up in her, an' she's out there now, rarin' to go.'

'Thank you so much,' Charlie answered. 'Miss Beaton, would you perhaps enjoy brief spin on lake?'

She leaped to her feet. 'I'd love it.'

'Air ain't so good to-night,' suggested

Cash, his smile vanishing. 'Kinda damp. Rain or snow, mebbe.'

'I'd love that, too,' Leslie Beaton added.

'Things is pretty dull down to the Tavern,' Mr Shannon persisted. 'Couldn't recommend it as no gay party.'

'I'll be ready in a moment,' the girl called to Chan from the stairs.

Cash continued to stand, gazing sadly at his hat. 'Sit down, Shannon,' Dudley Ward suggested. 'You're to stay here until they return, I take it.'

'Seems to have worked out that way.' Cash admitted. He looked at Charlie. 'What ideas you do git,' he added.

Chan laughed. 'Sheriff's orders,' he remarked.

'Oh — I begin to see it now,' Cash replied. 'An' I broke a date with a blonde to come down here.'

Leslie Beaton reappeared, her face flushed and eager above the collar of a fur coat. 'Hope you won't be long,' Cash said to her.

'There's no telling,' she smiled. 'You mustn't worry, Mr. Shannon. I'll be in the best possible company. Are you ready, Mr. Chan?' Out on the path, she looked aloft. 'What — no moon?' she cried. 'And not even a star. But plenty of sky. And such a joy to get a breath of fresh air.'

'I fear our friend Cash does not approve

our plans,' Chan ventured.

She laughed. 'Oh, one afternoon of Cash is sufficient unto the day. You know, I think there's a lot to be said for the strong silent men.'

She got into the launch, and Chan took his place at her side. 'Trust my avoirdupois is not too obnoxious,' he remarked.

'Plenty of room,' she assured him. He started the motor, and swung in a wide circle out on to the lake. 'It is a bit damp and chilly, isn't it?' the girl said.

'Some day,' he replied, 'I should enjoy privilege of escorting you along Honolulu water-front, accompanied perhaps by lunar rainbow.'

'It sounds gorgeous,' she sighed. 'But I'll never make it. Too poor. Always too poor.'

'Poverty has its advantages,' Chan smiled. 'The rats avoid the rice boiler of the lowly man.'

'And so does the rice,' nodded the girl. 'Don't forget that.'

They sped along the shore, great black houses, bleak and uninhabited, at their left. 'You have learned, I take it, that your brother is not to inherit the estate of Landini,' Charlie said.

'Yes — and it's the best news I've had in years. Money that came that way wouldn't have done Hugh any good. In fact, it would probably have ruined his career.'

Chan nodded. 'But now — his precious career is safe. You must not be offended, but Landini's death is, I suspect, a great relief to you.'

'I try not to think of it as such. It was, of course, a terrible thing. And yet — we're frank in these days, aren't we, Mr. Chan? — it has released my brother. Even he, I believe, feels that.'

'You have talked with him about it?'

'Oh, no. But I knew, without being told, that he was heart-sick over his predicament. He never really intended to become engaged to her. She sort of — well, jollied him into it. She had a way with her, you know.'

'I know,' Chan agreed.

'Somehow, I couldn't help feeling sorry for her at times, in spite of everything. She was still seeking romance — she needed it, you might say, in her business. And she was thirty-eight years old!'

'Incredible!' cried Chan, with a secret smile at the young girl beside him. 'Poor foolish Landini.' The lights of the Tavern popped up ahead. 'One question I would like to ask, if I may,' he continued. 'You said last night you had met Doctor Swan before. Could you tell me the circumstances?'

'Surely. It was over in Reno. Some people had taken me to a gambling place — just for a lark, you know. Doctor Swan was there, playing roulette.'

'Did he have aspect of confirmed gambler, please?'

'He seemed pretty excited, if that's what you mean. One of our party knew him, and introduced us. Later, he joined us at supper. He sat beside me, and I talked to him about Landini. I wish now I hadn't.'

'You still believe he placed your scarf in Landini's hands?'

'He must have.'

Chan nodded. 'He may have. I can not say. But should you meet him to-night, please do me one vast favor. Assume that he did not try to involve you, and be cordial to him.'

'Cordial to him? Why, of course — if you ask it.'

'That is so good of you. It happens that I have small plan forming in rear of my mind, and I shall require your help. This much alone I need tell you now — I am eager to watch Doctor Swan while he gambles.'

'I don't know what it's all about,' the girl smiled. 'But rely on me.'

They were now beside the pier. Chan tied up the launch, and walked with the girl up the steps of the terrace to the Tavern. The lights were blazing in the big lounge, Charlie pushed open the door and followed the girl inside.

Don Holt at once came forward and took charge of Leslie Beaton, with that shy manner of his which was at the same time full of authority. Moving on to the fireplace, Chan encountered Dinsdale, the manager, Doctor Swan, Sam Holt and a small nervous man in a black suit.

'I don't know as this is any picnic for you,' the young sheriff was saying to the girl. 'Jes' thought maybe you'd like to come for the boat ride.'

'That part of it was fine,' she assured him.

'But this don't look so gay, does it?' he said, his eager look fading.

'Oh, I don't know. Who's the little man in black?'

'Well — he's the coroner.'

'Good. I've never met a coroner. Having new experiences all the time. Up to last night, I'd never met a sheriff. And I got through that all right.'

'You sure did, as far as the sheriff's concerned,' Don Holt said. 'Now — er — Mr. Chan an' I got a little business, an' then I guess I'll be free for — the rest of the evening. I'm afraid that's about all that's goin' to happen — jes' the rest of the evening.'

'That sounds exciting enough for me,' she smiled.

He left her with Dinsdale and Swan before the fire and walked down to the far end of the big room, whither Charlie had already led Sam Holt and the coroner. 'Well, Inspector,' he said, 'I reckon you've already met Doctor Price?'

'I have had that pleasure,' Chan returned. 'He assures me that Landini was murdered by person or persons unknown. He has, you will observe, caught up with us in our search.'

'The usual verdict, of course,' the physician remarked. 'Unless you gentlemen have some evidence of which I am not aware.' He waited for an answer.

Chan shook his head. 'It is now less than twenty-four hours since the killing,' he remarked, looking at his watch. 'Our researches in that time have been amazingly extensive, but lack definite results. It is the same old story. Like pumpkins in a tub of water, we push one suspect down, and another pops up. However, we do not despair. Tell me, Doctor — what of the course of the bullet?'

Doctor Price cleared his throat. 'Ah — er — the bullet, which was of thirty-eight caliber and obviously from the revolver of the deceased, entered the person of the deceased four inches below the left shoulder, and after that pursued a downward course — '

'Then it was fired from above?'

'Undoubtedly. The deceased may have been struggling with her assailant, she may have fallen to her knees, and the assailant, standing above her, fired — '

'How close was weapon held?'

'I can not say. Not very, I believe. At least, there were no powder marks.'

'Ah, yes,' Chan nodded. 'One thing more interests me. Could the dec — I mean, the lady, have taken any step after the wound was received?'

'Which I asked him myself,' put in Sam Holt. 'He don't know.'

'There might be two schools of thought on that problem,' the doctor said. 'You see, the human heart is a hollow muscular organ, more or less conical in shape, situated in the thorax between the two lungs. It is enclosed in a strong membranous sac, called the pericardium — '

'He jes' runs on like that,' Sam Holt explained. 'The sum of it all is, he don't know.'

Charlie smiled. 'At least, you have the bullet?' he inquired of the sheriff.

'Yes — Doc gave it to me. I got it over there in Jim Dinsdale's safe, along with

Landini's revolver.'

'Excellent,' Chan nodded. 'And who would have the combination to this safe?'

'Why — nobody but Dinsdale and his bookkeeper.'

'Ah, yes. Dinsdale and his bookkeeper. Presently we may give more thought to the safe. Mr. Coroner, I thank you so much.'

'Don't mention it,' returned Doctor Price briskly. 'I am staying here with Jim overnight — anything more I can tell you, you have only to ask. Glad to have met you. I'm turning in now — want to get an early start in the morning.'

He went down the room, said something to Dinsdale and disappeared toward a distant corridor. Charlie and the two Holts joined the little group by the fire.

'Draw up and sit down, gentlemen,' Dinsdale remarked. 'I was just telling Miss Beaton how glad we'll be to have her come down here to-morrow. Of course, the Tavern isn't officially open, and things are a bit dull, but we can show her a little excitement, I reckon. There's a few newspaper reporters coming up from San Francisco on the morning train, and they'll stir things up. They usually do.'

'Newspaper reporters,' cried Don Holt in dismay.

'Yes — and that Reno bunch will be back here to-morrow. They've been prowling round the neighborhood all day. Claimed they wanted to find Mr. Chan.'

'Well, I hope it's Mr. Chan they find,' Holt said. 'Lord, I wouldn't know what to say to 'em.'

'The secret,' Charlie told him, 'is to talk much, but say nothing. Not your specialty, I fear. Leave them to me — I will act as buffer. I have the figure.'

'To-morrow sounds interesting,' Leslie Beaton remarked, 'but how about to-night? Where's the night life around here?'

Dinsdale laughed. 'Night life? I'm afraid you'll have to come back later in the summer.'

'Oh — but I've heard the gambling wasn't all on the other side of the state line,' the girl continued, and Charlie gave her a grateful smile. 'There must be a few places — '

'There ain't any in my county,' Don Holt said firmly.

'Well, let's get out of your old county, then. I feel like going places and doing things. Surely there must be a city, or a town, or at least a village, nearer than Reno.'

'Well, there's Truckee,' Dinsdale ventured dubiously. 'Summers we sometimes run over there in the evening. Not much doing now,

I'm afraid. But there's two or three restaurants, and a movie — and you might dig up a game.'

'Not if it's in Sheriff Holt's county,' the girl said mockingly.

'But it ain't,' replied the sheriff. 'It's over the county-line, so you can't tell — it might turn out to be the modern Babylon you're longing for. Get your coat, an' we'll have a look at it.' His manner was gay enough, but there was a note of disappointment in his voice.

'That'll be grand,' the girl cried. She went over to Sam Holt's chair, and bent above him. 'You're coming with us, you know,' she said.

'Shouldn't do it,' he answered. 'But say — I like your voice. Sounds lively. Full o' spirit, which young folks' voices is generally too tired nowadays to suit me. Sure, I'm coming. Fresh air never hurt nobody.'

Leslie Beaton turned to Swan. 'Doctor — you don't mind a little game, as I recall.'

'Well, really — I think I'd better stay here,' Swan replied. But his eyes had brightened.

'Nonsense — we won't go without you,' the girl said, while Don Holt stared at her in amazement.

'Oh — in that case — ' Swan stood up at once.

Dinsdale felt he should stay at the Tavern — a guest is a sort of responsibility, he explained, and there was no one about to take his place in the office. He offered his car for the trip, along with certain vague suggestions of the 'So you're going to Truckee' order.

But Truckee, when they had covered fifteen miles of snowy road and rolled on to its startled main thoroughfare, responded with the gloomiest welcome imaginable. Even the spirits of Leslie Beaton drooped at the prospect. Tired old store-fronts listing, it seemed, with the wind, a half-darkened drug store, the lighted windows of a few restaurants dripping with steam. Don Holt drew up to the curb.

'Here you are, folks,' he smiled. 'Night life in these parts; I don't know what you're looking for, but it ain't here.'

'Isn't that a light in the Exchange Club, over the Little Gem Restaurant?' Doctor Swan inquired.

'It might be, at that. I'm afraid you have the gambler's instinct, Doctor. Maybe we are in Babylon, after all. Anyhow, it won't hurt to inquire.'

Holt led them into the Little Gem. An odor of fried fish and other delicacies of the lake country nearly bowled them over. The proprietor of the establishment, a swarthy

Greek known locally as 'Lucky Pete,' was shaking dice with a customer.

'Hello, Pete,' Holt said. 'What's the big excitement in these parts to-night?'

'Dunno,' returned Pete, stifling a yawn. 'Is there any?'

'Jes' dropped in to find out,' Holt said. 'A few friends of mine — from Reno.'

Pete nodded. 'Pleased to meet them. The slot machines are over in the corner.'

'Nothing doing up-stairs?' Holt asked.

'Not these days — no. Tables all covered — times is bad. A few members of the Club — prominent gentlemen of the city — they play poker.'

Chan stepped forward. 'Is this a private game — or can anybody enter?'

Pete surveyed him critically. 'You can go up an' ask,' he suggested.

'Doctor Swan — what do you say? Shall we purchase small supply of chips?' Charlie inquired.

'We'll take a look, first,' Swan replied cautiously.

It appeared there was an inner stairway, which identified Lucky Pete as the real steward of the Exchange Club. The five, led by Don Holt, ascended. Charlie and old Sam Holt brought up the rear.

'Watch what you do in this place,

Inspector,' Holt said. 'A Greek! How did a Greek find Truckee — unless they closed all the other towns to him?'

'Greek people,' Charlie answered, 'appear to be born with geography of the world in one hand.'

In the big bare room above, half hidden in darkness, were numerous gambling tables, covered with brown canvas. Under the solitary light, five men played poker with soiled cards.

'Evening, gentlemen,' said Don Holt. 'Things don't seem to be prospering around here right now.'

'Not much doing,' one of the players responded. 'Unless you'd like to sit in on this game.'

Holt looked around the faces at the table and shook his head. 'I hardly think so. We've got jes' a few minutes — '

'Small contributions gratefully received,' said another player, who had the pale face and artificial-looking hair of a croupier.

'We might take brief turn to try luck,' remarked Charlie. 'Doctor Swan — what is your reply? Ten dollars spent in chips by each — and leave in one half-hour, win or lose?'

Swan's eyes glittered, his cheeks were flushed. 'I'm with you,' he replied.

'Good,' Charlie replied. 'It is now nine-thirty. Gentlemen — we drop out at ten precisely. May we squeeze in?'

Don Holt gave Chan a dazed look. 'All right,' he agreed. 'Miss Beaton and I will wait down-stairs. Father — '

'Git me a chair, son,' the old man said. 'I sure do like to hear the sound of them chips again. What is it, boys — straight, whisky or draw?'

'Draw,' answered one of the boys. 'How about you, Dad? Oh — excuse me.'

'I'll jes' listen in,' explained Sam Holt. 'That's all I'm doin', nowadays.'

'Would you be so good, gentlemen,' remarked Chan, 'as to explain to me the value of these chips? I am, you understand, a novice.'

'Yeah,' returned the man with the pale face. 'I've met them novices before.'

Don Holt and the girl returned to the aggressive odors of the room below.

'Like something to eat?' the sheriff inquired.

'Never wanted anything less in my life,' she smiled.

'Well, I guess we better order something, anyhow. It'd look better. You can't go huntin' night life, an' not spend any money. A table, or the counter?'

She walked past several tables, studying the cloths. 'The counter, I believe,' she told him.

He laughed. 'That's pickin' 'em,' he nodded. They sat up to the counter. 'Now, what would you like? Wait a minute — I meant to say, what will you take?'

'How about a sandwich and a glass of milk?'

'Well — you're fifty per cent right, anyhow. Stick to the sandwich — that was an inspiration. But as for the milk — '

'No?'

He shook his head. 'No. It don't do to pioneer in the West anymore. Jes' play safe an' make it what's known in these parts as a 'cup cawfee.''

'I'm in your hands,' she told him.

Pete appeared, and Don Holt ordered two ham sandwiches and two cups of coffee. As the man departed, the sheriff glanced toward the stairs. 'Well, Inspector Chan is sure havin' fun to-night,' he remarked. 'Some people, you jes' can't keep 'em away from a gamblin' table.'

The girl smiled. 'Is that what you think?'

'Why shouldn't I think it? Say, I hope he's good — those boys up there invented the game. At ten o'clock we leave — if I have to draw a gun. Your big fling at night life ends then, so make the most of it while you can.'

She gave him a quick look. 'You're not so very pleased with me this evening, are you?' she inquired.

'Who — me? Why — why sure I am. Maybe I'm a little disappointed — you see, I been tellin' myself perhaps you would like the county-seat, after all. It's quite a busy little town, but of course — '

'Of course — what.'

'I don't mean that you're to blame. It ain't your fault. You're jes' like all the other girls, that's all. Restless, always wantin' excitement. I see it on the parties I take out from the Tavern. What's got into the women nowadays? The men are O.K. They'd like to relax, an' take a look at the mountains. But the girls won't let 'em. Come on, boys, is their slogan. What'll we do now? I want to go places, an' do things.'

'Don't you?'

'Don't I what?'

'Want to go places, and do things?'

'Sure — when there's somewhere to go, an' something to do. But when there ain't, I can sit all the way back in my chair, an' not have any nervous breakdown.'

'Everything you say is pretty true,' the girl replied. 'Women are a bit restless — and I'm as bad as any of them, perhaps. But I've got too much spirit to sit here on this very

242

unsteady stool and be unjustly accused. It wasn't my idea — coming out to find a gambling house to-night.'

'But — but you suggested it.'

'Of course I did. However, it was only to please Mr. Chan. He told me he was eager to watch Doctor Swan while the doctor was busily engaged in gambling.'

A look of perplexity clouded Don Holt's fine eyes. 'He did? Well, then — say, I reckon there's a pretty humble apology due from yours truly.'

'Nothing of the sort,' the girl protested.

Pete appeared with the repast, and she smiled at the thickness of the sandwich that stood before her. 'I wonder if I could really open my mouth that wide,' she went on. 'It's worth trying, don't you think?'

The young sheriff was still puzzling over her news. 'So Mr. Chan wanted to watch Swan gamble,' he mused. 'It's too much for me. I wonder what the inspector's got on his mind.'

In the room above the inspector appeared to have much on his mind, including a rapid, tense and deadly game of poker. Scarcely once since it started had he taken his eyes from Doctor Swan. Every move of the latter's hands as he made his ante, pushed out his bet, lost or raked in the chips and sorted them, he watched with extreme care. Either because of this absorption or due to inexperience, Chan played badly, and his stack of chips was close to the vanishing point.

'Ah,' he murmured, 'how true it is that dollars going into a gambling house are like criminals led to execution. Doctor, might I trouble you — would you exchange ten white chips for a blue?'

'Gladly,' nodded Swan, 'but — pardon me — you are offering me a red chip, Mr. Chan.'

'Forgive the error,' smiled Charlie, correcting it. 'Not for worlds would I cheat you, my dear Doctor.'

When Don Holt came to get them at ten o'clock, Charlie held up one white chip. 'Behold,' he said, 'my stack has melted like snow under stream of hot water. I use my last chip to ante.' He took his five cards, glanced at them, and threw them down. 'No cards,' he said. 'The situation is hopeless. I withdraw.'

Swan remained in for the hand, lost it and also stood up. 'I'm about even,' he remarked. 'A lot of hard work for nothing.' He counted his stack, and pushed it toward the banker. 'Seven dollars and twenty-five cents,' he added.

'Better stick a little longer, gentlemen,' the banker said in a hard voice.

'No,' Charlie said firmly. 'We go along now — with the sheriff.' The five hard-boiled gamblers looked up with sudden interest. 'Ten o'clock — is that not correct, Sheriff?'

'Jes' ten,' Don Holt returned. 'Time to get goin'.'

There was no further protest against their doing so from the gamblers, who appeared to have lost all interest in the noble sport themselves. Presently the little group from Tahoe was out in the car, and the sleeping town receded rapidly behind them.

'I think it was lots of fun,' Leslie Beaton cried. 'So quaint and unusual.'

'But not very profitable,' muttered Doctor Swan. 'Eh, Mr. Chan?'

'Profit and pleasure so seldom found on same street,' Charlie answered.

When they reached the Tavern, Swan said good night and retired to his room down the same corridor as that into which the coroner had disappeared. Dinsdale suggested that Miss Beaton come and look at the suite he was preparing for her. 'There's a small sitting-room, with a fireplace — ' he was saying, as they moved away.

Chan turned quickly to the Holts. 'Humbly suggest you owe me ten dollars,' he said. 'The amount of money invested in poker game just now. Place it on your expense account for county to pay.'

'Hold on a minute,' Don Holt replied. 'I ain't getting this. I'm glad to pay the ten, of course — but what did we get for it?'

Chan smiled. 'We eliminated Doctor Swan from list of our suspects.'

'What!'

'I am, perhaps, getting a few paces ahead of myself,' Charlie conceded. He took galley one hundred and ten from his pocket, and gently unfolded it. 'Tonight, I am perusing the autobiography of Landini, and happy luck smiles upon me. Will you be so good as to read aloud to your honorable father, the first paragraph of Chapter Twenty-Eight?'

The young sheriff cleared his throat. ''After my marvelously successful season in Berlin, I came for a rest to — to Stresa, on lovely Lago' — Lago — say, what language is this, anyhow?'

'It is Italian,' Chan told him. 'Lago Maggiore — the second largest of the Italian lakes, I believe.'

'' — Lago Maggiore,'' continued Holt uncertainly. ''It is here, on a balcony of the Grand Hotel et des — des — more Italian — that I write the concluding chapters of my book. Where could I have found a more beautiful setting? I gaze in turn at the aquamarine waters, the fierce blue sky, the snowcapped Alps. Not far away, I am enraptured by Isola Bella, with its fantastic palace, its green terraces of orange and lemon trees rising a hundred feet above the lake. The dining that has always made life worth while for me is color — plenty of color, in personality, in music, in scenery. I have pitied many people in my time, but none more so than one I knew who was color-blind — ''

'By the Lord Harry!' cried old Sam Holt.

'' — color-blind,'' repeated his son doggedly, '''a poor luckless soul to whom all this gorgeous beauty would seem as a mere monotonous prospect of dull gray; lake, mountains, trees, sky — all the same.' What a tragedy!'

'Color-blind,' Don Holt said again, as he laid down the galley.

'Precisely,' nodded Chan. 'A person, who, sent for a green scarf, comes back with a pink one. A poor luckless soul who, having murdered Landini and desiring to give semblance of order to desk, places on the yellow box the crimson lid, and on the crimson box, the yellow.'

'Mr. Chan,' old Sam Holt said, 'you've sure struck the right lead now.'

'Who was this person?' Chan went on. 'That remains to be discovered. One thing I know — it was not Doctor Swan, who for one half-hour to-night sorted so carefully the chips, blue, red and white. He is eliminated, but we proceed with high heart now, for we may be pretty sure that the person Ellen Landini pitied — the one who would not have enjoyed to sit with her on the balcony of the Grand Hotel et des Îles Borromees — that is the person who murdered her.'

'So you think,' Don Holt said slowly, 'that she was killed near the desk? By someone who was in the room with her at the time?'

'I am certain of it.'

'Then why all that talk about pine trees, and pieces of bark lying on the ground?'

Chan shrugged. 'Might it not be that I am truly amateur student of trees? But what is the use? Can you make public believe that policeman is something more than dumb brute thinking only of man-hunt? Can you convince it that he may have outside interests of gentler nature? Alas — can you borrow a comb in a Buddhist monastery?'

# 13

## Footsteps in the Dark

Dinsdale and the girl returned at that moment, and Charlie hastily restored galley one hundred and ten to his pocket.

'Sorry I can't put you higher up,' the hotel man was saying. 'The view would be better, of course. But I'm using only the ground floor at present, and just the one wing, at that.'

'It's awfully good of you to take us at all,' Leslie Beaton assured him. 'Now, Mr. Chan, hadn't we better be going? I just remembered poor Cash.'

'For whom, perhaps, time does not travel so rapidly as it did this afternoon,' Chan replied. 'You are quite right, we must hasten.' Don Holt and the girl went outside, and Dinsdale followed. Charlie turned to the old sheriff. 'Good night, sir. We have something to work on now. As I recall — you once enjoyed camping journeys with Sing — '

'Funny,' said Sam Holt, 'the way you an' me — we always come back to Sing. I was jes' thinkin' of him myself. Yes, I camped with him, but I don't recollect he was color-blind. Leastways, he never showed it ef he was.'

'You are quite sure? An unusual number of Chinese are.'

'Doggone it, Mr. Chan,' cried the old man, 'let's try not to think about Sing. Why should we? Fine character, he's always been. Model of all the virtues.'

'Ah, yes,' nodded Chan, 'the real virtues. But was murder any great vice in era from which Sing dates? I think not — if the motive was good. The motive — that was what counted then. And would count to-day, with Sing, I think.'

'I ain't listenin',' Sam Holt replied grimly.

Charlie smiled. 'I can not find it in my heart to blame you. It will, you may well believe, pain me deeply if I have traveled all this distance to put an ornament of my own race in hangman's noose. But let us not anticipate.'

'Good advice, that is,' the old man agreed. 'But hard to follow, at my age. I said this afternoon I'd sleep better tonight — but — I dunno. Don't seem to need much of it at my age — an' it ain't so easy to sleep when you kain't tell the daylight from the dark. Somethin' tells me this case is goin' to change the world — fer a few of us. My boy — '

'One of finest young men I have had the

honor to meet,' Chan put in.

'I know. I wouldn't tell him, Mr. Chan, but I know. Ain't never paid much attention to girls, Don ain't. But I heard somethin' in his voice to-night when he was talkin' to the Beaton girl — '

Chan laid his hand gently on the old man's shoulder. 'A splendid young woman. Most of her life so far has been devoted to her brother. She knows the meaning of loyalty.'

Sam Holt sighed with relief. 'Then that's all right. Ain't nobody's opinion I'd take before yours, Mr. Chan. Yes, that's all right — but that boy Sing! By the lord, Inspector, I'll be a happy man when we git out o' the woods on this case — even ef I kain't see the mountaintops myself.' He held out his hand. 'Good night.'

There were deep understanding and sympathy in their hand-clasp. Chan left the old man standing by the fire, his sightless eyes turned toward the open door.

Dinsdale spoke his farewell on the terrace, where flakes of snow were beginning to sift gently down. 'More of it,' the hotel man grumbled. 'Is spring never coming? Seems to me the weather's all haywire these last few years.'

Miss Beaton and the sheriff were waiting beside the launch. 'Water's churning pretty lively,' the latter remarked. 'I'll take you back.'

'Ah, yes,' nodded Chan. 'But I am sorry to remind you that, though we walk a thousand miles along the way with a friend, moment of good-by is still inevitable.'

'For which remark,' Don Holt replied, 'you draw the back seat, an' the snow that goes with it. Hop in.'

The pier lights faded suddenly behind them as they nosed into impenetrable dark. From out the soft blackness of the night came the drifting snow, thicker now, cool and refreshing. Chan lifted his face, delighting in the touch of the whirling flakes, so different from the liquid sunshine of steamy Honolulu days. Again a feeling of renewed energy swept over him.

Unerringly Don Holt found the lights of Dudley Ward's pier, and they moored the boat. Sing let them in, muttering vaguely on the ways of people who never knew when to come home, and the steadily multiplying labors in this house. Romano and Cash were alone in the living-room, the latter in the midst of a rather conspicuous yawn.

'Here we are — back already,' remarked Don Holt.

'Thought you'd all been drowned,' said Cash. 'Maybe we might as well stay on fer breakfast now.'

'Wait till you've been asked,' suggested Holt. 'All serene, I take it?'

'Sure — everybody in bed hours ago — except me an' the perfessor, here. He's been tellin' me all about music. I reckon I'll be a wow on my ukulele from this on.'

'Most exciting to meet you, Mr. Shannon,' Romano remarked. 'Always I have deep interest in Wild West cinemas.'

'I don't know what you're calling me, Mister,' returned Cash. 'Don't sound very complimentary, but I'm too sleepy to care. Well, Don, do we hit the down trail now?'

It appeared that they did, and the two departed. Miss Beaton said good night and hastened up-stairs. Chan was hanging his hat and coat in the closet at the rear, when Romano approached him. 'If possible, I would enjoy word with you,' he said.

'The enjoyment would be mutual,' Charlie returned. 'Shall we sit here by the fire? No. Sing, I perceive, is annoyed — we will retreat to my room.' He led the way upstairs, and politely proffered a chair before the fireplace. 'What, my dear Mr. Romano, is hovering in your mind?'

'Many things,' Romano replied. 'Mr. Chan, this news I have heard to-day — this fortune that has dropped into my lap — it works a vast difference in my life.'

'A pleasant one, no doubt,' Chan replied, also taking a chair.

'Naturally. From a pauper I ascend suddenly to the position of a man of property. What is my first reaction? To get away from this spot, lovely as it may be — to hasten to New York — to realize on my inheritance, and then to move on to the continent, where alone I feel at home. I shall sit in the twilight while the band plays in the Piazza at Venice, and I shall be grateful to Landini. I shall climb the stairs of the Opera in Vienna — but I perhaps move too quickly. What I am asking, Mr. Chan, is — how far has this matter of Landini's murder traveled to solution?'

'So far,' Charlie told him, 'we have been ringing wooden bell.'

'Which, if I interpret correctly, means you are nowhere?'

'In that neighborhood,' Chan replied.

'Alas, it is unfortunate,' Romano sighed. 'And we unlucky ones who are unable to give satisfactory account of ourselves — how long must we languish here, waiting?'

'You must languish until guilty person is found.'

'Then we may go?' asked Romano, brightening.

'All those of you who are not concerned

— yes. All those who will not be required to give evidence at trial.'

For a long moment Romano stared into the fire. 'But one who had such evidence — one who had, perhaps, assisted in the arrest of the guilty — such a one would be forced to linger here?'

'For a time. And he would undoubtedly be commanded to return for the trial.'

'That would be most unfortunate for him,' replied Romano suavely. 'But long ago I find there is no justice in this American law. Ah, well — I must be patient. Paris will be waiting, Vienna will still be the same, and I shall sit again in the Opera at Milan. Perhaps direct once more — who knows? Yes — I must — what you call it? — bide my time.' He leaned forward and whispered. 'Did you, also, hear a noise outside that door?'

Chan rose, went softly over and flung it open. No one was there.

'I think you are unduly nervous, Mr. Romano,' he said.

'And who, I pray, would not be nervous?' Romano replied. 'All the time, I feel I am watched. Everywhere I go — every corner I turn — prying eyes are on me.'

'And do you know why that should be?' Chan said.

'I know nothing,' Romano answered loudly.

'I have no part in this affair. When Landini was murdered, I was in my room, the door closed. I have testified to that. It is the truth.'

'You had nothing else to say to me?' Chan inquired.

'Nothing whatever,' Romano said, rising. He was calm again. 'I merely wished to tell you I am very eager to go to New York. It means nothing to you, of course, but I am praying for your sudden success, Mr. Chan.'

Charlie's eyes narrowed. 'Sometimes success comes like that. Suddenly. Who knows? In this case it may happen.'

'I hope with all my heart it will,' bowed Romano. His eyes were on a table by the fire. 'Is it that you have written a book, Inspector?'

Charlie shook his head. 'Landini has written book,' he replied. 'I have been perusing galley proofs of same.'

'Ah, yes. I knew of Landini's book. As a matter of fact, I assisted occasionally in the writing.'

'Were you, by any chance, present when last chapter was written? Same was composed, I believe, at Stresa, on Lago Maggiore.'

'Alas, no,' Romano answered. 'I was detained in Paris at the time.'

'But you know Stresa? I understand it is beautiful spot.'

Romano raised his hands. 'Beautiful, Signor? Ah, the word is not enough. Oh, belle, belle — Stresa is heavenly, it is divine. Such coloring in the lake, the sky, the hills. Beloved Stresa — I must not forget — it is one of the places to which dear Ellen's money shall take me. I really believe I shall have to make a list. There are so many lovely places.' He moved toward the door. 'I hope I have not troubled you, Signor,' he said. 'Good night.'

But he had troubled Charlie slightly. What did this interview mean? Was Romano concealing important evidence? Was his door, after all, not quite so tightly closed as he pretended at that moment when Ellen Landini was shot?

\* \* \*

Or was he merely seeking to divert suspicion to others? Always he gave the impression of slyness; what could be slyer than for a guilty man to hint that perhaps he could tell something if he chose? And that play-acting about a noise at the door — rather hollow, rather unconvincing.

Charlie stepped quietly into the hall. All was silent below, and cautiously he crept down-stairs. No one seemed to be about, so with only the flickering fire to show him the way, he went to the closet and removed his hat, his overcoat, and those strange arctics which had come into his life when he decided to take this simple little trip to Tahoe. Returning to his room, he placed all these articles within easy reach, got out his flashlight and inspected it, and then — settled down to read the autobiography of Ellen Landini.

At one o'clock Charlie stopped reading, put down the galleys and stepped to his window. Pines, lake, sky, all had disappeared; the world seemed to end three feet away in a mixture of white and black. The outlook appeared to give him immense satisfaction; he was smiling as, with some difficulty, he got into the arctics and fastened them. He donned the unaccustomed overcoat, put his black felt hat securely on his head and took up his flash-light with a steady hand. Extinguishing all but one of his lights, he went into the hall and closed the door silently behind him.

It was the back stairs he chose to-night, and all down their length and along the passageway to the back door, he half expected to encounter the ubiquitous figure of the aged Sing. But no Sing loomed in his path. He let himself out on to the snowy back porch, and started toward the garage where only a few hours before he had come upon a ladder. The amateur student of trees was again immersed in thoughts of his favorite line of research.

But fate intervened, and Charlie did not visit the garage that night. For, flashing his light cautiously along the path, he suddenly perceived that there were fresh footprints ahead of him. Some one else had left Pineview by the back way tonight — and not so long ago.

To one who had hitherto known footprints only as something to be found in sand along a sunlit beach, the idea was fascinating. Almost unconsciously he followed the trail, up the flight of outdoor stairs that led to the road, which was some distance above the house. There he paused, and considered.

Who had left this house since eleven o'clock, which was about the time the snow had begun to fall? Had one of his charges escaped from his care? The falling snow was rapidly covering these tracks, but they seemed fresh ones, none the less. The quickest answer appeared to lie ahead.

He began to travel, as rapidly as his girth permitted, down the road that led in the direction of the Tavern. The wind howled through the long fragrant aisles of the pines, the storm wrapped him in a damp embrace. But he made speed, for his energy was great, and the languor of the semi-tropics was far-off and forgotten.

About half a mile down the road he came to the house of Dudley Ward's nearest neighbor. He remembered having seen it from the water — a great rambling barracks built of wood. Its windows were closed and shuttered for the winter, no sign of life was anywhere about it. And yet — the footprints which Charlie followed unmistakably turned off at this point. Turned off, and went unerringly down the path to the rear door.

A bit skeptical now, Charlie did the same. Perhaps, he reflected, he was merely on the trail of a watchman, or some equally harmless person. For a moment he stood on the rear porch. Then he reached out and tried the back door of the deserted house. A little thrill ran down his spine — for it opened at his touch.

At any rate, this was not housebreaking, he thought as he went inside. He found himself in a passageway, similar to the one in Ward's house, and again he stopped alert for some sound of human habitation. The wind rattled the windows and sighed around the eaves, but nothing moved or seemed to live in these empty rooms. Yet at his feet, Chan's flashlight showed him, was a trail of loose snow leading off into the dark.

He followed this trail, out of the passage into a front hall. Great shadows danced about him on the walls; in distant rooms he saw ghostly chairs and sofas swathed in white.

Undaunted, he pushed on, up the carpeted stairs where the fresh snow lay. It led him to a closed door at the rear of the second-floor hall, and there it stopped. He tried the door, quietly, and found it locked.

A brief examination of the sill decided him, and he had raised his hand to knock, when he thought he heard the closing of a distant door. He waited. Undoubtedly stealthy footsteps were crossing the polished floor of the down-stairs hall. Charlie was thinking very fast.

He had been in somewhat similar situations before, and had learned that all the advantage lies with the side which attacks suddenly and unexpectedly. Putting his flash-light in his pocket, he moved softly and swiftly to the stairs and began to descend. Half-way down he stopped and so, almost, did his heart. For the person in the hall below had lighted a match.

Charlie crouched close to the wall, the shadows flickered about him, but the life of a match is brief, and evidently he was still safe when the flame expired. Safe — in a way — except for the fact that the unknown intruder was coming rapidly up the stairs.

He had the top position, and there was nothing else for it — Charlie gathered all his strength and leaped, straight into the surprise of his life. For it was obviously a giant upon whom he fell, a giant who kept his footing and took Chan, avoirdupois and all, into his arms. In another second the plump detective from the islands was engaged in a struggle he would long remember. They staggered together down the stairs; their swaying forms hit the newel post, and an old-fashioned lamp that had been established there for thirty years crashed down in a million pieces. Next they were rolling on the floor, Charlie grimly determined to keep in so close an embrace that this terrible stranger would have no chance to square off for a blow. One blow from that source, he felt, would ruin him for ever.

Not in such good condition as he used to be, Chan reflected, as the fight went doggedly on. Getting on in years, easily winded — ah, youth, youth. No use pretending, it left one day, never to return. About this struggle now — he was losing it. Unmistakably. He was on his back, the stranger's hands were at his throat, he sought, vainly, to tear them away. A flash of the little house on Punchbowl Hill, the bougainvillea vine hanging over the veranda — then the dark, slowly enveloping his senses.

Then the stranger, sitting down violently on Charlie's generous stomach, and the voice of Don Holt, crying, 'Good Lord — is that you, Mr. Chan?'

'Alas,' said Chan. 'At night all cats are black.'

Holt was helping him to his feet, deeply solicitous. 'Say — I sure am sorry about this, Inspector. Of course — I never suspected. I hope I haven't hurt you much. How do you feel?'

'How does sparrow feel when hit by cannon-ball?' Charlie returned. 'A little disturbed. However, I expect to survive. And I am delighted we have met, though I must disparage the details of our meeting. For there is something strange afoot in this house to-night.'

'I reckon there is,' Holt answered. 'I was sound asleep when the coroner came to my room — '

'One moment, please,' Chan interrupted. 'I will hear that later. Just now I think it important that we investigate a certain door up-stairs. Without delay.' He got out his flashlight and, to his surprise, found it still working. 'Will you be kind enough to follow me?'

Quickly he led the sheriff to the locked door on the second floor. 'Track of snow brought me here,' he explained. 'And behold.' He pointed. On the doorsill was more snow, a portion of a heel-print where a foot had recently trod.

'Then somebody's inside,' said Holt, in a hushed voice.

'Somebody,' nodded Chan. 'Or something,' he added.

The sheriff raised a great fist, and the sound of his blow against the panel echoed loudly through the house. 'Open up here!' he shouted.

In the dead silence that followed there was something sinister and disturbing. Holt rattled the knob, and then moved back a few feet.

'Well,' he said, 'we already owe for that lamp downstairs. Might as well add a little damage here. Will you turn the light this way, Inspector?'

Charlie illuminated the scene, and the sheriff lunged forward. There came the sound of splintering wood as the lock gave way and the door swung open. Chan's flash swept the room inside. An ordinary bedroom, it seemed to be, as one after another the articles of furniture emerged from the shadows. An ordinary bedroom — and on the floor beside the bed, the motionless figure of a man.

As they stood for a moment in the doorway, Chan thought suddenly of Romano. Romano sitting nervously in that other bedroom, asking what would happen to one who — perhaps — assisted in the arrest of the guilty. Had there been real fear in the Italian's eyes when he whispered: 'Did you, also, hear a noise outside that door?'

Kneeling, the sheriff turned the figure on the floor face up. Chan joined him with the lamp — and they were looking into the dead eyes of Doctor Swan.

# 14

## Thought is a Lady

For a moment, while the yellow glare of Chan's flash-light rested idly on the face of the dead doctor, there was no sound save that of the storm roaring about the old house.

'Exit Doctor Swan,' said the sheriff grimly. 'I wonder what this means?'

'I believe,' Chan answered, 'it means that blackmailer has met with obvious finish. Was Doctor Swan enclosed safely in room last night when fatal shot was fired at Landini? It never did seem probable. Suppose he hovered about in hall, desiring one final word with his former wife. Suppose he learned who killed her. Would such a man report at once to police? Or would he, instead, see new delightful path for blackmail opening up before his dazzled eyes?'

'Sounds reasonable,' Holt agreed.

'I think it happened. Suppose he is summoned down here to-night to receive first installment of his wickedly earned money. And receives instead the bullet of a desperate person who can not pay — or, knowing that the demand will be endless, will not pay. Ah, yes, from murderer's standpoint, this would be wiser course. I can not truthfully say I disagree. But you were about to tell me how you chance to be here?'

'The coroner had the room next to Swan's at the Tavern,' Holt replied. 'He was waked up about twelve-thirty by the banging of a shutter. The noise seemed to come from Swan's room. The coroner stood it as long as he could, and then he rapped on Swan's door. Well, to cut it short, nobody answered — an' that was how I come into it.

'We saw right away that Swan had left by the window. I followed his footprints to the road, where they turned in this direction. It looked like the doctor was staging a getaway. Say, I didn't stop for anything — I jes' hurried along on his trail. Didn't even have a flash-light — not so strong on preparedness as you are. But I did have a full box of matches — jes' used my last down-stairs.'

'You walked the two miles or more from the Tavern?'

'Sure — when I wasn't running. When I got to the point behind this house where Swan had turned off, I looked up and got the glimmer of a flash-light back of the hall shutters on the second floor — yours, I reckon. So I pushed open the back door, and came in.'

'The back door was still unlocked?' Chan asked thoughtfully.

'Sure.'

Charlie considered. 'The killer of Doctor Swan must have intended this house as temporary hiding-place for victim,' he reflected. 'Would he then have departed, leaving door unlocked for any passer-by to enter? I think not. The answer is, of course, he was still in house when we arrived. He may even be here now. Come — we waste valuable time.'

Hastily he led Don Holt down-stairs and through the passageway to the rear door. He turned the knob. But now the rear door was locked, and there was no key in sight.

'Haie!' Chan cried. 'Our friend has made his escape — perhaps while we were tumbling in mortal conflict in the hall. Where was he hiding when we entered?' He made an investigation of the plentiful snow along the passage. 'Ah, yes.' Pushing open the door into a butler's pantry, he sadly pointed out to Holt more snow on the linoleum inside. 'Let us place order for ample supply of sackcloth and ashes,' he remarked gloomily. 'You and I, my boy, both walked to-night within three feet of the murderer we so hotly seek. Alas, this winter climate is not so invigorating to the mental processes as I had hoped it would be.'

The sheriff returned to the back door and fiercely rattled the knob. 'He's got a fine start on us, too,' he said.

'Man inclined to exercise would not need to look farther for nice pair of dumb-bells,' Chan answered. 'Pardon vile slang, which I acquire from my children, now being beautifully educated in American schools. Come, we must seek new footprints leading away from this rear door. They are our only hope.'

They ran to the big front door, where somewhat rusted bolts again delayed them. After a struggle, however, they got it open, and hastened around to the back of the house. The snow was very damp now. 'Turning to rain,' Holt announced, looking up at the sky. 'This'll have to be a quick job.'

There were, indeed, new footprints in the snow at the back. They led away, not to the road, but around the house, on the opposite side from that which Chan and the sheriff had traveled. Breathlessly the two representatives of the law followed them — straight to the pier. At the edge of the restless water beneath the pier, the footprints stopped abruptly.

'That ends that,' sighed Holt. 'This guy had a rowboat, I reckon.' He stared at the wild waters. 'Wouldn't care to be traveling out there to-night,' he added.

Charlie was bending eagerly with his flashlight above the last visible prints just before they entered the water. 'No use,' he said, sighing ponderously. 'Fresh snow obscures any identifying marks. Snow, I fear, has been a little too highly spoken of as aid to detectives in hour of need.'

They returned to the front veranda of the house. Holt continued to study the lake. 'With this rain coming on,' he remarked, 'I don't believe a rowboat could keep afloat out there.'

'If man who killed Swan, and then escaped after we entered house, brought boat,' Chan said, 'then who was person whose tracks I followed down from Pineview by the road? Did he perhaps carry boat on back?'

'Oh — you followed somebody down here, too?'

'I assuredly did, and I believe he was the man we seek.'

'Perhaps he took a boat from this place.'

'No — I observed boat-house intact. Might I make another suggestion?'

'By all means. I'm through.'

'Might he not have stepped into water and

run along shore for some distance? Beach is flat here.'

'By golly, that's right,' agreed the sheriff. 'He could travel by that method for a while in either direction. Of course, he'd probably leave the water as soon as he thought himself safe. There's an idea — we could follow the shore — '

'In which direction?'

'Why — you take one way, and I'll take the other.'

Charlie shook his head. 'No use,' he said. 'Already this gentleman has had twelve minutes' start. As for me, my avoirdupois precludes success — and even your thin legs, I think, would fail.'

Holt sighed. 'It seemed the only chance,' he said.

Charlie smiled. 'There will be other chances,' he replied. 'Do not despair. Our quarry will be caught — but by subtler means than running alongshore in the rain. For I perceive we now have rain.'

'Yes, spring has come,' Holt answered. 'And here I am, too tangled up in murder to enjoy the thought.'

'From the black sky, white water falls,' smiled Chan, looking aloft. 'This may yet prove very pleasant spring for you.'

'Oh, yeah?' the sheriff replied. 'Well, in the

meantime, what next? Here we are, stuck down here, in a deserted house with a dead man — no telephone, and nothing but our feet to get away on. Here's my suggestion. I'll go back to the Tavern and get the coroner, while you go and see what's doing at Pineview.'

'So sorry to disagree,' Chan said. 'Everything would no doubt be quiet at Pineview — every one in bed and asleep by the time I reached there. No change — save that I might possibly find back door, which I left unfastened now locked. In such case, I must raise row, or stand in rain until morning. Besides, is it wise to leave this place unguarded? We might return to find our dead man gone. Suppose the killer still lurks among the trees, sees us both depart, and proceeds to follow out hastily the plan I am sure he intended to pursue at leisure — to drop body of Swan far out in lake, to hide it in hills, to dispose of it in some manner. No. Plan for yourself is excellent, but I shall linger here, awaiting return of the honorable sheriff, the coroner and light of another day.'

'Well.' Holt looked back into the dim empty house. 'It's no job I would rise in meeting to ask for, but if you want it, it's yours. But what in Sam Hill will you do with yourself? I'll be gone quite some while.'

'There is no need of hurry on your part. First, I shall open front door very wide, seeking to exchange stale air of long-closed house for fresher breath of first spring night. Then, I shall find comfortable chair in parlor, repose in it and think.'

'Think?'

'Precisely. Thought is a lady, beautiful as jade, so do not fear I shall be lonely. Events of to-night make me certain I must not neglect the lady's company longer.'

'Well, look out for yourself, if you stay here,' Holt remarked. 'That's not a pretty picture you painted — the killer creeping back. I haven't got my gun with me, or I'd loan it to you.'

Charlie shrugged. 'I hold with Mrs. O'Ferrell — the less guns, the fewer gets killed. However, have no anxiety. The chair I sit in will be like seat for guest of honor at Chinese dinner. It will face the door, so I may note enemy's approach.'

'Then I'll be going — ' Holt began.

Charlie laid a hand on his arm, 'Already that lady inspires me — I see Doctor Swan, standing on pier to-night, just before you took him to the Tavern in your launch. What was it he desire so eagerly to know?'

'That's right,' Holt said. 'About Romano

and the will. Did Romano get Landini's property?'

'And was he, consequently, a good blackmail prospect?' Chan's eyes narrowed. 'It would seem to me Sheriff, that Swan came here to-night to meet a man of whom, physically, he had no fear. A small man — like Romano.'

Don Holt scowled. 'But Romano. If he had done either of these killings wouldn't he have been more likely to use a knife?'

'Ah — excellent reasoning,' Charlie cried. 'I am proud of you. However, you forget — or perhaps you do not know — that Romano, like Ireland, served in the war. An Italian officer — he must have known well the use of the revolver. But no matter — I merely continue to marshal facts for the storehouse of my mind. A pleasant journey to you.'

'Yeah — in the rain, on foot,' smiled Holt. 'Well, good-by — and good luck.'

He ran down off the porch and disappeared toward the road in the rear. Chan retired inside, leaving the door open, and moved on into a large living-room. A pleasant place this must be, he thought, on summer nights, with its splendid view of the lake. He removed a sheet from a large chair and placing the latter in what seemed the safest corner, dropped into it. Then he shut off his light, and put it in his pocket.

The rain beat against the house, the wind roared, and Charlie thought back over this wintry case upon which he, detective of the semi-tropics, was now so unexpectedly engaged. First of all he thought of people: of Sing, whose beady little eyes even Chan could not read; of Cecile, jealous and angry last night when she heard the airplane over the lake; of Ireland, clumsy and uneasy when out of his plane, but so expert when in it. He considered Romano, broke and according to his own confession, desperate — but now come into money through Landini's sudden passing. Hugh Beaton, sick of the bargain he had made; his sister, jealous as Cecile, but in a different way — a high-strung, impetuous girl. Dinsdale — since he was including them all — evidently so aloof from all this — but an old friend of the singer, none the less. Ward, who had started it all and encountered two tragedies. Ryder, with the scornful blue eyes above the blond beard, and Swan — dead now in that room above. Had it been, after all, attempted blackmail that led to Swan's death? How young Hugh Beaton had raged at the doctor last night after the murder — and how Michael Ireland and Swan had snarled at each other.

The rain outside seemed to increase in

fury, and Charlie decided he had had enough of the open door. He crossed over, closed it and returned to his chair. Once more, he decided, he would take things from the beginning — the sudden shot upstairs, Landini on the floor, the boxes with the mixed lids — ah, he had been over all this a hundred times. But — and he started up suddenly in his chair — there was one thing he had forgotten. Not yet had he carefully considered the events before the murder.

He was back, then, on the train, repeating from memory his talk with Romano; he was riding up from Truckee to the Tavern; again the icy spray of the lake stung his cheeks, he was going ashore at Pineview, the ex-husbands of Landini were drinking before the fire. Then followed dinner — his excellent memory recalled vividly every incident at the table, nearly every word that had been spoken. He heard again the bark of the dog announcing the arrival of the singer — felt again the vibrant, colorful personality of Landini — ah, what a pity her brilliant career was so soon to end.

But beyond the shot that ended it, Chan did not trouble now to explore. He gazed around this strange room, listened for a moment to the spatter of rain at the windows, and then, oblivious to any killer who might

276

return, he curled up comfortably in his chair, drew his overcoat closer and fell into a deep and peaceful sleep. After all, a man must sleep.

He awoke with a start to find the sheriff bending over him. A semblance of dawn seemed to be floating through the house, but the rain still beat against the windowpanes.

Beyond Don Holt stood the coroner.

'Sorry to disturb you,' Holt said. 'We just dropped in.'

Charlie yawned, sat up and was about to step to the window for a look at his beloved Honolulu. Then he remembered.

'Anything exciting happen?' Holt wanted to know.

'I — I think not,' Chan said. 'No — as I recall now — nothing happened. Ah, yes — the coroner. He will want to go upstairs.'

He leaped briskly to his feet, and led the way to the room above. The others followed, not so briskly. They could all see, in the semi-darkness, the body of Swan, lying as it had been left by Charlie and the sheriff the night before.

'We need more light here, I think,' Chan said. 'I will admit some, such as it is.' He went to the window opened it and threw back the blinds. For a moment he stood leaning over the window-sill, then Don Holt was surprised to see him climbing through the window.

'What are you doing?' the sheriff inquired.

'Small polar expedition of my own,' Chan replied. He had dropped to a balcony some two feet below the window. It was covered by about twelve inches of snow, now melting rapidly. At one side of the window, close to the house wall, was a spot which had melted more rapidly than the rest, leaving a small hole. Charlie bared one arm to the elbow, and plunged it deep into the crevice. With an expression of triumph on his face, he held up an automatic pistol so those inside the room could see.

'Man who buries his treasure in the snow,' he said, 'forgets that summer is coming.'

# 15

## Another Man's Earth

Chan handed the revolver to the sheriff and began a rather cumbersome climb back into the room.

'Guard weapon well,' he suggested. 'It may prove valuable — who knows? How many cartridges exploded, please?'

'Why, one, of course,' the sheriff replied.

'Ah, yes — the bullet from which, now reposing in poor Doctor Swan, the coroner will later obtain for us. You may handle pistol freely, Sheriff. The killer we deal with does not leave finger-prints — even with his footprints he is careful man. In spite of his care, however, his discarded weapons may yet tell us much.'

'You think so?' inquired Holt.

'I hope so.' For a time Charlie stood studying the revolver as it lay in the sheriff's hand. 'This one has somewhat old-fashioned look,' he suggested.

'Sure does,' Don Holt agreed.

'You are, of course, too young to have fought in the war?'

'Too young by six years — I tried it,' smiled the sheriff.

Charlie shrugged. 'No matter. All sorts of weapons were issued in the war — on many fronts. We must seek other path.'

Doctor Price stood up. 'All right,' he said, 'that's all I can do now. We may as well take this man down to the village.'

'What would you deduce?' Chan inquired.

'I believe he was shot at close range, and without a struggle,' the coroner replied. 'Certainly there was no struggle here — though he may have been killed elsewhere, and carried to this room.'

'Very probable,' Chan nodded. 'For that reason, I make no extended examination of the place.'

'I don't believe the poor devil had any inkling of what was about to happen to him,' Doctor Price continued. 'That's just a guess, of course. The bullet entered his side — it may have been fired by some one who was walking close to him — or slightly behind him. All things that we'll never know, I reckon.' There came the honk of a horn behind the house. 'That's Gus Elkins. I told him to follow us with his ambulance.' He yawned. 'Gosh — I expected to be on my way back to the county-seat before this.'

While Doctor Price and Mr. Elkins

attended to the removal of Swan's body, the sheriff and Charlie made a tour of the house, restoring it to order, in so far as they could.

'You an' me — I reckon we'll take my old flivver and get over to Pineview,' the sheriff said. 'We come up by road — lake looked pretty choppy. But say — wait till you hit the road.' He kicked aside some broken glass in the lower hall. 'Hope you ain't feelin' any ill effects from our friendly tussle.'

'He who goes out on the hills to meet the tiger must pay the price,' returned Charlie.

Holt laughed. 'Sure was a mix-up. I was wonderin' when I walked back to the Tavern what we ought to do next. Somebody had a key to the back door of that house, I said. So I sent a wire down to the owner in San Francisco an' asked him who that would be.'

'Excellent,' Charlie returned. 'It was what I was about to suggest. But now you are moving a little ahead of me on our rocky path.'

'I ain't so sure about that,' Holt said. 'How did you get on with your home work while I was away? Going to do a lot of heavy thinkin', I believe you told me.'

Charlie's eyes narrowed. 'Alas,' he answered, 'I fear that, like my little son Barry, I toppled in sleep on to my books.'

'Oh, yeah?' Don Holt answered.

In a few moments the ambulance had gone, and Chan climbed into the flivver beside the sheriff. 'Feel at home in such seat,' he commented. They started with a jerk. 'But not on such road. Not much melting snow on Punchbowl Hill.'

Daylight had come, but a sullen counterfeit daylight. The rain beat down on the top of the car, and on Don Holt's two-gallon hat as he leaned far out to follow the road — the windshield wiper, he explained, was not working. The wind had died, the pines were silent and dripping; they plowed on through slush a foot deep.

'Wonder how we'll find all the folks at Pineview,' the sheriff said presently. 'Including the murderer. I guess there ain't much doubt he'll be there, waiting for us.'

'He may be,' Charlie agreed.

'Well — let's have a check-up. Who's there now? Romano, Ryder and Ward. Hugh Beaton — and his sister.'

'A charming lady, Miss Beaton,' Chan suggested.

'Yeah — she's all right. But don't get me off the track — I'm countin'. Let's see — well, that's about all — except Sing and Cecile — I sort of had that French dame on my mind, but after this, she don't look so good. That's the list.'

'And Mrs. O'Ferrell,' Chan added.

'Yeah — I can see her plowin' down through the snow to put a bullet in Swan. Say — I never been able to figure out what you meant — about Trouble bein' a clue.'

'So sorry,' Chan replied. 'But we all have our little mysteries to sting us, as summer flies pester the horse. For example, in own mind I am convinced blow received by Sing in defenseless face on night of murder was vastly important clue. But — I can not figure it. However, we must be patient. You and I — we will both learn in time.'

They left the car on the road above and descended the steps to the back door of Pineview. Sing was shaking a duster on the porch. He gave Charlie a slightly startled look.

'Wha's mallah you?' he demanded. 'My think you upstair in bed, you come home back step, plenty wet.'

'I was called away on business,' Charlie explained.

'Hello, Sing,' the sheriff said. 'Don't worry about Mr. Chan. I've been taking care of him. Anybody up yet?'

'Nobody, only me,' Sing replied. 'My get up sunlise, woik, woik, woik. Too much woik this house. No can do.'

Inside, they found Sing's statements

somewhat inaccurate. Mrs. O'Ferrell was busy in the kitchen, and gave them a cheery greeting. Proceeding to the living-room, they found Leslie Beaton, reading a book.

'Hello — you're up early,' Holt remarked.

'The same for you,' she replied, 'and as for Mr. Chan — I don't believe he ever sleeps. Was that he — or should I say him — I saw in the road behind the house in the night?'

'It may have been,' Charlie said quickly. 'Again, it may not. Elaborate the statement, if you will be so good.'

'I couldn't sleep very well,' the girl went on. 'Can any one — in this house? My room is in an ell in the rear, close to the road. I went to the window and looked out. I saw a shadowy figure, hurrying up the steps, and fairly running along the road.'

'Sounds pretty active for the inspector,' smiled Holt. 'Do you know what time this was?'

'Yes — it was precisely ten minutes after twelve. I looked at my watch.'

Chan leaned toward her eagerly. 'Describe this person,' he urged.

'Impossible,' she answered. 'It was snowing hard. It might have been anybody — even a woman, for that matter. I was somewhat worried. I went into my brother's room — he's right next door — and wakened him.

But he told me to go back to bed, and forget it.'

Hugh Beaton at that moment appeared on the stairs. His face seemed paler than usual; there were dark circles about his eyes, and his manner was extremely nervous. He saw Charlie and the sheriff.

'What's happened now?' he cried. 'For God's sake — what is it now?'

'It is nothing,' Charlie replied soothingly. 'You arise early.'

'Why shouldn't I? My nerves are all shot to pieces, in this God-forsaken place. When are you going to let us out of this prison? What right have you — '

'Please, Hughie,' his sister cut in. 'Mr. Ward might hear you — and he's been so kind to us.'

'I don't care if he does hear me,' the boy retorted. 'He knows I don't want to stay here. When do we go to the Tavern? You promised to-day — '

'And it will be to-day,' Holt said, looking at him with a trace of contempt. Temperamental artists were not in the sheriff's line. 'Brace up.'

'Tell me,' Chan said. 'When your sister came in to wake you last night — '

'When she — oh yes. I remember now. What was that all about?'

'You remember, Hughie,' said the girl, 'I told you I'd seen somebody leaving the house.'

'Oh, yes. Well, did somebody leave? Is some one missing?'

'Somebody did leave,' Charlie explained. 'We think he returned, however. But not until, in an empty house down the road, he had shot and killed Doctor Swan.'

There was silence for a moment. 'Doctor Swan,' gasped the girl. Her face was as white as her brother's. 'Oh, that's too terrible.'

'It's no more terrible than the killing of Ellen,' her brother said, and his voice sounded hysterical. 'We've got to get out of here, I tell you. To-day. This minute.' He rose and stared wildly about.

'A little later,' Holt remarked calmly.

'But I tell you — my sister — she's in danger here. So are we all — but I have to look after her — '

'A natural feeling,' Chan said. 'Your sister will be taken care of — and so will you. I presume you heard nothing in the night — save, of course, your sister's entrance. You can throw no light on this?'

'None. None whatever,' the boy answered.

'Most unfortunate.' Charlie rose. 'I go to my room to freshen up drooping appearance. I return soon,' he added to the sheriff.

He went up, leaving the three young people in the living-room. Cecile was standing just inside his door.

'Ah, Monsieur,' she cried. 'Your bed is untouched.'

'I know,' he replied. 'I did not sleep last night. Just a moment, if you will be so kind. Do not go.'

'Yes, Monsieur.' She regarded him with troubled eyes.

'Your husband, Madame? When did you see him last?'

'When he left here just before dinner. Surely you recall? He took the little dog in his plane.'

'He did not return to this neighborhood last night?'

'How could he? Such a night. He could not fly in such weather.'

'But is he not an expert chauffeur? He could return in automobile.'

'If he returned, I did not know it. I do not understand of what you speak, Monsieur.'

'He and Doctor Swan — they were not the best of friends?'

'Michael hates him, as you saw yourself. He despises him, and with many good reasons. But why do you ask?'

'Because' — Charlie keenly watched her face — 'because, Madame, Doctor Swan was murdered in this vicinity last night.' Still he watched her. 'Ah, that is all. You may go now.'

She left without a word, and after hastily washing his hands and his as yet unshaven face, Charlie went out and knocked on Romano's door. The conductor let him in; he was partly dressed, his face was covered with lather, and he held a razor in his hand.

'Enter, Inspector,' he invited. 'You will pardon my condition. The hour — it is an early one.'

'Events conspire to give me no rest,' Chan told him. 'Continue, please, to shave. I will repose here, on edge of bathtub. There is a word or two — '

'What do you wish, Signor?'

'You heard no one about this house last night? You saw no one leave by the rear door?'

'I am a sound sleeper, Inspector.'

Quickly Chan told him what had occurred. He wished the Italian had removed more of that lather before hearing the news. But — wasn't the swarthy forehead now somewhat more in harmony with the white lather?

\* \* \*

'Swan, eh?' said Romano slowly. 'Ah, yes — he knew too much, that one, Inspector.

288

Him, he could not hold his tongue. Only yesterday, when we were having long day together, he spoke indiscreetly to me.'

'He said — what?'

'Nothing definite, you understand. I could not give you words. But already I thought his greedy fingers counted fresh bank-notes. That is dangerous business — blackmail.'

Chan studied the Italian's face. From the first, this man had baffled him.

'And in my room last night,' he said, 'you, yourself, hinted at knowing something, too.'

An expression of vast surprise crossed Romano's face.

'I, Signor? The day is young — you are still dreaming.'

'Nonsense. You spoke of — '

'Ah, my English — it is not good. You do not understand me when I speak it.'

'You asked if any one who could give information in this case would have to remain here after giving it.'

'Did I say that? I must have been thinking of Doctor Swan.'

'Unusual, if you were,' Chan answered. 'I should not say you devoted much thought to others. Of yourself, you think. Then consider this — if you have information which you withhold, it will go hard with you when matter is discovered.'

'I have no information,' Romano answered suavely. 'All I can say is, I trust this new murder will speed your search, for speed is what I most desire. In the meantime you are permitting Miss Beaton and her brother the privilege of changing their residence to the Tavern to-day. Can you deny the same to me? You can not. I will not stay in this house another day.'

'Ah — you begin to remember, now,' Chan smiled. 'You are afraid here. You do know something, after all.'

'Signor,' cried Romano passionately, 'you insult my honor. Ellen Landini was dear to me — her memory is dearer still — would I conceal the name of her assassin? No! A million times, no! Anyhow,' he added more calmly, 'I do not know the name. Must I tell you again?'

'For the present — no,' bowed Chan, and left the room.

Down-stairs, he found Hugh Beaton nervously pacing the floor, while his sister and the sheriff sat before the fire. The latter's conversational powers seemed to be ebbing fast, and Charlie was happy to help him out. In a few moments John Ryder came down the stairs, carefully groomed as always, remote and aloof.

'Beastly day, isn't it?' he remarked. He

glanced at the sheriff. 'Hello, Mr. Holt. Anything new?'

'Nothing unusual,' Holt said. 'Another murder, that's all.'

'Another what?' It was Dudley Ward who spoke, from the stairs.

Charlie Chan explained, watching both men alternately as he did so. Ryder's expression never altered; Ward looked only a little older, a little more worn, as he listened.

'A nasty bounder, Swan,' Ryder said coldly. 'But, of course — murder is a bit extreme.'

'None too kind to Ellen,' Ward remarked thoughtfully. 'But then — I guess none of us were, for that matter.'

'Speak for yourself, Dudley,' answered Ryder warmly. 'Don't begin to idealize the woman, just because she's dead.'

'I'm not idealizing her, John,' Ward returned. 'I'm just trying to keep in mind her virtues — and they were many. And it has occurred to me these last few days, that she was not too lucky in her choice of husbands.' His eyes were on Romano, sleek and dapper, who was now coming down the stairs.

'Breakfast ready now,' announced Sing, from the rear.

'Come on, Don,' Ward said. 'You're eating with us.'

'That's — that's mighty good of you,'

replied the sheriff.

'Nonsense. Sing — set another place.'

Sing muttered something about the amount of work in this house, and retired. But when they reached the dining-room, the old Chinese was there ahead of them, briskly and efficiently making a place for Holt.

The meal was eaten for the most part in silence. When it was ended, and they were back in the living-room, Holt informed Leslie Beaton and her brother that he would send his launch for them at nine-thirty, and that they should be packed and ready for the move to the hotel.

'You bet I'll be ready,' young Beaton cried. Seeing his sister's eyes on him, he added: 'Of course, Mr. Ward, I appreciate your hospitality. And the way Leslie's looking at me, I suppose I ought to add, I had a nice time.' His tone was childish and disagreeable.

'Hardly that,' Ward replied amiably. 'But I shall miss your sister and you very much, and I hope you may some day return for a stay under happier conditions.'

'You've been wonderful,' Leslie Beaton told him. 'I shall never forget you. The perfect host — at the most imperfect moment.'

Ward bowed. 'I shan't forget you,' he said.

Romano popped to the front. 'There will be a place in your launch for me?' he asked.

'What do you mean?' inquired Holt.

'I mean I also — with deep regret, Signor Ward — am leaving here to-day for the Tavern. Inspector Chan has agreed.'

Holt glanced at Charlie, who nodded. 'All right,' the sheriff said. 'You can have Swan's room. You've heard what happened to him.'

Romano shrugged. 'Ah — he wandered too far away. Me — I stick close to the hotel.'

'Well, see that you do,' Holt replied.

Charlie followed the sheriff into the passage at the rear. 'Pardon me,' he inquired. 'You have revolver we discovered in snow?'

'Sure. You want it?' Holt produced the weapon.

'I will take it brief while. When our friends come down to Tavern, I will be with them. Tell me, is there train to Oakland this morning?'

'Yes — there's one about ten-thirty. Say' — an expression of dismay spread over the sheriff's face — 'you ain't leaving, are you?'

'No. Not at this date.'

'Who is?'

'We will discuss the matter later.'

'So long, then.' Holt lowered his voice. 'Well, we had a nice breakfast, didn't we? But that's about all we got, eh?'

'Not quite.' Chan's eyes narrowed. 'We received also, from Miss Beaton, very pretty

293

alibi for her brother at twelve-ten last night.'

'My gosh,' the sheriff said. 'I never thought of that.'

'I did not think you would,' smiled Charlie.

He went at once to his room where, for a time, he experimented with lampblack and brush on the automatic pistol. Then, leaving the weapon on his desk, he hurried at last to the refreshing solace of his morning bath. He had just finished shaving when Sing appeared in his room with a supply of wood. Chan came out from the bath to find the old man staring at the pistol.

'Hello, Sing,' he remarked, 'you see that before, maybe?'

'I no see him.'

'You are quite sure?'

'I no see him — tha's no he, Boss.'

Charlie's eyebrows went up at this unexpected tribute of respect. 'Mebbe you catch 'um killer — hey, Boss?' the old man added.

Chan shrugged. 'I am stupid policeman — my mind is like the Yellow River.' He paused. 'But — who was it said — even the Yellow River has its clear days?'

'No savvy,' responded Sing, and started out.

Charlie laid a hand on the thin old arm.

'Delay one moment, if you will be so good,'

he said in Cantonese. 'You and I, honorable Sing, are of the same race, the same people. Why, then, should a thousand hills rise between us when we talk?'

'They are hills you place there with your white devil ways,' Sing suggested.

'I am so sorry. They are imaginary. Let us sweep them away. How many years did you have when you came to this alien land?'

'I had eighteen,' the old man replied. 'Now I have seventy-eight.'

'Then for sixty years you have carried another man's heaven on your head, and your feet have trod upon another man's earth. Do you not long to return to China, ancient one?'

'Some day — ' the old man's eyes glittered.

'Some day — yes. But a man takes off his shoes tonight. How does he know he will put them on again in the morning? Death comes, Ah Sing.'

'My bones return,' Sing told him.

'Yes — that is much. But to see again the village where you were born — to walk again on the soil where your bones are to rest — '

The old man shook his head sadly. 'Too much woik this house,' he said, lapsing into English. 'No can go. No can go.'

'Do not despair,' Charlie returned, dropping his somewhat rusty Cantonese. 'Fate settles all things, and all things arrive at their appointed time.' He took a clean white shirt from his bag and proceeded to put it on. 'A very dull day, indeed,' he added, stepping to the window and gazing out at the dripping pines. 'On such an occasion, the attire of man should compensate. You understand what I mean — I should wear gay clothes, happy clothes. My brightest necktie, perhaps.'

'Tha's light,' nodded Sing.

'I have a very red necktie — my daughter Evelyn gave it to me on Christmas, and she herself put it in my bag when I left. It is, my dear Sing, the reddest necktie the eyes of man have seen. And this, I believe, is the fitting day for it.' He went to his closet, removed a tie and drew it around his neck. For a moment he faced the mirror, and while he tied the knot, he watched the expression on the old man's withered countenance. He turned about, to give Sing the full effect.

'There,' he beamed, 'that will brighten this gloomy day. Eh, Sing?'

'Velly good,' agreed Sing, and walked slowly from the room. Charlie stood looking after him, his eyes narrowed, his face very thoughtful.

# 16

## That Boy Ah Sing

At half past nine, Cash Shannon appeared with the sheriff's launch. When it came to brightening the day and atoning for the weather, Cash took second place to no man. Indeed, at the mere sight of his colorful costume, the weather seemed to be giving up the struggle; the rain had stopped, and the clouds raced madly through the sky as though seeking to give the sun an opening. There was no doubt that the storm was over, nature would soon be smiling but not, probably, as brightly as Cash at the sight of Leslie Beaton.

He appeared slightly surprised at the number of passengers he was to carry, for Romano added himself and his luggage to the group on the pier, and Charlie made it known that his not inconsiderable person was also to be included. However, once they were started, Cash paid no attention to any one save the girl.

'Well, I guess you might call this the opening day at the Tavern,' he remarked to her. 'If I was the management — which I ain't

— there'd be tea on the terrace, music in the casino, an' flags hanging all over the place.'

'What are you talking about?' she inquired.

'Any time a girl like you comes to a hotel, ought to be some sort of celebration. That's the way I figure it. Say — how do you get on with a horse?'

'I ride a little.'

'Well, we'll change all that. You'll ride a lot, the next few days. Some of the trails are open now an' say — the plans I got — '

'If you will be so kind,' called Chan, from behind him. 'Please make utmost speed.'

'What for?' inquired Cash.

'I have some plans myself,' smiled Charlie.

The instant the launch had landed, he leaped ashore and hurried to the hotel. Old Sam Holt was seated by the fire, and greeted Chan with every evidence of pleasure.

'Been waiting to talk to you,' he said. 'Sorry I wasn't with you last night up the road.'

'We have much to discuss,' Charlie answered. 'But first there is a matter that requires great haste. Where is your son, please?'

'I reckon he's out to the stables. I'll send one of the boys.' The old man made his way to the desk, gave the order and returned. 'What's on your mind now, Inspector?'

'You will denounce me bitterly when I tell

you,' Chan replied.

''Tain't easy to picture that,' the old man said. 'You mean — '

'I mean I propose to call into this case some one we both agree is absolutely worthless. A scientist.'

Sam Holt laughed. 'Wal — gener'ly speakin', Mr. Chan. Gener'ly speakin'. O' course, mebbe I'm a leetle unreasonable. An' if you cave in oh th' point, I reckon I kin cave with you.'

'A gentleman I met in San Francisco a few weeks ago,' Charlie explained. 'An instructor of physics at the University of California, in Berkeley. I had a serious talk with him, and I thought — ' Don Holt approached and Chan leaped to his feet. 'Mr. Sheriff, tell me — have you bullet from body of the recent Doctor Swan?'

'Sure — I got it,' Holt replied, producing it. 'Another thirty-eight. The coroner — '

'Haste is required,' Chan cut in. 'Pardon the abrupt manner. But inform me — can we place some one on the ten-thirty train at Truckee — and if so, whom?'

Cash had just entered with Leslie Beaton and her brother. The deputy was loaded with bags, and eternal adoration of the fair sex gleamed in his eyes. Holt laughed.

'I'll say we've got some one we can put on

that train,' he chortled. 'And good riddance, too. Hey — Cash.'

Cash dropped the luggage and came over. 'What is it, Chief?'

'Get a bag packed, kid. You got to catch the Oakland train at Truckee, an' you got to step.'

'Me?' cried Cash in dismay. 'But say, I just made a date with Miss Beaton to exercise a couple horses at three o'clock — '

'Thanks a lot,' smiled Holt. 'I'll be glad to take care of that for you. Get a move on, boy. I'm tellin' you.' Cash hurried out toward the stables. 'Now, Mr. Chan — that's the best idea you've ever had in your life. Where's he goin', and why?'

'To begin operations,' Charlie said, 'kindly bring me from safe of Mr. Dinsdale, Landini's revolver, and along with it bullet from same which killed her. Also, please obtain for me one very large and strong Manila envelope.' He sat down at a writing-desk, and took the pistol which had slain Swan from his pocket. This he laid on the desk. The bullet he had just received from the sheriff, he put in an envelope and marked. Then he took a sheet of note paper and hastily began to write.

He had finished the letter when young Holt returned and placed before him the pearl-handled pistol that had been Landini's property, and the other bullet. The latter was put into a second small envelope and marked, and Charlie then proceeded to insert a marked piece of paper in the barrel of each gun. He took the big envelope Holt handed him, wrote a hasty name and address on the outside, and put into it the two weapons and the two small envelopes. He then sealed the flap, and handed the big envelope to the sheriff.

'It bears, you will note, an address in Berkeley. Tell the good Cash to alight at Oakland and visit this man at once. He is to obtain answer to question in my letter — tonight if possible — and wire same to you instantly. Impress upon him great need of speed.'

'Fine,' answered Holt, looking at his watch. 'I'll let him take my car, and he can just about make it. He can leave the car in a garage near the station in Truckee.'

He hurried out. Sam Holt, who had been listening, came up. 'And this perfessor at Berkeley, Mr. Chan,' he said, 'what does he claim he kin do?'

'He claims,' Charlie replied, 'that if he has both pistol and bullet, he can tell how far latter has traveled.'

'He's a liar,' said Holt promptly.

'Perhaps,' smiled Chan. 'But the wonders

of science — who are we to question them? And I have some curiosity to know how far these bullets traveled — especially that one found in poor unhappy Landini. My friend also claims that many times, from portion of thumb-print found on head of shell, he can reconstruct full print of person who had pushed same into carriage. That would be useful in other instance.'

'He's a colossal liar,' insisted the old sheriff.

'We shall see,' Chan told him. 'If you will pardon me for one moment, I have telephone call to make.'

He went into a booth, and in a few minutes he was greeting Miss Meecher in her Reno hotel.

'So sorry to disturb you,' he said.

'That is quite all right,' she answered. 'Is there any news?'

'None save that of Doctor Swan's unexpected passing, about which you have no doubt heard.'

'Yes — a bell-boy just told me. It seems rather terrible.'

'Entire case is terrible. Miss Meecher, you are in receipt of Trouble?'

'Oh — you mean the dog? Yes, Mr. Ireland brought him in last night. Poor little fellow — he just roams about the apartment, looking for his mistress.'

'That is very sad. However, he is in kind hands, I know. There is a question, Miss Meecher, which I must ask you.'

'I'll tell you anything I can.'

'Naturally. You have told me that you and Madame Landini worked on her biography together. Do you recall beginning of last chapter, written on balcony of hotel at Stresa, where she spoke of knowing color-blind person?'

'Why, yes, I do,' Miss Meecher replied.

'Did it chance that she mentioned to you the name of this person?'

'No, she didn't. I remember she wrote that herself, and when I came to type it I was slightly curious. But she wasn't about at the moment, and though I meant to ask her later, it slipped my mind. It didn't seem important, anyhow.' There was a brief pause. 'Is it important, Mr. Chan?'

'Not even slightly,' replied Chan heartily. 'I was, like you, somewhat curious. But it does not matter. My real intention in calling up — I would ask has anything developed you think I should note?'

'I believe not. There's a wire from Madame's attorneys in New York asking me if it is true she never signed the will. It seems Romano is already in touch with them.'

'Ah, he is no wastrel of time, this Romano.'

'Shall I wire them the truth?'

'By all means. And kindly give my best regards to the anxious little dog. I have great likeness for him.'

'Thank you so much,' Miss Meecher replied.

As Charlie emerged from the booth, two young men entered the hotel lounge from the terrace. One of them — tall, lean, a bit graying at the temples — rushed forward eagerly.

'As I live and breathe,' he cried. 'My old friend. Charlie Chan. You remember me — Bill Rankin, of the San Francisco Globe?'

'With a pleasant glow,' Chan replied. 'You were my very good ally when Sir Frederic Bruce was killed.'

'And here I am, all ready to be an ally once again. Oh — this is Gleason of the Herald. He thinks he's a newspaper reporter, too. What ideas these youngsters get!'

'Hello, Mr. Chan,' Gleason said. 'We just missed you down at Pineview. But we had a nice ride on the lake.'

'Let's get down to cases,' said Rankin. 'This sheriff up here, Inspector, is a swell guy, but he won't talk. That was never your trouble, as I recall.'

'Talk was my weakness,' grinned Chan.

'Of course, you never said anything, but it made copy. Now, what's the dope? Who bumped off Landini?'

'Surely you do not think I have solved such a problem already?'

'Why not? You've had over twenty-four hours. Not slowing up on us, are you? Getting old — no, I can tell you're not by looking at you.'

'The case,' said Chan, 'has many angles. We labor hard, but it will not be brought to solution in a day. No tree in the forest bears cooked rice.'

'Yeah,' smiled Rankin, 'I'll remind my managing editor. Might make a head-line. 'Inspector Chan Says No Tree in Forest Bears Cooked Rice.''

'Look here, Mr. Chan,' Gleason said solemnly, 'surely you have some results to report to our readers. That's what they want. Results.'

'Ah, this American passion for results,' Charlie sighed. 'Yet the apple-blossom is so much more beautiful than the dumpling.'

'And can we send back an armful of apple-blossoms?' laughed Rankin. 'You met my editor once. He wants a pan of dumplings, warm from the oven.'

'So sorry,' Chan apologized. 'I suggest first of all, you get lay of land.'

'We got it,' Gleason replied. 'Say, what was in that big envelope you just sent the drug-store cowboy flivvering off with? We asked him — but of all the nasty tempers — '

'Ah,' nodded Chan, 'perhaps it was Landini's will.'

'Carried it with her wherever she went, eh?' Rankin grinned.

'Just a suggestion,' Chan told him. 'Who inherits her property? Merely one of the angles.'

'By gad — we never thought of that,' Gleason cried. 'How about it, Bill?'

'What was the name of her lawyers in Reno?' Rankin inquired. 'Thanks, Inspector. There might be a story in that. I think I'll take a run over there for lunch — '

'I'm right with you,' Gleason assured him. 'We'll see you later, Mr. Chan. Thanks for the tip.'

'It was nothing,' Charlie smiled. As the two went out, he walked over and sat down beside Sam Holt. 'Ah, the reporters — they are upon us,' he murmured.

'Like the pest of the locust,' the old man said. 'I could hear what ye told 'em. Gave 'em somethin' to think about, eh?'

'I did,' Charlie replied. 'While we think of something else. Your son has told you all concerning last night, I presume?'

306

'He did — in a terrible hurry. You think this Swan knew too much about who killed Landini?'

'I'm certain of it. I also, Mr. Holt, think there is one other who knows something concerning the matter.'

'Yes, Mr. Chan?'

'Romano, the Italian, fourth and final husband of great singer — he hinted to me that his door was not too tightly closed on night of murder. Vast numbers were about on that second floor when Landini died. This morning, Romano's courage fails him. He will say no more. We should get together, sir, and put bolster under that courage.'

'He's up at Pineview, ain't he?'

'No — he came down with us, and took Swan's room. Your son is approaching — the three of us will descend on this man. We may conquer by numbers.'

Five minutes later the representatives of the law were facing Romano in his small bedroom. The conductor, frightened and nervous, sat on the edge of his bed and protested.

'I tell you I know nothing, gentlemen. Mr. Chan, he mistakes what I say. If — I told him. If a person knew, I said. Observe that if, please.'

'Look here,' said Don Holt, 'you know something — don't deny it. You don't want to tell because you're afraid it will delay you in getting back to the bright lights an' spending Landini's money. Well, it might — I can't promise. If I can fix things so it don't, I will. But one way or the other, Mister, you're tellin'. Or I lock you up. Get that, an' get it quick.'

'I am — I am so upset,' wailed Romano. 'This American law — it is confusing. What I saw — it was nothing, really. But I will tell. You understand, I am in my room, looking upon snow of flying field, I see plane alight, and for a time I watch it. Then — it comes to me — Landini will be going now. Have I accomplished my purpose? No. A few bills, thrown to me like I am a beggar — I, who have every right to demand. Am I not the husband? I go to my door. I will demand from Landini a definite appointment in Reno.

'I open that door, you understand. I am on point of moving into the hall. Opposite is the study door, now closed. Before I can move, it opens, and — a man — he steps into my view. I watch him, with stealthy look around he slips silently into the room beside the study — the one at my left as I stand.'

'Landini's old sitting-room,' Chan nodded.

'Something in that man's manner — it gives me pause,' continued Romano. 'Me — I am not easily suppressed, but for the moment

I am just that. And then, suddenly — from the study rings out — what? A shot, gentlemen. The shot that means Landini's death.'

'All right,' said Don Holt. 'But who was the man?'

'The man I saw,' replied Romano, with drama. 'The man who slips so slyly from one room to another. That man was Sing.'

In the silence that followed, Charlie heard Sam Holt sigh wearily.

'Fine,' remarked Don Holt. 'You keep that to yourself now, an' you'll be all right.'

'Me — I will keep it,' Romano cried. 'And I hope — so much — I will be all right.'

Charlie and the old sheriff walked together down the corridor. 'It keeps comin' back to Sing,' Sam Holt said. 'Fer all we kin do, Mr. Chan — it keeps comin' back to him.'

'Quite true,' Chan replied, 'but consider. Romano is the man who profits most by Landini's death. A man who may well have killed her. And a sly one, like a thief amid the fire. One of the slyest I have ever encountered. Suppose he sought to turn attention from himself? His eye lights on — '

'Poor old Sing,' finished Holt, slapping his thigh. 'Which is the first it would light on, I reckon. Sing, that looks helpless, an' not so quick on the come-back.' He stopped. 'Still

— I ain't so sure, Inspector.'

'No?' inquired Chan.

'No. If Romano was cookin' up a story about Sing, would he ha' done it so doggone well? Wouldn't he say he seen Sing creepin' into the study, an' then heard the shot? Would he say he seen him creepin' out o' the study, an' then the explosion came? No, Inspector — I got a sort o' sick feelin' Romano's story sounds like the facts. Sing brings th' blanket, an' finds Landini alone. He goes out, into her old room, opens the windows fer a way of escape, runs back to the study by way of the balcony, kills her an' then gits out the way he came. If he killed her, that's the way he done it, an' Romano is too close to it fer comfort, the way I feel.'

'Romano is sly and clever,' repeated Charlie. 'He studied situation, maybe.'

The old man laid his hand on Charlie's arm. 'Don't it beat all,' he said, 'the way that boy Sing keeps poppin' back, an' the way you an' me, we jest go on makin' excuses fer him? What I want to know is — how long kin we keep it up?'

Don Holt was waiting for them in the lounge. 'Well, what do you think of that story?' he inquired. 'Something behind it, if you ask me. Why, I've knowed old Sing since I was a baby. Reckon I'd better keep a sharp

310

eye on that Romano, after this.'

'There ye are, Inspector,' Sam Holt said. 'One more vote for Sing.'

'Won't you stay here for lunch?' Don Holt invited.

'You are very kind,' Charlie replied. 'But I fear we leave Pineview too much alone. I believe it wiser to return.'

'Maybe you're right,' agreed the sheriff. 'Tell that boatman on the pier I said to run you up to the house. I — '

A young woman summoned him into Dinsdale's office. Chan said good-by to Sam Holt and hurried toward the pier. He was stepping into a launch when Don Holt ran across the terrace and called to him.

'Just took a wire from San Francisco,' the sheriff said as he reached Chan's side. 'From the owner of the house where we found Swan. He says there's just one person up here has a key to that rear door. He leaves it here in case of an emergency.'

'Ah, yes. And he leaves it with — '

'He leaves it with Sing,' Holt answered. 'You'd better look into the matter when you get to Pineview.'

Charlie sighed. 'The man who would avoid suspicion should not adjust his hat under a plum tree. He is always adjusting his hat — that Sing.'

311

# 17

## The Net Closes In

Chan found the living room at Pineview deserted and walked rapidly through it to the kitchen. There conditions appeared to be somewhat chaotic. Sing and Mrs. O'Ferrell seemed to be jointly preparing lunch, and the latter was red of face and evidently quite flustered.

'Sing,' said Chan sternly from the doorway, 'I must speak with you immediately.'

'Wha's mallah you?' Sing replied. 'My velly busy. You go 'way, Boss.'

'I'll say he's busy,' cried Mrs. O'Ferrell indignantly. 'It was understood whin I come to this house I was to do the cookie', an' no wan else. An' here he's been all mornin', stirrin' up hivin knows what. Sure, an' it's me notice they get after this — '

'Sing,' Charlie repeated, and his voice was firm, 'come here!'

The old man inspected a pot at the rear of the stove, dropped the lid hastily and came to the door.

'Wha's mallah, Boss? This velly bad time fo' talk — '

'This plenty good time. Sing — you got key to big house down the road?'

'Sure, my got key. All time got key. Plumber come, light man come — they want key. My got 'um.'

'Where you got 'um?'

'Hang on hook, in hall, outside.'

'What hook? Show me.'

'My velly busy now. All time woik this house. No can do — '

'Show me, and be quick!'

'All light, Boss. Keep collah on. My show you.' He came into the passage and pointed to a hook beside the rear door. It was empty. 'Key all gone now,' he commented, without interest.

'Gone — where?'

'No savvy, Boss.'

'When did you see it last?'

'No savvy. Yeste'day, day befo' — mebbe las' week. My got to go now.'

'Wait a minute. You mean somebody has stolen the key?'

Sing shrugged. 'What you think, Boss?'

'Do you know that Doctor Swan was murdered in that house last night? And the person who did it had your key?'

Mrs. O'Ferrell gave a startled cry.

'Too bad, Boss,' Sing answered. 'Solly — got to get back to kitchen now.'

313

Charlie sighed and let him go. 'Does it chance you had noticed that key, Mrs. O'Ferrell?' he inquired.

'Sing showed it to me whin I first come,' she answered. 'There was a tag on it, tellin' what it was for. Sure, I niver give it a thought from that day to this.'

'You wouldn't know, then, when it disappeared or who probably took it?'

'I would not, Mr. Chan. It's sorry I am I can't help you.' There was a clatter from the kitchen. 'Excuse me please, sir. Sure, I don't know whether it's me or Sing that's gettin' lunch.'

Charlie went to his room to freshen up. When he returned down-stairs, Ward and Ryder were in the living-room.

'Our ranks are somewhat depleted,' the host said. 'It's going to seem a little lonely from now on.'

'I'll have to be getting back on the job myself very soon,' Ryder told him. 'If there's nothing I can do for you, old man. I — I don't believe the sheriff can hold me here. Do you think so, Mr. Chan?'

'Seems nothing against you,' Chan admitted.

'I hear your business is even more prosperous than usual, John,' Ward remarked.

Ryder brushed an imaginary bit of lint

from the lapel of his beautifully tailored coat. 'I can't complain,' he admitted. 'If I've got nothing else from life, I've at least got money. More than enough.'

At the luncheon table, Sing appeared to be in a state of great excitement. He served Charlie and Ward first with chops and vegetables, meanwhile assuring Ryder that the latter was not forgotten. 'You wait. You see,' he said repeatedly. Presently he appeared, triumphantly bearing aloft an enormous bowl, which he set before the mining man.

'Rice!' cried Ryder. 'Sing — you old rascal!'

'Like ol' time,' chuckled Sing, patting him on the back. 'You wait now. You see.'

He fairly ran to the kitchen, reappearing almost at once with another bowl. 'Chicken gravy. You smell 'um, hey? Like ol' time — when you lil boy.'

'Sing — this is wonderful,' Ryder remarked, evidently touched. 'I've been dreaming of your rice and gravy for nearly thirty years. Nothing has ever tasted so good since those old days in your kitchen.'

'Sing goo' cook, hey?'

'The best in the world. Thank you a million times.' Charlie thought Ryder had never seemed so human before.

'Ah — er — ' Ward looked slightly embarrassed. 'It seems that you and I are rather out of things, Mr. Chan. You must forgive Sing's peculiar ideas of hospitality.'

'Not at all,' Chan replied. 'You and I will have plenty lunch. And I believe Sing's ideas of hospitality are excellent. With him, old friends are best friends. Who could place blame on him for that?'

'This is a real bowl of rice,' Ryder was saying. 'Not one of those little bowls. A real, big bowl. And the gravy — come to think about it, I don't know that I'll ever go home.'

After lunch, Chan retired to his room to finish the last few galleys of Landini's story. Nothing more of interest had cropped up, but the personality of the writer had steadily grown upon him, and now, as he finished, he was one of the singer's friends, he felt. More than ever, he was determined to find her slayer — wherever the trail might lead.

He went down-stairs again. Pineview was deserted. He put on his arctics, for though the spring sun was now warm in the sky, things were a bit damp underfoot. Going outside, for a time he wandered about among the sheds at the rear, trying various doors. All, save those of the garage, were tightly padlocked. At the latter spot he looked longingly for a moment at the ladder. Evidently the pine trees again intrigued him.

He moved around to the front of the

house. Much of the snow on the lawn had melted, leaving only a thin coating of slush. Now and again he stopped, to pick up a cone or a fallen branch; idly, aimlessly, the student of the pines seemed to be gathering data on a favorite subject. Murders, the stern realities of his trade, policemen and sheriffs, appeared to be far from his thoughts.

And at that moment, Charlie was surprisingly far from the thoughts of the sheriff. Don Holt was seated in the saddle on his favorite mount, and beside him along the narrow trail under the pines, rode Leslie Beaton. The magic air of Tahoe had brought into her cheeks a color that was not for sale in the beauty parlors of Reno, and her eyes were shining with a new enthusiasm for life.

'It sure was a grand idea Cash had,' the sheriff remarked. 'Inviting you to go on this ride.'

'Poor Cash! What a pity he, was called away.'

'He's the kind that's likely to get called away,' Holt responded grimly.

'He never even said good-by to me.'

'They wasn't time. You see, Cash's good-by is likely to be long an' lingering — like that guy Romeo's. I reckon you're missin' old Cash.'

'Cash is a fluent talker.'

317

'I'll say he is. By this time, he'd have told you all about — how — pretty you look.'

'Do you think so?'

'I know he would.'

'I mean — do you think I look — all right?'

'Fine. But I ain't got the words, somehow.'

'Too bad. Cash's absence begins to look like a great calamity.'

'I was afraid you'd feel that way. Always been cooped up in cities, ain't you?'

'Always.'

'This air is doin' you a lot of good. It would do you more good — if you stayed.'

'Oh — but I must go back East. I have to work for living, you see.'

The sheriff frowned. 'Cash would explain to you that you needn't go. He's pretty convincin', that boy.' They came into a clearing, and turned their horses about. Far below lay the lake, reflecting snow-capped peaks beyond. 'Mighty nice view, ain't it?' said the sheriff.

'If sort of takes my breath away,' the girl answered.

'Makes you a little dizzy, eh? This is where old Cash would have staged a big emotional scene. About how you was the loveliest girl he'd ever met — how he couldn't live without you — '

'Don't, please,' smiled the girl. 'I seem to

be missing so much.'

'Oh, you ain't missing a lot. Cash got engaged to three girls on this very spot last summer.'

'You mean he's fickle?'

'Well — you know — these fellows that talk a lot — '

'I know. But the strong silent men ought to strike a happy medium now and then — don't you think?'

'I reckon that's right, too.' The sheriff took off his hat, as though to cool a fevered brow. 'You — you think you could like this country?'

'The summers must be lovely.'

'That's jest it. The winters — I don't know. I wish you could come down an' look at the county-seat — before you go away. It ain't a very big town. I reckon you wouldn't like it.'

'No — perhaps not. Can we see Pineview from here?'

'It's over there — in that bunch of trees. Gosh — I'd plumb forgot. Pretty big job we got on our hands, at Pineview.'

'Does it mean a lot to you — to succeed?'

'I'll say it does. I got to live up to Dad's reputation. He kind of expects it, I guess. But I don't know. Even with Mr. Chan's help — we don't seem to be going very strong.'

For a moment the girl did not speak. 'I'm

afraid I haven't been quite fair with you,' she said at last. 'I wonder if you'll ever forgive me?'

'I reckon so. But what do you mean?'

'About the night of Landini's murder. I can't imagine why I was so silly — but it seemed quite terrible. Involving some one who might perhaps be innocent — getting involved myself — I — I just couldn't.'

'You couldn't what?'

'I wanted to think it over — I've done that — and I see I've been a fool. All the time I really wanted to help you — I do now. You know — I was in the bedroom next door when I heard the shot that killed Landini.'

'I know.'

'Well, somehow, the shot seemed to be on the balcony. So — I didn't just sit there dumbly. I ran to the balcony window, opened it and looked out. And I saw a man leave the study, run along the balcony and disappear through the window of the room beyond — a man with a blanket under his arm.'

'Sing.'

'Yes — it was poor Sing. It seemed incredible — I couldn't believe it. But Sing ran out of the study just after that shot was fired. I'm so sorry I didn't tell you before.'

'You've told me now,' Holt replied gloomily. 'Gosh — I'd rather be hung myself.

But there's nothing to it — duty is duty, an' I took the oath. I reckon we'd better be goin' back.'

They started down the trail along which they had come. Again on that homeward trek Holt was the strong silent man — oppressively silent, now. When they parted before the Tavern stables, the girl laid her hand on his arm. 'You forgive me for not telling sooner, don't you?'

He looked at her solemnly in the dusk. 'Sure I do,' he answered. 'I reckon, when I come to think of it, I'd forgive you for almost anything.'

As he led the horses into the stable, he saw his father sitting alone in the office, near the door. Presently he went inside and sat down.

'Ain't no more doubt, I reckon,' he said. 'Sing killed Landini. I got it straight from a reliable party this time.' He repeated Leslie Beaton's story. 'Mebbe I'd better go up an' get him now,' he finished.

'Hold yer horses,' Sam Holt replied. 'We got to consult Mr. Chan. Yes — I guess there ain't much doubt — but it don't do to jump too soon. We want to git all the evidence we kin, first. Wasn't the coroner goin' to hold an inquest on Doctor Swan about this time?'

The young man looked at his watch. 'Yes — that's right.'

'You go over there, son,' Sam Holt said. 'Pick up anything you kin. There's plenty o' time fer Sing.'

As soon as the sheriff had gone, Sam Holt's groping hands sought for the telephone on the desk. In another moment he was talking to Charlie Chan at Pineview.

'Yes,' he was saying, 'it's Sing, Inspector. The net is closin' in. Matter o' fact, it's about closed.'

'As I expected,' Chan replied softly. 'What do you suggest?'

'Git down here as quick as ye kin, Mr. Chan — an' fetch Sing with ye. Don't say nothin' to nobody — but have him bring his bag. Jest a little bag — about what a man would need — in jail.'

'Ah, yes — in jail,' Chan repeated thoughtfully.

'Ye'll find me in the office o' the stables,' Sam Holt went on. 'Them reporters drove me out o' the Tavern.'

'I understand,' Charlie replied. 'There is an old flivver here. We shall arrive most speedily in that.'

And they did. Twenty minutes later, Charlie pushed open the door of the over-heated little office.

'Hello, Mr. Chan,' Sam Holt said. 'Somebody with ye, ain't they? Well, tell him to wait in th' stable, You an' me needs a little talk.'

There was an air of tense expectancy about Charlie as he came in alone and took a battered old chair beside the roll-top desk at which Holt sat. 'New evidence has leaped to view?' he inquired.

'It sure has,' Holt answered. 'After we heard from Romano, Inspector, I got to thinkin'. Sentiment is sentiment, but duty is duty. So I got that doctor over here — the Tahoe doctor that helped Don bring Landini's body down to town the night o' the murder. I says to him, 'Sing brought you blankets,' I says, 'to wrap about Landini. Blue blankets. Do you remember,' I says, 'was they ever laid on a velvet chair in that room?'' Holt paused.

'And the doctor's answer?' inquired Charlie.

'Seems I was a better detective than I wanted to be. Mr. Chan,' Holt went on grimly. 'That doctor took them blankets from Sing at the door, an' laid 'em on the floor beside the body. They never touched a chair. He was dead certain about that. Yes, sir — that blue blanket was in the room before the murder — they ain't no doubt about it.'

'I congratulate you on keen deduction you performed that morning in the study,' Charlie said.

'Kick me, Mr. Chan, an' I'll be more obliged,' Holt replied. 'Yes, sir — jest as I thought — Sing fired that shot. We got the blanket evidence, the hurt knee from that dressing-table bench. We got Romano, that seen him slip through that room next door, jest before the shot. An' we got some one else — some one who seen him leave the study jest after it.'

'That is news to me,' Chan remarked. Sam Holt told him of Leslie Beaton's story. Charlie shook his head. 'Too many people on that floor at time,' he remarked sadly.

'Too many fer poor ol' Sing,' agreed Holt. 'Got him comin' an' goin', we have. Don wants to lock him up.'

'A natural course,' Chan nodded.

'I wonder,' said Sam Holt. Charlie looked at him keenly. 'I wonder,' went on the old sheriff. 'I've been thinkin', Mr. Chan. A blind man gits a lot o' time to think, an' I been at it this afternoon, at it hard.'

'You have been thinking of all the clues in this case, perhaps?' Chan suggested gently.

'I have. What you said to Don about the dog. An' all this interest of yours in the pine trees, Mr. Chan.'

Charlie smiled. 'Mr. Holt — the best clue of all, you do not know. I did not recall it myself until last night, while I waited alone in creaking house of death. I propose to make a slight narration. I intend to tell you, from start to finish, every event that occurred, every word that was spoken, at dinner my first night at Pineview. Before the murder, you understand.'

He moved close to the old man, and in a low confidential voice, he spoke for some ten minutes. When he had finished, he leaned back in his chair and studied Sam Holt's face.

Holt was silent for a moment, playing with a paper-knife on the desk. At last he spoke. 'Mr. Chan — I am seventy-eight years old.'

'An honorable age,' said Charlie.

'A happy one, too, because I am here, among my own people, in the country I've always known. But now — jes' supposin' — I was in some foreign country — what would I want more than anything — '

'You would wish to see again your native village — to walk upon the soil wherein your bones were some day to rest.'

'You're a smart man, Mr. Chan. You git me right away. Inspector — Don ain't never even made ye a deputy. You ain't got no real authority here.'

'I am well aware of the fact,' nodded Charlie.

Sam Holt rose and stood there, a distinguished figure, a figure of honor, of integrity. 'And I — I am blind,' he said.

Chinese do not easily weep, but suddenly Charlie Chan felt a stinging in his eyes. 'Thank you,' he said. 'I speak for entire race when I say it. You will pardon me now, I know. I have little errand to perform.'

'Of course ye have,' said Holt. 'Good-by, Mr. Chan. An' if it should so happen that I don't ever meet a certain friend o' mine ag'in — give him my love an' say I'm proud I knowed him.'

Chan stepped through the door and closed it after him. In the dim shadows several feet away, he saw the bent figure of old Sing. He went over to him. 'Come on, Sing,' he remarked. 'You and I got journey to make.' Suddenly he saw looming in the doorway the powerful figure of Don Holt. He seized the old Chinese and drew him back into the shadows.

Don Holt opened the office door. 'Hello, Dad,' he said. 'You know, I been thinkin' some. I reckon I ought to go down to Pineview now — '

'Step in, son,' came the voice of the old sheriff. 'Step in, en' we'll talk it over.'

The door of the office closed behind the young man and Charlie hurried Sing out to the car in which they had come down together from Pineview. He motioned to the old man to get in beside him, and they set off along the Tavern drive. When they came to the main entrance, Chan turned toward Truckee.

'Wha's mallah now?' ventured Sing. 'Mebbe I catch 'um jail, hey?'

'You're a wicked man,' Chan replied sternly. 'You have caused us much worry and suffering. Jail is what you richly deserve.'

'I catch 'um jail, hey, Boss?'

'On the contrary,' Chan replied, 'you catch 'um boat for China.'

# 18

## Rankin Drops a Bomb

A boat for China! Charlie could not see the face of the old man who sat at his side in the car that sped along the road to Truckee, but he heard a tremendous sigh. Of relief?

★ ★ ★

'All light, Boss,' Sing said.

'All right?' repeated Chan with some bitterness. 'Is that the extent of your remarks? We are doing you a great favor, a tremendous kindness, and you reply, all right. The courteous man, Ah Sing, would not permit his tongue to stop at that.'

'My velly much obliged.'

'That is better. It still appears inadequate, but it is slightly better.'

They traveled along the wet road in silence. Chan's face was grim and determined. This next hour, he reflected, was not to be the happiest of his career. All those years on the Honolulu force, beset with temptations, but always honest, always irreproachable. And now — to come to the mainland, to do what he was doing — would his conscience ever be clear again? Ah — thank the gods — the lights of Truckee were twinkling just ahead.

Chan drove at once to the station. 'Train for San Francisco arrives in twenty minutes,' he announced. 'I have consulted time table.' They entered the waiting-room, Sing carrying his small bag. 'You got money, Ah Sing?' Charlie asked.

'My got 'um,' the old man answered.

'Then purchase for yourself a ticket,' Chan ordered. 'I am sorry, but we do not also furnish fare.'

As Sing returned from the ticket window, the detective noted that he was limping,

'Your knee still troubles you?' Chan inquired.

'Velly bad knock,' Sing admitted. He put his foot on a bench, and rolling up his wide trousers, exhibited a considerable expanse of black and blue.

'Ah, yes,' Chan said. 'The wound you acquired when you bumped into dressing-table bench in Landini's old sitting-room?'

'Tha's when. Aftah my shoot — '

'Enough!' Charlie cried. He glanced uneasily around at the other people in the room and spoke in Cantonese. 'Do not poke your finger through your own paper lantern.

The luck is running high for you to-night, ancient one. Be cautious, lest the heart of the law yet harden against you.'

Sing appeared to be properly impressed. They sat down side by side on the narrow bench, and for a time, neither spoke.

'The government has fallen upon evil times,' Chan said at last. 'You understand, it can not even afford to squander small piece of rope on man like you. Old man who will die soon, in any case. So it says — return to China — '

'I will go,' Sing remarked in his native tongue.

'I envy you. You will walk again the streets of the village where you were born. You will supervise the selection of your own burial place. I myself will see that your trunk is prepared and sent to you while you await the boat. Where shall I send it?'

'To the establishment of my brother, Sing Gow, in Jackson Street. The Fish Shop of the Delicious Odors.'

'It shall be done. For you, the past died this afternoon. The future is born to-night. You understand?'

'I understand.'

'I am the bearer of an affectionate message for you, ancient one. Mr. Sam Holt has sent it. He is proud to have known you.'

Sing's face softened. 'An honorable man. May the four nails of his coffin be of purest gold.'

'To match his heart,' Chan agreed. His own heart stirred with relief as he heard the approach of the train. 'Come,' he said, rising. 'Your vehicle draws near.'

They stepped on to the platform. In another moment the train thundered up to the station. Charlie held out his hand.

'I am saying good-by,' he shouted in Sing's ear. 'May your entire journey be on the sunny side of the road.'

'Goo'-by,' Sing answered. He took a few steps toward the train, but turned and came back. Removing something from his pocket, he handed it to Chan. 'You give 'em Boss,' he directed. 'My fo'get. Tell 'um Boss too much woik that house. Sing go away.'

'I will tell him,' Charlie agreed. He led Sing back to the steps of a day coach and helped him aboard.

Retiring to the shadows close to the station, Chan stood watching. He saw the old man drop into a seat and remove his hat. In the dim gas-light the wizened face was stolid, emotionless. The train gathered momentum, and Ah Sing was swept quickly from view. Still Chan hesitated, deep in thought. For the first time in his life — but this was the

331

mainland, strange things happened here. And after all, Inspector Chan had no real authority.

When he got back to Tahoe, Chan again turned in at the Tavern gate. The stables were dark and deserted, and leaving the Pineview flivver parked in the drive, Charlie entered the hotel. Dinsdale was alone beside the office desk.

'Good evening, Mr. Chan,' he said. 'Warming up a bit after the rain, isn't it?'

'That may be,' Charlie replied. 'I fear I had not noticed.'

'No — I suppose you're a pretty busy man,' Dinsdale returned. 'By the way — of course it's none of my business, but — er — are you getting anywhere?'

'So sorry. There is nothing yet able to be announced.'

'Well, of course, I didn't mean to butt in.'

'Ah, but you are naturally interested. You were old-time friend of poor Madame Landini, I believe?'

'Yes. I knew her even before her first marriage. A beautiful girl — and a fine woman. I hope you haven't been judging her entirely from the view-point of her discarded husbands.'

'For a time, I made that error,' Chan replied. 'Then I read Madame's own life-story, and my opinion changed. I agree with you — a splendid woman.'

'Good!' cried Dinsdale with unexpected vehemence. 'I'm glad you feel that way. Because if you do, you'll be almost as eager to see her murderer hang as I am. By the way, well be having dinner in half an hour. Please stay, as my guest.'

'I will be only too happy,' Chan bowed. He indicated a youth who had just come in and taken his place behind the desk. 'Would you be so kind as to have this young man call Pineview, and inform whoever answers that I will not dine there to-night?'

'With pleasure,' Dinsdale answered.

'And now — if you can tell me the number of Mr. Sam Holt's room?'

'It's number nineteen — at the end of that corridor over there.'

At Charlie's knock, Sam Holt called for him to come in. He entered to find the old sheriff standing in the middle of the room, adjusting his necktie.

'Hello, Mr. Chan,' he said, as he reached unerringly for his coat, which lay on the bed.

'Ah, you know my step,' Charlie remarked. 'It indicates, I fear, the heaviness of my person.'

'Nothin' o' the sort,' Holt replied. 'It's the lightest step in the whole shebang, except mebbe that Miss Beaton's.'

'But my weight — ' Chan protested.

'I don't keer about yer weight. You step like the tiger, Inspector Chan.'

'Yes?' sighed Charlie. 'But a tiger who lets his prey escape.'

'Then I take it ye've gone an' done that errand?'

'I have done it — yes.'

'Ye ain't regrettin' it, are ye?'

'Not unless you are, Mr. Holt.'

'Which I reckon I'm never goin' to do, Mr. Chan. Howsomever, I'm glad to see ye first — before ye've talked to Don. I ain't told Don anything yit.'

'The wisest course, no doubt,' Charlie agreed.

'It sure is. Ye know, Don really is in authority here. 'Taint with him like it was with you an' me. He's took the oath, an' he's honest, the boy is. Reckon he'd feel he'd jest have to go after a certain party, an' bring him back. An' ye kain't depend on juries no more, Inspector.'

'I fear you are right.'

'In the old days — wa'al, it would ha' been different. But — they's women on the juries now, Mr. Chan. An' women ain't got no sentiment. They're hard, women are — since they took to runnin' the world.'

'I have noticed that myself,' Charlie nodded.

'Yes, I jes' figured we better give that certain party all the start we could.' The door of the room beyond the bath opened, then slammed. 'It's Don,' Sam Holt whispered.

'I will await you both in the lobby,' Chan whispered back. 'It happens I am dining here to-night.'

He made a guilty sort of exit, aided by old Sam Holt, who was looking rather guilty himself. Reaching the lounge, he selected a chair and sat down by the fire. In a few moments, a door from the terrace opened and Leslie Beaton entered.

'Hello, Mr. Chan,' she cried. 'Glad to see you again. I've been out admiring the view. It's marvelous.'

'You like this mountain country?' Chan asked.

'I love it.' She urged him back to his chair, and took the one beside it. 'You know — sometimes I believe I'll stay here. Would that be a good idea, do you think?'

'Happiness,' Charlie told her, 'is not a matter of geography.'

'I suppose not.'

'Wherever we are, life is the same. The sweet, the sour, the pungent and the bitter — we must taste them all. To the contented,

335

even the cabbage roots are fragrant.'

'I know,' she nodded. 'Would I be contented here?'

Chan shrugged. 'I seek to win reputation as philosopher, not as fortune-teller,' he reminded her. 'If I were assaying latter role, I would say it would depend on whether you have a companion or not. You can not applaud with one hand.'

'Oh, well — I'm sorry I brought the matter up,' laughed the girl. 'Let's change the subject — shall we? Looking around for a new topic my eye lights — inevitably — on your necktie, Mr. Chan. I'm not accustomed to making personal remarks, but somehow that's the sort of necktie one just can't ignore.'

'Ah — one might call it red,' he replied.

'One couldn't very well call it anything else,' she admitted.

'It was present from my young daughter, Evelyn, on recent Christmas,' he told her. 'I had forgot I was so brilliantly adorned. But I remember now — I put it on this morning. For a purpose.'

Young Hugh Beaton came up at that moment, in a rather cheerful mood for him. Even one day at the Tavern seemed to have proved good medicine. He greeted Charlie in friendly fashion, and led his sister off to the dining-room. Presently Romano appeared, arrayed in evening clothes as though he were about to conduct an opera.

'Mr. Romano — how do you do,' Charlie remarked. 'You quite confound me by your formal attire. When I — I must disgrace dining-room with necktie such as this.'

'What is wrong with the necktie?' Romano responded. 'Me, I dress not for others, but for myself. You should do the same. Attired as I am now, I feel I am already back in some metropolitan center, such as New York. The thought — it gives me great happiness. The reality — it will be sublime.'

'Patience,' Chan counseled. 'In time, the mulberry leaf becomes silk.'

Romano frowned. 'Not so comforting, that. The process sounds complicated. But in the meantime, one may still eat.' He moved away.

Don Holt and his father appeared. 'Hear you're staying for dinner,' the former said. 'Fine. You'll sit with us, of course.'

'But I am Mr. Dinsdale's guest,' Charlie protested.

'That's all right — we'll take a table for four,' Dinsdale said briskly, coming up just then. He led them into the dining-room. Don Holt looked a bit disappointed, for he knew discussion of the case must now be postponed until later. Chan, however, was deeply relieved. He had no desire for such a discussion with the sheriff of the county at the moment. Indeed, he did not look forward to it at any moment.

Toward the close of the dinner, Dinsdale was called away. Don Holt lost no time.

'I reckon Dad's told you about my talk with Miss Beaton this afternoon,' he began. 'The way I see it, that puts the murder of Landini right in old Sing's lap. It's like I told you at the first — I've knowed Sing ever since I was a kid. Always been fond of him, too. But when I took the oath of office, there wasn't anything in it about protecting my friends. I got my job to do, and — '

He was interrupted by the arrival of the amiable Bill Rankin, who leaned suddenly above the table. Chan sighed with relief.

'Hello,' cried the reporter. 'All the forces of the law, breaking bread together. Gosh — think of the poor criminals on a night like this. Well, what's the good word to send down to the yawning presses?'

'You must find your own words,' Charlie told him. 'Has your day disclosed nothing?'

Rankin dropped into Dinsdale's empty chair. 'We had a nice time in Reno. Called on Miss Meecher. I suppose you know this sleek boy named Romano stands in line for all Landini's property?'

'We do,' said Don shortly.

'Well, Romano was at Pineview the night of the murder,' Rankin went on cheerily. 'Sort of puts the lad in the running, doesn't it? He knew the singer — and the money — was slipping away from him in a couple of weeks. He knew Landini had a pistol in her hand-bag. Need I say more?'

'Thank you so much,' grinned Chan. 'Gentlemen, our case is solved. Odd we did not think of this ourselves.'

'Oh, you thought of it all right,' Rankin laughed. 'But what I'm getting at is — wouldn't you like to think of it all over again, just for to-morrow morning's paper?'

'Has libel law been repealed?' Charlie asked blandly.

'Libel? Innuendo, Mr. Chan. A game at which I am probably the most expert player west of the Rockies. Well, if that little point doesn't interest you, maybe you'll answer me a question.'

'I must hear it before I can answer it,' Charlie replied.

'You'll hear it, all right. Why did you take that old Chinese servant, Sing, over to Truckee this evening in a flivver, and put him on a train for San Francisco?'

Charlie Chan had known a long and active career, but never before had he encountered such an embarrassing moment as this. In the dead silence that followed the innocent dropping of Rankin's bomb, Chan looked across and saw the fine eyes of Don Holt ablaze with sudden anger. Old Sam Holt's hand trembled as he hastily set down his water glass. Charlie did not speak.

'You can't keep that dark,' Rankin went on. 'Gleason ran over to file a couple of stories with the telegrapher at the station, and he saw you. What was the big idea?'

The reporter looked directly at Chan, and was amazed at the answering look he received from one who had, a few moments ago, appeared so glad to see him.

'I took Sing to Truckee as a favor — from one Chinese to another,' Charlie said slowly. He rose to his feet. 'Sing desired to make a visit to San Francisco, and as there were several points I wanted investigated down there, I decided to permit that he go. The matter means little, one way or the other, but I prefer that for the present you write nothing about it.'

'Why, sure — if you say so,' Rankin returned pleasantly. 'It just seemed rather queer, that's all.'

But Charlie was already walking rapidly away from the table. Don Holt and the old sheriff followed closely at his heels. He moved on, straight through the lobby and into

Dinsdale's small private office. As he expected, the others did the same.

Don Holt came in last and slammed the door shut behind him. His face was white, his eyes dangerously narrowed.

'So,' he said, through his teeth, 'you took him there as a favor — from one Chinese to another? Some favor — if you're asking me!'

'Hold yer horses, Don,' his father cried.

'I've been double-crossed,' the boy went on. 'I've been made a fool of — '

'Wa-al, ef ye have, son — I done it. I told Mr. Chan to take Sing to Truckee. I told him to help him git away — to China.'

'You!' cried Holt. 'To China! An' all the time ye knew he was guilty as hell. You knew he went into that room — you knew he fired that shot — '

'I knew all that, son.'

'Then how could you let me down like this? Get out o' my way!'

'Where you goin'?'

'Goin'? I'm goin' after him, of course. Am I sheriff of this county, or ain't I? You two sure have took a lot on yourselves — '

Dinsdale opened the door. 'Telegram for you, Don,' he said. 'They're phoning it from Truckee. I've switched it in here.' He looked in a puzzled way at the young sheriff's face, then withdrew and closed the door.

Don Holt sat down at the desk and took up the receiver. Chan looked at his watch and smiled.

'Hello! Hello! This is Don Holt. What! What! Say that again. All right. Thanks. Mail it up to me here, if you will.'

Slowly the young man swung around in the swivel chair, and his eyes met Charlie's. 'What was it you asked that bird down in Berkeley about them pistols?' he inquired.

'It was a simple question concerning the bullets,' Chan replied calmly. 'What does he say?'

'He — he says both them bullets came from the gun that killed Swan,' Don Holt answered perplexedly. 'He says neither one of 'em came from Landini's gun.'

'Wa-al,' drawled Sam Holt, 'them scientists kain't always be wrong. Now an' then one of 'em's bound to strike the right lead.'

Don Holt stood up, and gradually the puzzled look faded from his face. He smiled suddenly at Charlie.

'By the Lord Harry!' he said. 'Now I know why you was always talkin' about the pine trees.'

# 19

## Chan Climbs a Ladder

Don Holt walked up and down the small room excitedly. 'It's beginning to straighten out,' he continued. 'The dog — I'm gettin' that, too.'

Charlie nodded. 'Good little Trouble. It was he who set me on correct trail that very first night. Already I had experienced my first doubts. Of the five unaccounted for at time of killing, not one offered alibi. You will recall I commented to you on that. Strange, I thought. The guilty, at least, usually has alibi ready and waiting. I wondered. Could it be that the guilty was not among those five? Could it be he was among those standing in my sight when supposedly fatal shot was fired?'

'Then we went out and talked with Mrs. O'Ferrell,' the young sheriff said.

'Correct. Landini had remarked she would take dog with her in the plane. 'He loves it,' she had said. But according to story of Mrs. O'Ferrell, Trouble had wailed and cried most pitifully when plane arrived over house. No happy barks of anticipation such as I reported to you when, on subsequent evening, he heard sound of plane. Instead, every evidence of grief. Why did he grieve? I considered. As all those who know me have learned to their distress, Chinese have proverb to fit every possible situation. There is one — I recalled it as I talked to Mrs. O'Ferrell.'

'What is it?' son Holt asked.

'The dog, wherever he is, knows his master's mood,' Charlie quoted. 'Poor little Trouble — did he know that, at moment plane was over house, Landini was dying? Yes, I cried inwardly, that was it. Why not? In terrific din made by airplane, a dozen shots might have been fired and gone unheard. But by some sixth sense which we can not explain, the dog was aware. He knew that when the airplane had landed, and we all stood with the aviator in the living-room and Ryder strolled down the stairs, Ellen Landini was already dead. She was dead some time before the firing of that shot which brought us all to her side.

'The shot we heard, then, had been merely to mislead. Who had fired it? Sing, probably. From the first I suspected him — last night I was sure. For I recalled the dinner on the evening of my arrival at Pineview — before I had even seen Ellen Landini. I recalled what

Ryder had said: 'Always a friend in need, Sing was.''

Holt nodded. 'So Ryder said that, did he?'

'He did, and his statement was quite correct. A friend in need. All the way from chicken gravy and rice, to the firing of a deceiving bullet from the study window into the pines.'

'Do you know what was in that letter Landini wrote to Ryder?' Holt asked.

'Alas, no. There are several things which I must yet accomplish at Pineview. The message from professor at Berkeley is important, but our evidence is not complete. I propose to go now and complete it. But first, I must ask a thousand pardons. When I set Sing on road to China, I was, I fear, law-breaker myself.'

'That's all right,' Sam Holt remarked. 'Don't you apologize, Mr. Chan. I ain't goin' to. We saved this young hothead here from a mighty embarrassin' situation.'

'I reckon you did,' Don Holt agreed. 'I'm sorry for anything I said.'

Charlie patted the boy on the arm. 'You were remarkably restrained. And you will note, I did not answer back. I recalled our conflict last night in hall of empty house. With most complimentary intention, I add that the man who has once been bitten by a snake, fears every rope in the roadway.'

The sheriff laughed. 'Well, I'll take it as a compliment, anyhow. And I'm glad you got Sing out of the way. I don't suppose he thought he was doin' anything wrong, but if he was around here now, I'd sure have to arrest him as an accessory. By the time I'm through with this business, I probably won't know where he is.'

'You certainly will not,' Chan smiled, 'if you are depending on your honorable father for help. Or on my humble self. I go now to Pineview to investigate those matters which I mentioned. After brief talk with your father, you will know precisely how to act.' He glanced at his watch. 'Give me, however, one hour.'

Holt nodded. 'One hour, exactly,' he agreed.

The moon was shining and a warm breeze was blowing through the pines as Charlie traveled the lonely road back to the house where he had been a guest for several days. Now his moment of triumph was drawing close, but he was not in a mood to gloat. As in so many other cases, he found it impossible to view things from the standpoint of a scientific machine. Always he thought of people — of the human heart. For that reason, his own heart was never to know elation in moments such as this.

But by the time he had driven into the Pineview garage, he had put aside his regrets. He was brisk and businesslike. Now at last he lifted that ladder at which he had only this afternoon cast longing eyes, and boosting it to his shoulder, he cautiously carried it around the house to the front lawn. A light streaming from the dining-room windows indicated that Ryder and his host were still lingering over dinner.

Placing the ladder against the tall tree from which, Chan was sure, that piece of bark had fallen, he climbed aloft, his plump figure finally disappearing among the thick branches. There, for a time, his flash-light played like a will-o'-the-wisp. Finally he found what he was seeking — what he sought in vain that afternoon on the ground — the bullet Sing had fired from the open window of the study, in order to provide an alibi for a friend. This bullet would complete the story told by the two pistols down at Berkeley; he took out his pen-knife and began to dig it from its resting-place.

With the slug securely in his pocket, he lowered himself from among the branches and found the ladder. He had gone half-way down it when he was aware of a tall, able-bodied man waiting for him in the darkness below.

'Oh — is it you, Mr. Chan?' said Michael Ireland. 'Cecile seen somebody from the window, and she sent me out to get him — whoever he was. Her nerves ain't none too good, you know.'

'So sorry I have disturbed her,' Charlie replied, stepping on to the ground. 'Assure her, please, that there is no cause for alarm. I merely pursue my harmless investigations.'

'Sure,' remarked Ireland. 'Can I give you a hand with that ladder? Kinda heavy, ain't it?' They carried the ladder back to the garage.

'I was not aware that you were with us to-night,' Charlie said. 'Did you make the journey by plane?'

'Yes. An' I was wantin' to talk to you, Mr. Chan.'

'I am a great believer in the here and now.'

'Well — it's Cecile. Always kinda nervous an' flighty — you know women. Since this Swan business she's all on edge ag'in — an' she telephoned me to come over 'n' take her home. I says, I ain't so sure the sheriff will let you leave — but she just set off the fireworks — you know how it is. So I said I'd ask.'

'I know how it is,' nodded Charlie. 'But you are now asking the wrong person.'

Ireland shook his head. 'No, I ain't, Mr. Chan. I called up the sheriff a little while ago, an' he said everything down here was in your hands. He said you would tell me when Cecile could go.'

Charlie considered. He glanced at his watch. 'Ask me again in half an hour — if you will be so kind.'

'O.K.,' Ireland answered. 'In half an hour.' He started away, but suddenly stopped. 'Say — what's going to happen in half an hour?' he demanded.

Chan shrugged. 'Who shall say? If you will pardon me now, I remain in open for few more minutes.'

He waited while Ireland went reluctantly up the back steps and reentered the house. Then he removed from his pocket an enormous bunch of keys. With this in his hands, he disappeared among the sheds at the rear of the garage.

Some ten minutes later, Chan went into the house by the rear door. Mrs. O'Ferrell, Cecile and Ireland were in the kitchen, and they regarded him with anxious eyes as he passed. He went on up the back stairs, walking as quietly as the tiger to whom Sam Holt had compared him. Reaching the hall above he leaned over the stair-rail and listened; far in the distance, in the dining-room, he heard voices. He went into his room and locked the door behind him.

For a short time he was busy at his desk,

and it was obvious that finger-prints concerned him. Then hastily he began to pack his suitcase. When everything was accounted for, he stood the case in the hall, placed with it his overcoat and hat, and again listened. The sound of voices still came from the dining-room. After a brief visit to the study, he returned to the hall, gathered up his things and went down-stairs.

The firelight flickered in friendly peaceful fashion on the walls of the great living-room. Chan set down his luggage and stood for a moment, looking musingly about him. He was reliving a scene; the scene in that room at the moment, two nights ago, when Michael Ireland came in for a drink. He pictured Beaton and Dinsdale beside the fire, Ward preparing the highball, Ireland waiting expectantly in that big easy chair, Ryder strolling nonchalantly down the stairs. Five men in all; six if you included Chan himself.

The picture faded from his mind. He walked slowly through the passage that led to the dining-room, and stood there in the doorway.

Ward and Ryder were seated at the table, coffee cups before them. Impelled by his innate sense of hospitality, the former leaped to his feet.

'Hello, Mr. Chan,' he cried. 'We missed

you at dinner. Won't you have something now? Sing!' He stopped. 'Damn it, I keep forgetting. Sing, Mr. Chan, has disappeared.'

'No matter,' Charlie answered. 'I have eaten a sufficiency, Mr. Ward. But I appreciate your kindness, none the less.'

Ryder spoke. 'Perhaps Mr. Chan can throw some light on the disappearance of Sing?' he suggested.

Charlie drew a chair up to the table. 'I can,' he nodded. They waited in silence. 'I am grieved to tell you, Mr. Ward, that all evidence uncovered has pointed with painful certainty to Sing as the person who fired that shot at Landini — the shot that took us up to the study to find her dead body on the floor.'

'I don't believe it,' Ward cried hotly. 'I don't care where the evidence points. Sing never did it — '

'But if Sing himself admits he did — '

Ward stood up. 'Where is he? I'll go to him at once.'

'That, I fear, is impossible,' Charlie replied. 'The sheriff was about to arrest him when — he dropped from sight.'

'He got away?' Ryder cried.

'For the time being,' Chan answered. 'He may yet be apprehended.' He turned to Ward. 'I am so sorry, Mr. Ward. This must be a great shock for you, I know. I have paused for brief moment only to inform you that with deep regret, and with warm glow of thanks for your hospitality, I leave this house at once. There is nothing more I can do.'

'I suppose not,' Ward replied. 'But you must not go until one thing is settled. I promised you a thousand dollars to undertake the search for my boy — '

'But the search was so brief,' Chan protested.

'No matter. There was nothing about that in our agreement. Wait here just a moment, please. I shall write you a check.'

He left the room. Charlie turned to see an unaccustomed smile on the face of John Ryder.

'You find only pleasure in the escape of Sing,' the detective remarked.

'Need I conceal that, Mr. Chan?'

'Sing was a very good friend of yours.'

'One of the best I ever had.'

'Ah, yes — chicken gravy and rice,' nodded Charlie.

Ryder made no answer. In another moment Ward returned, and handed Charlie a check.

'I accept this with crimson cheeks,' Chan said, and having placed it in his pocketbook, he looked at his watch. 'It is time I am going,' he added, and rose to his feet.

'Won't you have a farewell drink?' Dudley

Ward suggested. 'But you don't drink, do you? It's just as well because, come to think of it, there's nothing to drink. Poor John and I have been sitting here with parched throats all evening — you see, Sing had the keys to the sideboard, and the cellar, too.'

'Thank you so much for reminding me,' Chan cried. 'I was on the point of forgetting.' He took from his pocket a great key-ring, on which hung more than a score of keys. 'This was entrusted to me by your servant — just before his escape.'

'That's a bit of luck,' Ward answered. He took the keys and stepped to the sideboard. 'What will it be, John? A cordial with your coffee?'

'I don't mind,' Ryder said.

From the sideboard Ward took four cut-glass decanters, and set them on a tray. He placed the tray before his friend. 'Help yourself,' he suggested. He secured a larger and heavier decanter, and put it at his own place. 'Mr. Chan — you won't change your mind?'

'I am great believer in proper ceremony,' Charlie answered. 'In old days, in China, refusal to drink parting libation would be slur on hospitality of the host. A small taste — if you will be so good.'

'Fine,' Ward cried. He placed another glass

before Ryder. 'John — give the inspector — which do you prefer, Mr. Chan?'

'A little of the port wine, please.' Suddenly Chan's voice grew louder. 'One thing more. In China, in the old days, refusal of the host to pour the parting libation himself might well have been regarded as a slur on the guest.'

There was a sudden silence in the room. Charlie saw Ryder hesitate, and look inquiringly at Ward. 'But I do not press the point,' Charlie continued, with an amiable smile. 'You understand, I recall my first dinner at this table. I recall how courteous you were, Mr. Ward — how you served the cocktails yourself — how nothing was too much trouble — until that tray of decanters was put before you. And then — how you shouted for Sing — how Sing had to return from the kitchen before the cordials could be served. Ah — these little things — they register in the mind of a detective. Many hours later I remembered, and I said to myself — can it be that Mr. Ward is color-blind?'

He paused, and another tense silence filled the room.

'It was an interesting question,' Charlie continued. 'Only to-night I answered it once and for all. There were two varieties of ink on your study desk up-stairs, Mr. Ward. Black on the right, and red on the left. A moment ago I slipped in and took the very great liberty of changing the position of the ink-wells. You will forgive me I hope.' He tapped the pocket into which he had put his purse. 'The check you just gave me was written in red ink Mr. Ward. So you are color-blind after all.'

'And what if I am?' Ward asked.

Charlie leaned back at ease in his chair. 'The person who killed Landini was first sent by her for a green scarf. He returned to her bringing a pink one. Later, in vague impulse to straighten the desk and alter the look of affairs, he put a crimson lid on a yellow box, and a yellow lid on a crimson one. No, thank you, Mr. Ryder.' He waved aside the glass Ryder was holding out. 'I could not quite bring myself to drink with a man I am about to arrest for murder.'

'Murder!' cried Ward. 'Are you mad, Inspector?'

'No — it was you who went mad — night before last in the study.'

'I was in the living-room when the shot was fired. You saw me there.'

'Sing's shot into the pine trees — yes. But alas, Landini was actually killed in noise and confusion of the moment when airplane was roaring over the house.'

'At which moment I was turning on the lights of the landing field. You heard what the aviator said — '

'That those lights flashed on while he was above the house. And he was correct — they did. But you, Mr. Ward, did not turn them on.' Charlie took an envelope from his pocket and held up, very carefully, the wooden handle of an electric light switch. 'Short time ago, aided by a bunch of keys from Sing, I entered shed at rear of hangar from which light was managed. I removed this article from its place. On it are two sets of finger-prints. Each set is from the fingers of your faithful servant, Ah Sing.' He dropped the switch back into its envelope. 'Two very good alibis,' he added. 'Sing's shot into the trees — your claim of having turned on the lights. Both gone. Both useless now.'

Looking up, he saw that a terrible change had come over the usually genial Ward. He was trembling with rage, his face was purple, his mouth twitching. 'Damn you!' he screamed. He snatched up the heavy decanter from the table, and his muscular arm drew back to strike. Then his eyes strayed to the door at Charlie's back, his purpose faltered, and, as suddenly as it had come, his fury passed.

'Cool off, Dudley,' said the voice of old

Sam Holt from the doorway. 'I told you when you was a kid that temper of yours would finish you some day.'

Dudley Ward slumped into his chair, and covered his face with his hands.

'I guess you were right, Sam,' he muttered. 'I guess you were right, at that.'

# 20

## After the Typhoon

The old sheriff stepped into the room, and
Don Holt followed. Charlie looked at his
watch.

'One hour, to the minute,' he remarked to
the younger Holt. 'Fortunate you are man of
your word. I feared I was about to lose a most
important piece of evidence.'

'Then you got what you came after?' Don
Holt inquired.

'I got it.' Chan handed an envelope to the
sheriff. 'Handle of light switch from shed at
rear of hangar,' he explained. 'On it,
finger-prints of Sing who turned off lights on
landing field when unhappy evening had
ended. Also, more finger-prints of Sing, who
evidently turned them on in first place.'

'So Dudley Ward never went near them
lights,' nodded Holt.

'Such is the inference we must naturally
draw,' Chan agreed. 'I am handing precious
cargo over to you. Also, in this other
envelope, bullet from Landini's gun, which I
have recently dug from pine tree.'

Ryder pushed forward, his expression unpleasant and contemptuous as usual. 'And you expect to convict my friend on evidence like that?' he cried.

'It will all help,' shrugged Chan. 'We will in addition trace the owner of a revolver which now reposes in Berkeley.'

'That may not be so easy,' sneered Ryder.

'Perhaps not.' Charlie turned and looked at Ward. 'If difficulties arise, we can still bring back to this scene the accessory to the crime, Ah Sing. Of course, in such case, he also would suffer punishment — '

Ward leapt to his feet.

'Oh, stop it,' he cried passionately. 'What's the use? Let Sing alone. Let him go. I killed Landini, and I killed Swan, too.'

'But look here, Dudley — ' Ryder protested.

'What's the use I say?' Ward went on. 'Forget it, John. I've nothing to live for — nothing to fight for. Let's get on with it. Let's get it finished. That's all I want now.' He sank back into his chair.

'I am so sorry, Mr. Ward,' Chan said gently, 'that visit to your home must finish in such manner. Let us, as you say, get on with it. I will detail a few happenings in this house night before last, and perhaps if I am wrong, you will correct me. You and I went with

Madame Landini to the study. You accused her of hiding from you knowledge of your son. She denied it, but you were not satisfied. The airplane appeared, you left presumably to turn on the lights of landing field. When you left, Landini was wildly seeking to communicate with John Ryder.

'You could not turn on lights until you located Sing, who had keys of everything about this house. You found him on rear porch, on his way to manage lights himself. You sent him along, telling him that later he must bring blanket to study for Landini's dog.

'With more questions for Landini, you returned to study. She, meanwhile, has written letter to Ryder, who has refused to see her. When you enter, she is on balcony waving to aviator. 'Oh, it is you, is it?' she says. 'I'm freezing — get me my scarf. It's on the bed in the next room. The green one.' The great Landini, giving orders as of old. You go into next room, return with pink scarf. She snatches it from you. Did she chide you then? Did she say, I had forgot you were color-blind? No — the questions are only rhetorical. They do not matter. She decides Miss Beaton's scarf will do. And then — your eye lights on the desk — on the letter she has written and addressed to John Ryder.'

Charlie paused. 'I wonder what was in that letter?' he said slowly.

'You seem to know everything,' Ward answered. 'What do you think was in it?'

'I believe that news of your son's death was in it,' Chan replied.

Ward did not speak for a moment. He sighed wearily. 'You do know everything,' he said at last.

'You were curious about that letter,' Charlie continued. 'Always a little jealous of Ryder, perhaps. You asked Landini what it meant. Your unhappy temper grew hot. You snatched up the envelope, ripped it open, and read. Landini was asking Ryder, your best friend in the house, to break to you gently the news that your boy had died.

'Died — and you'd never seen him. Your temper was terrible then. Murder was in your heart. From the drawer of your desk you removed a revolver — an automatic — and turned on the woman. She screamed, struggled with you above the desk, the boxes of cigarettes were upset. The aviator was once more just overhead, the din was terrific. You cast Landini from you, she fell, you fired at her from above. And the roar of the plane died away in the distance. Just as the roar of your frightful anger was dying away in your brain.

'You were dazed, weak, unsteady. A neat man, always, you unconsciously sought to straighten things on the disordered desk. It came to you that perhaps it might help to pretend Landini had been shot from the balcony. You dragged her to the window — and from her hand-bag, opened in the struggle, her own revolver fell. You examined it — the same caliber as yours. At that moment, Sing entered the room, beneath his arm, a small blue blanket.

'What happened then? Whatever it was, it happened quickly. Whose idea was it — the alibi of the shot to be fired by Sing? Yours or his — that does not matter. He was your loyal servant. You knew that he would protect you as he had protected you from your childhood. He was your keeper of the keys.'

'That says it,' old Sam Holt cried. 'Keeper of the keys. For sixty years Ah Sing had been slammin' the doors on the Ward family skeletons, an' turnin' the keys on them. I know all about it — don't I, Dudley? An' he'd a' done it this time — only Inspector Chan had his foot in the door.'

'I'm afraid he did,' Ward admitted.

'So you left it all to Sing,' Charlie went on, 'and hurried down to the landing field to greet a new guest. Ah, your manners, Mr. Ward — they were always so perfect. But a

362

golden bed can not cure the sick, and good manners can not produce a good man. You made the aviator welcome, and we came inside. While up above, Sing kept the faith. As my friend, Inspector Duff of Scotland Yard, would say — he carried on.'

Charlie rose. 'We need no longer shade the scene with dark pictures of the past. I do not dwell on murder of Swan. It is not for his death that you will be tried.'

'I'm sorry I won't,' Ward answered grimly. 'Because I rather imagine I did the world a service there. A dirty blackmailer — he was at the door of the study when I — when Landini died. When I went to him later on to take him things for the night, he threatened me, demanded money. I told him I would get him some the next day in Reno, and I did. Last night I telephoned to him he could get it if he'd meet Sing at the house down the road. Then I got to thinking — he would suck at me, like a leech, for ever. So I didn't send Sing — I went myself. And when Swan came, eager for his first drop of blood — I finished him. Yes — I'm rather proud of what I did to Swan.'

'And I am very grateful,' Chan said. 'We needed that revolver of yours, Mr. Ward — as cherry trees need the sun. I wondered at first why you did not toss weapon into lake, but remembering the famous clarity of Tahoe waters near the shore, I applauded your wisdom. You planned to come back later with boat, and carry both Doctor Swan and the pistol far out — but ah, the best-laid plans — how often they explode into disaster.' Charlie nodded at Don Holt. 'Sheriff — I am turning this man over to you. With only one question in my mind — who, on the night of Landini's murder, struck the loyal and faithful Sing that cruel blow in the face?'

Ward confronted the detective, and a red dangerous light was gleaming in his blood-shot eyes. 'What's that got to do with it?' he cried. 'My God — don't you know enough now? Are you never satisfied? What's that got to do with it?'

'Nothing, Dudley,' old Sam Holt put in soothingly. 'Not a thing in the world. Mr. Chan, I reckon we won't insist on knowin' the answer to that.'

'Of course not,' answered Charlie promptly. 'My connection with the case is now completely finished. I go to procure my things.'

Ten minutes later the two Holts, Chan and the now silent Ward, stepped into the sheriff's launch. Ryder had been left in charge at Pineview, and Don Holt had also persuaded Ireland to remain overnight. The little boat cut its way through the silvery water; on distant peaks gleamed the snow that was still a nine days' wonder in the eyes of the detective from Hawaii.

They walked up the Tavern pier toward the hotel. 'I asked the coroner to be ready,' Don Holt remarked to Chan. 'We're driving down to the county-seat right off, an' takin' Ward with us. By the way, I'd like to stop at the Tavern for just a minute. I wish you and Dad would take Ward around to the drive. That is — if you think I can trust you.'

'We have enjoyed brief lapse,' Charlie replied, 'However, I believe we are now quite safe custodians.'

'Yes — I reckon you are. An' that lapse — I'm grateful for it. Sixty years of loyalty an' love — say, jail would have been a fine reward for that.'

As young Holt entered the Tavern lounge, the two newspaper men from San Francisco leaped upon him. It appeared that the coroner had been a trifle indiscreet, and a torrent of questions was the result.

'Nothin' to say,' the sheriff replied. 'Only this. I just arrested Dudley Ward, an' he's confessed. Nothin' more — only — give all the credit to Charlie Chan.'

Rankin turned to his companion. 'Did you hear what I heard? A mainland policeman giving the credit to Charlie Chan!'

'They grow 'em different up here in these mountains,' Gleason answered. 'Come on — the phone's in the office. I'll match you for the first call.'

As they disappeared, Holt saw that Leslie Beaton was seated near by.

'Fine,' he cried, as she rose and approached him. 'You're the very person I wanted to see.'

'Dudley Ward,' she remarked, her eyes wide. 'Why — that's incredible.'

'I know — but I can't discuss it now. I'm in an awful rush. I want to say — Cash will probably turn up here early in the morning.'

'You mean — he'll be company for me while you're away?'

'Yeah — I'm afraid he will. I wired him to take a little vacation in San Francisco, but he's the sort who will see through that. Yes — he'll pull in here at dawn. And the first thing he'll do — he'll want you to take a ride up to that clearing where we was this afternoon.'

'Will he really?'

'Sure. An' I wish — as a sort o' favor to me — I wish you wouldn't go.'

'But what shall I tell poor Cash?'

'Well, you might tell him you been there already.'

'Oh! But Cash isn't the sort to be put off with an excuse like that.'

'No, I guess he ain't.' The sheriff turned his

hat about in his hands, staring at it as though it were something that caused him much embarrassment. 'Well, then — you might — just as a favor, too — tell him you're going to — to marry me.'

'But would that be the truth?'

'Well — I know you ain't seen the county-seat yet — '

'I haven't — no. But I've seen the sheriff.'

He looked at her, his fine eyes glowing. 'By golly. Do you mean that?'

'I guess — that is, I reckon I do.'

'You'll marry me?' She nodded. 'Say,' cried Don Holt, 'that's great. I'll have to run now. But I'll be seein' you.'

He started off. 'Just a minute,' said the girl. 'Let me get this straight. Is it you I'm going to marry — or Cash?'

He came back, smiling. 'Yeah — I don't wonder you're sort o' mixed.' He took her in his arms and kissed her. 'I reckon that might help you to remember,' he added, and disappeared.

Charlie and Sam Holt were waiting beside the car, in which the coroner was already at the wheel. A dim figure huddled in the rear seat. 'Mr. Sheriff,' Chan said. 'Your prisoner informs me he will plead guilty.' He took out his pocketbook and removed a narrow slip of paper. 'So I imagine you will not require this

367

check for evidence at the trial.'

'What is it?' Holt inquired.

Chan explained.

'No, we won't need it,' said Holt, handing it back. 'You jes' keep it — an' use it.'

But already Charlie was tearing it slowly across and across. He tossed the pieces into the air. Dudley Ward leaned suddenly forward from his place in the rear of the car.

'You shouldn't have done that,' he protested.

'So sorry,' Chan bowed. 'But I could not enjoy spending the money of one whose association with me ended in disaster for him.'

Ward slumped back in the car. 'And I always thought,' he murmured, 'that Don Quixote was a Spaniard.'

The sheriff had seized Chan's hand. 'You're a grand guy, Charlie,' he said. 'Will you be here when I come back tomorrow?'

'If you come early — yes.'

'Don't go till I see you. By that time, maybe I'll be able to think up some words that'll tell you what your help has meant to me.'

'Not worth mentioning,' Chan replied. 'In this world, all sorts of men could help one another — if they would. The boat can ride on the wagon, and the wagon on the boat.

Good night — and my best wishes for — for ever.'

Charlie and the old sheriff watched the car start, then walked around the Tavern and out upon the pier. Near the end of this stood a sheltered group of benches, and on one of these they sat down together.

'Kinda hard case,' remarked old Holt.

'In many ways,' Chan agreed. He contemplated the snow-capped mountains, gorgeous in the moonlight. 'From the moment I made up my mind that shot we heard was but empty gesture, I was appalled at possibilities. Did Hugh Beaton climb to balcony and kill Landini, and did his sister fire shot to protect him, as she had protected him all her life?

'I wondered. Or did Michael Ireland shoot Landini from plane, and did Cecile fire again to save her husband? It was intriguing thought, and for a time I played with it. But no — I told myself sadly that jealous wives are not so obliging. Then I recalled the serving of the cordials that first night at dinner — and at last my eyes turned toward the guilty one.'

'He never was no good, Dudley wasn't,' mused Sam Holt. 'I knowed it from the days he was a kid. Terrible temper, an' a born drunkard. Yes — even the giant redwoods — they got rotten branches. The family of

Ward had theirs, an' Dudley was the last — an' rottenest. If his name had come up sooner — I could ha' told ye. That time long ago Landini run away from him — he was tryin' to beat her. Sing stepped in — good ol' Sing — locked him in his room — helped Landini git away. I tell you, Mr. Chan, when Landini hid the news of that baby from Dudley Ward, she knew what she was doin'. She knew he wasn't fit to care fer it.'

'Poor Landini,' Charlie remarked. 'What unlucky fate she had when matter of husbands comes up. Romano — grasping as he was — I imagine he was the best — and the kindest.'

'I reckon he was,' nodded Holt.

'I presume it was Ward who struck Sing that night of the murder?'

'Sure it was. I didn't think we needed to humiliate him no more — but sure, he struck Sing. An' why? Because Sing had the keys to the sideboard, an' Ward wanted booze. He wanted to git drunk an' fergit what he done, but Sing had sense enough to know how dangerous that would be. So he refused to give up them keys, an' Ward knocked him down. I used to see him in them tempers as a boy. He's no good, Mr. Chan. We don't need to waste no sympathy on Dudley Ward.'

'Yet Sing would have died for him. Would

never have left him, if he hadn't seen Ward's pistol on my desk this morning, and thought his master was in danger. When, as he thought, we blundered and selected him as the murderer, he was delighted to go away. I believe he would have gone to the gallows just as cheerfully.'

'Of course he would. But Sing never saw Dudley Ward growed up. He saw him allus as a little boy, beggin' fer rice an' gravy in the kitchen.'

They rose and walked back along the pier, the waters lapping peacefully beside them.

'After a typhoon there are pears to gather,' Charlie mused. 'From this place I take away golden memories of two men. One was loyal and true beyond all understanding. Of my own race — I shall recall him with unseemly pride. The other — yourself, Mr. Holt.'

'Me? Oh, hell, Mr. Chan, I ain't nobody. Never was. Jes' been goin' along fer seventy-eight years, doin' the best I kin.'

'The greatest of Chinese emperors, being asked to suggest his own epitaph, replied in much the same vein,' smiled Charlie.

In the Tavern lounge, he bade the old man good night. As he turned, he saw Leslie Beaton approaching.

'Ah,' Chan remarked, 'I perceive my necktie now has serious competition. I refer

371

to your cheeks, Miss Beaton.'

'Excitement,' she explained. 'You see, I'm engaged. At least — I think I am.'

'I know you are,' Charlie told her. 'I also knew you were going to be, from the moment I saw the young sheriff's eye light upon you.'

'You really are a great detective, aren't you?' she replied.

Chan bowed. 'Three things the wise man does not do. He does not plow the sky. He does not paint pictures on the water. And he does not argue with a woman.'

We do hope that you have enjoyed reading this large print book.

Did you know that all of our titles are available for purchase?

We publish a wide range of high quality large print books including:
**Romances, Mysteries, Classics**
**General Fiction**
**Non Fiction and Westerns**

Special interest titles available in large print are:
**The Little Oxford Dictionary**
**Music Book**
**Song Book**
**Hymn Book**
**Service Book**

Also available from us courtesy of Oxford University Press:
**Young Readers' Dictionary**
**(large print edition)**
**Young Readers' Thesaurus**
**(large print edition)**

For further information or a free brochure, please contact us at:
**Ulverscroft Large Print Books Ltd.,**
**The Green, Bradgate Road, Anstey,**
**Leicester, LE7 7FU, England.**
**Tel: (00 44) 0116 236 4325**
**Fax: (00 44) 0116 234 0205**

*Other titles published by*
*The House of Ulverscroft:*

## THE BLACK CAMEL

### Earl Derr Biggers

In Hawaii the beautiful Hollywood actress, Shelah Fane, rents a house in Waikiki, but when she is found dead in the garden's pavilion, it sparks a murder investigation. It seems that this case is linked with another murder — three years before — of a Hollywood actor, and involves a psychic named Tarneverro. Chan, in his position as a detective with the Honolulu Police Department, untangles the deception, lies and mystery surrounding the case, hoping to find the murderer who brought the 'Black Camel of Death' to her door.

# BEHIND THAT CURTAIN

## Earl Derr Biggers

In San Francisco, former head of Scotland Yard Sir Frederic Bruce pursues the long-cold trail of a murderer. Sixteen years previously, a London solicitor had been killed. The only clue — the Chinese slippers he wore. At the same time there was another mystery: a series of women around the world had vanished — and all were linked to the disappearance of a woman in India, named Eve Durand. But then, at a dinner party attended by important guests, Inspector Bruce is killed — and he had been wearing a pair of Chinese slippers. Now it's left to Chan to solve the case . . .

# THE CHINESE PARROT

## Earl Derr Biggers

When heiress Sally Jordan is forced to sell
a valuable set of pearls, they are sold to
the Wall Street financier P. J. Madden
through a local jeweller named Alexander
Eden. The pearls are to be delivered to
Madden in New York by Charlie Chan
and the jeweller's son, Bob. However,
plans change and the pearls must be
taken to Madden's ranch in the Califor-
nian desert. But there, mysteriously, a
Chinese speaking parrot dies, followed
closely by a member of the household.
Chan goes undercover to investigate and
solves a number of crimes . . . whilst Bob
Eden meets a beautiful young woman . . .

# THE HOUSE WITHOUT A KEY

## Earl Derr Biggers

John Quincy Winterslip, a young lawyer from Boston, travels to Hawaii to visit his wealthy uncle, Dan Winterslip. John had failed a request to retrieve and destroy a certain box from his uncle's house in San Francisco — but others are also eager to find it. He arrives in Hawaii and learns that his uncle has been murdered. When Charlie Chan offers to help solve the killing and the mysteries surrounding the box, the detective's main clue is a wristwatch with an obliterated number 2 . . . whilst John, much interested in the chief suspect's daughter, assists Chan in solving the mystery.

# PUPPET ON A CHAIN

## Alistair MacLean

Paul Sherman of Interpol's Narcotics Bureau flies to Amsterdam on the trail of a dope king. This assignment was never going to be easy, but before he's even left Schiphol Airport, his key contact is gunned down. He finds himself targeted by an assassin and tangles with the local authorities. Then, as betrayal severely hampers his investigation, he must resort to increasingly violent tactics . . .